WARRIORS OF
WINTER

Amidst Snow and Shadows, Christmas Heroes Rise

Published by Radiant Leaf Publishing
Paperback ISBN: 978-1-7395576-0-7
eBook ISBN: 978-1-7395576-1-4

WARRIORS OF
WINTER

Amidst Snow and Shadows, Christmas Heroes Rise

J R BOLAKY

To Debbie,

Your unwavering belief in me fuelled my journey. Though you're gone, your faith remains my guiding light. This book is a tribute to your enduring spirit and love.

Forever in my heart.

PROLOGUE

Snow fell over the city of London, and the sleigh fell with it.

It whipped back and forth in the sky. The reindeer brayed in panic, their reins loose and flapping. Sleigh bells tore loose and *plinged* on one of the parapets of the Norman Tower, whitewashed to stand out as a beacon of power for miles around in times gone by, before being scooped up by the black-winged shadow of a raven.

The grizzled figure at the front of the sleigh swung his fist into thin air. There was a sound like a meat hammer on a steak, and then, where there had been no one, there was a shadow.

The shadow fell back. "Lucky swing," it said in a voice that personified evil, a voice that would send a chill to your very bones and make you want to start throwing punches or run for your life.

"I don't believe in luck," the old man said showing no fear; he had chosen to throw punches. Snow spun between them.

Then the shadow figure was beside him. It held a knife.

He barely turned the first slash aside. It caught in his red wool coat, slicing through to the white undershirt beneath. Then the shadow was on his other side, jabbing. The old man vanished and reappeared on the far side of his sleigh. He held up shaking fists.

"I thought you believed in everything," the shadow figure said. Snow hissed and crackled as it touched his skin. The scent of smoke filled the sleigh.

"Kindness, goodness, miracles—" the grizzled man stopped, for the shadow had moved again, too fast to be seen. It struck, disappeared, and struck again. The grizzled man tried to respond in kind, but his every move was half a second too slow, more defensive than offensive. He took a hit to the stomach, then the jaw. His cheek cracked against his teeth, and he tasted blood.

Bent over and gasping, he thrust out a hand. It glowed but the light was flickering and weak. The shadow figure uttered a laugh that pierced the howling wind around them.

The sleigh lurched, and the grizzled man was flung to the side. His reindeer screamed as they tore around the top of the Shard.

"Bloody modern architecture," he said. The thought that King Charles had been right all along about the destruction of the London skyline flashed across his mind. Then the shadow figure was beside him again.

The stone knife sank deep into his chest, piercing the wool coat, the undershirt, the skin, the lung. He gasped. Snowflakes dusted his coat, melting in the spread of deep, deep red.

The shadow pulled him in and held him in an embrace like a brother until the last of his breath steamed in the air. The reindeer screamed and broke apart in a pattering of bones and magic.

"Miracle your way out of this," the shadow said, and disappeared. Then there was nothing but the snow and the echo of manic laughter on the wind as the sleigh tumbled down.

CHAPTER ONE

Arthur Stowe's mobile rang before he was two pints deep. Which, by his own rules, meant that he had to pick up.

"This is Stowe," he said, trying to sound less sulky and more professional. It was his night off, but Commander Montague had given him more than his fair share of grace. He pushed a thick fringe of reddish sandy hair back from his forehead and leaned on the bar.

Arthur could barely hear Montague over the sound of a group of lads at the other end of the bar. "I need you down at St. Paul's."

Arthur stared hard at his half-finished Guinness. If he concentrated hard enough, perhaps it would disappear from the glass and reappear in his body, making him too intoxicated to come in. "St. Paul's Cathedral? Now?"

"Did I stutter?"

"St. Paul's isn't our jurisdiction, sir." Arthur fumbled a coaster off the edge of the bar. "I'm a bit confused—"

"Snell has asked for you personally."

That explained things. "I'm on my way, sir." Stowe ended the call and rubbed at the red-gold stubble on his chin. Snell would tell him he was poorly representing the Met, but Arthur had been off-duty and he didn't have time to shave twice a day. He didn't even have time to sit with a pint.

He'd paid good money for that pint. He glared at it as he pulled on his navy double-breasted wool coat and dark leather gloves. "I guess you can finish it," he told the barman.

The barman was a giant of a man named Lew, with more tattoos than teeth and a lack of love for the Met. "A Guinness? You must be joking," he laughed as he took it away.

Arthur checked reflexively that his dad's trusty wooden

truncheon was still in the inside pocket of his coat. That truncheon had seen a lot of action with his dad in the 1960s when a police officer commanded respect on the streets of London and was not feared and despised like they are today. Although it was not police issue anymore, he always felt better knowing it was there and he felt his dad was with him in some way; his passing had been a blow to him and wished he were around now to talk to. Arthur set off.

The Blue Whale wasn't far from Lewisham Station. Arthur stalked along the pavement, all but invisible to the few other pedestrians on their way to parties. With his thin nose and chin and cheeks, he resembled a scarecrow that had somehow come to life and regretted it. His figure concealed a muscled runner's frame, good for catching crooks but not so good at keeping them down.

Arthur wandered through to the platform and rubbed at his temple while he waited for the train. A busker played *Joy to the World on* his violin, and Arthur moved down the track. He wasn't interested in soppy carols that inspired a feeling of nostalgia and hope that only came once a year. *What about the rest of the year?* he thought. He just wanted the chance to be alone and miserable on Christmas.

Maybe this was a good thing, he told himself. Maybe Snell wanted him to come because he'd found a lead. Arthur doubted it. The only thing Snell ever seemed to be able to find was someone else to blame for his problems.

He squeezed into a tube car with a whole platform of revellers. It was the twenty-third of December, uni was out, and students were getting in one last party before going home to Mum and Dad. The lads wore fine coats and felt reindeer antlers on their heads. The girls were in high skirts and higher spirits. The train car stank of perfume and sweat. Arthur tried not to look at them wistfully. They had so much life ahead of them. And most of it was downhill from here.

The girl in front of him had her phone out. She nudged the boy next to her and tilted the screen. "Look at this." Arthur caught the start of a TikTok. A girl stood in front of a ditch, holding up a dirty cardigan. A caption read: *#savethekidslondon NEW EVIDENCE??*

Arthur turned away.

The 'Save the Children' initiative was Arthur Stowe's worst ever case, and currently his entire reason for being. Over thirty children had been abducted straight from their beds. Sometimes their parents had even been awake in the next room. The case was a top priority and high profile—which meant that every political figure and every superior in the London Metropolitan Police Force was up his arse, all the time. It meant that every kid who watched *Sherlock* went trekking through crime scenes on social media. And it meant that if Arthur solved the case, his career was made. Secretly he wished he had a Sherlock Holmes in his pocket to solve all this in a heartbeat. And he could be Watson just watching it all unfold.

Of course, if he didn't solve the case, he'd lose his job. Again.

Arthur and half of London spilled out of the train car twenty minutes later. Someone down the line started a rousing rendition of *All I want for Christmas,* and a fellow Scrooge's, "Shut it!" did nothing to swell the tide of off-key song. Bells jingled from silly little hats and laughter pealed up the escalators and out into the night. Girls screamed as the snowstorm assaulted their bare legs and shoulders. As Arthur headed up to the road, he kept his head down against the stinging wind, half wishing he had a hat. He slid through a crowd of shoppers, barely avoiding assault by a multitude of shopping bags as late-night panic buyers staggered for home under the weight of half a dozen bags each carrying the promise of commercial happiness on the morning of Christmas Day.

London was full of garlands and baubles and light and noise. Every pub was done up in festive fairy lights and showcased menus offering Christmas morsels and drinks and, it seemed, had their speakers retro-fitted to play music as loudly as possible so that the revellers in the street had to shout to be heard.

Bloody Christmas bloody cheer, thought Arthur. It was giving him a headache. He set off for the cathedral.

His phone buzzed with a barrage of texts that hadn't come through underground. Two missed calls from the Commander, with a *Hope you're on your way detective.* A text from Detective Inspector Izzy Blair, his partner: *call me asap pls.* And a text from

Missy.

David fell on his skateboard, think his arms broken. Taking him to A&E.

Arthur's fingers hovered over the reply. *Oh dear. Hope he's all right. Feel better soon. Sorry.* All shit responses, coming from a shit father.

He'd left them for a reason. He was saving up money to move them all here. He'd make up for it soon. The usual slate of excuses ran through his head. And, as usual, he knew better than to think next year would be better than this one. He put the phone in his coat pocket. David didn't need his meaningless words. Missy was there for him, and she was more comfort than Arthur could ever be.

Blue and red flashed over the white marble of St. Paul's Cathedral. The shrieks of partygoers chasing each other through the snow faded as Arthur rounded a corner and approached. Police tape stretched across the edge of Cannon Street, guarded by a Met officer who stood with his arms crossed against the cold. Arthur recognized the pencil moustache and wrinkled nose and heaved a sigh. Of all the blokes on duty tonight, it had to be Charles Waylan.

Maybe if he waited until Waylan was distracted, he could slip under the cordon without having to talk to him. Arthur phoned Izzy and leaned against the wall of an Information Centre, nervously tapping the top of his truncheon lying in his pocket.

She picked up on the first ring. "We found something," she said.

Arthur's stomach jolted. "What was it?"

"Some—some clothing. Shorts and a T-Shirt. They match the description of one of the missing boys." Her voice started to wobble. "Geordie Jones."

"I remember." Arthur remembered all the kids. He remembered Geordie's mother, too, silent and crying as he interviewed her at the station over a year ago.

"They found it in the Thames… Arthur, we're going to have to call his mother."

Izzy had lucked into the campaign, if you could call it luck. She was a new recruit, young and eager and ready to make a difference. But two years with almost no leads had started to wear on her. Now she sounded closer to broken than ever.

"Look, I'm just down at St. Paul's," he found himself saying. "Snell's asking for me, so I'll come in after that. I'll talk to Geordie's family."

"You would?" She sounded too grateful.

"Yeah. Go home and chill with Netflix, or whatever it is the kids do these days."

Izzy chuckled, though she still sounded a little watery. "Don't ever use that phrase, Art."

"Don't ever call me Art, Izzy." He hated being called Art. He hung up and dropped his smile. Why had he offered to make his night even worse?

Because Izzy Blair still had optimism. She still thought there was some good in this world. Why break a woman before her time?

No one had come to provide Waylan with a convenient distraction. Arthur steeled himself and stepped away from the shadows. Then he stopped, staring up.

The dome of the cathedral looked like a cracked egg. Before he could make sense of this, a shout was aimed at him.

"Oi. You can move along, please."

Waylan obviously didn't recognize Arthur in his plain clothes and the snow was causing a distortion in his line of sight. Arthur trotted across the street, holding out his badge and trying not to slip on the slick road. "Evening, Charles."

Waylan's face fell even further as he realized who was speaking. "Arthur. What're you doing here?" He sniffed, then leaned back. "You supposed to be on the clock?"

Arthur ground his teeth together. "Was my night off," he managed casually. "But I got called in special."

"Should've called in sick," Waylan said.

I'll give you something to be sick about, Arthur thought, but before he could think of something to say without costing himself his badge, another familiar—if no less unwelcome—voice raised a greeting.

"There you are! Been waiting for a good forty minutes, my chum. I told Montague he needs to focus on punctuality in the force.

Where's your car?"

The man who said this said it all while striding toward Waylan and Arthur, holding an umbrella against the snow, and without pausing for breath or reply. Antonius Snell was tall, with the good looks of a classic Oxford boy. His dark hair came together in a widow's peak above his smooth brow and small, sharp nose. His dark eyes glittered with anticipation. He stuck out a gloved hand and Waylan shook it, mumbling something about the honour. Snell was still talking, in a strangely hypnotic and smoky voice, the sort of voice you couldn't help but listen to. "I got the call and I had to come see for myself. It looks promising, Art."

"Arthur," Arthur said, not expecting Snell to pay attention.

He didn't. "The timing couldn't be better. Terrence has been up my arse about the campaign. With the energy crisis and the opposition's school budget obsession, we need a win. My job's on the line, mate. Which means your job's on the line. And good Lord, what's that on your face? When d'you last shave?"

Arthur eyed Snell's pinstripe suit as he mumbled something about having shaved this morning. That suit probably cost more than a month's rent. If Snell lost his job, chances were he'd be reshuffled into some other government position. If Arthur lost his job, he'd be out on the street.

He loathed most politicians, but Snell was a special item. Antonius Snell, the face of the Save the Children campaign, loved the way he looked on camera far more than he loved any kids. He was the kind of man to get into Arthur's face and demand the kids back by the end of the year, no excuses, as though Arthur had them hidden in a cupboard under the stairs. And if they did find the kids, alive and well, what would happen then? Snell would pat himself on the back, give each of them a hug, then turn around and slash school funding the very next day. Last year he'd even promised a Christmas care package to every under-funded school in Britain. Hard times, he'd said before the flashing cameras. Britain's most vulnerable. Everyone deserves a little Christmas cheer.

Naturally, that care package never materialized.

Presentgate was a short-lived scandal. There was always

something else—an affair come to light, embezzlement of funds, the Prime Minister saying something stupid on television. Most people forgot. But not Arthur. Arthur watched his neighbours go without heat last Christmas, and the best he could offer their kids was a couple of extra blankets. He knew the oldest lied about his foot size so that his mother didn't have to buy new shoes. And Antonius Snell wore patent leather shoes and a Rolex watch and said he didn't know where to find the money for Britain's most vulnerable children.

Snell slapped him on the back, and he came back to now. "I really have a good feeling about this one. It's going to make you, my friend."

"So, what is this lead?" Arthur said.

Antonius Snell smiled, and there was an unsettling fire in his eyes. "A body," he said.

Snell led him up the marble stairs and between the columns at the front of St. Paul's. At the door stood another uniform and Snell's assistant, Carl Kuiper. Kuiper was a good head shorter than Snell himself and looked like a half-finished watercolour of a man. Everything about him looked washed out, from his dull blond hair to the limp way he held out his gloved hand for a shake. He was sweating despite the cold.

"Minister Gemmel rang," he began.

"Tell her to piss off," Snell laughed. He sounded like a braying donkey.

Kuiper opened the door to St. Paul's and Snell breezed through. Kuiper and Arthur took a moment to exchange resigned looks. Arthur hated most politicians, but at least Kuiper knew he was working for an idiot. Kuiper half bowed. "After you, Detective Inspector."

Arthur had never been in St. Paul's before. It was one of those things that tourists do, and Londoners don't. He tried not to gape as he walked up the long nave, but his eyes were drawn to the ornate columns, the vivid ceilings, the glittering gold chandeliers. No doubt they'd been turned on for the investigation. The click of his boots echoed as he crossed the checkerboard floor, passing among the

15

marble columns like an ant in the grass. Soft red velvet adorned the pulpit and garlands dotted with Christmas stars marked the start of the choir. A fir tree twice Arthur's height glowed and glittered with red and gold baubles.

A policewoman stood in front of the transept. As Arthur approached, she came forward to block his way. "Sorry, sir, not sure how you got in here. But this is a police investigation."

Arthur showed her his badge. "I've been asked to look at the body."

She examined the badge with pursed lips. "We've already got detectives on site. So, thank you for your offer to assist, Detective Inspector Stowe, but it won't be necessary. We'd like to keep this within jurisdiction."

"He's with me," Snell said, leaning over Arthur's shoulder to smile his oily politician's smile. "It's vitally important that this man has the chance to inspect the body. It's part of an ongoing campaign I run: 'Save the Children'."

The policewoman turned those pursed lips on Snell. Finally, she stepped back and waved them through. "Don't touch anything. And please let the officers do their work."

"Thank you *so* much, Chief Inspector." Snell pumped her hand and strode forward.

Arthur nodded to her as he followed, though resentment coursed through him. What world did he live in when Antonius Snell had to vouch for him to other officers of the London Met?

The body lay on its back in front of the pulpit, boots turned out to either side. One arm was thrown out to the side, while the other rested on his prodigious belly. He was—*Father Christmas,* thought Arthur, and then he thought, *No, stupid,* but the man did look like he belonged in a Coca-Cola commercial from the fifties. His trousers and coat were spot-on in colour and cut, trimmed with white fur. His leather boots were scuffed but looked to be of good quality. His lined face spoke of a hard life, and his unkempt beard said *homeless* more than *Father Christmas.*

There was a dark spread over his coat.

"Already bag the weapon?" he said. The nearest detective gave him a dirty look. "No," she said, as though his very presence were a criticism of her ability.

So perhaps whoever had killed him had kept the knife. The homeless Father Christmas, as Arthur was starting to think of him, was dusted with plaster as fine as snowflakes. Larger chunks lay over the floor in a scattered radius. Arthur looked up at the gaping ceiling and the blackness beyond it. Around them, several officers worked and conferred in low voices. They were placing a little tag next to something that looked like bone. Human or animal, Arthur couldn't tell.

Arthur stared at the body for a long time. Then he turned to Kuiper. "All right. Why am I here?" Kuiper raised one eyebrow. His eyes were so pale it was hard to tell their colour. "You brought me out here to investigate the murder of a homeless Father Christmas? I thought he said this had something to do with the campaign."

"Oh, but it does." Snell picked at a bit of lint on his jacket. "This man is almost certainly connected to the disappearances."

"How, exactly?" Arthur said.

"He's been wanted in connection with other child-crime cases," Snell said.

"Who is he?"

"Just get his information, Stowe." Snell sounded bored. Arthur pressed his mouth together before he said something he'd regret and exchanged another sympathetic look with Kuiper.

Arthur checked with the Chief Inspector. The man had been discovered around seven o'clock when a caretaker had heard a crash. So far, the police had found little. No identification on the man, no evidence of a struggle. "It's like he just... fell from the ceiling," she said.

Arthur looked up again. The richly painted figures on the dome seemed to stare at the gaping hole. Flecks of gold gilt were scattered over the choir and halfway down the nave. "No man falls from that height and looks like that," he said.

"Can't argue. But he didn't get stabbed and then walk in here, either. No blood trail and the doors were locked."

Arthur went back to the body. They must be missing something.

He crouched next to it, thinking. Looking at the dark stain on the suit and looking at the man's face. That was the thing about bodies: the old man didn't look like he'd died falling from a great height or bleeding out from a stab wound. He looked... he looked like he'd fallen asleep, and never woken up. Maybe after one too many bottles of the bad stuff. A shiver crawled down Arthur's spine. For a moment, he saw himself in the corpse's face. And truth be told, it only made him need a drink more.

Then he frowned. Something glittered amongst the plaster. He shifted a piece. Perhaps it was gold paint? No, it wasn't paint at all. The man was surrounded by long shards of something... glass? "What is this?"

The nearest officer leaned over to look. "Building materials," he said. "Insulation or something."

"I don't think so," Arthur said as the officer slouched off.

Snell peered as well, though he made sure to stay well away from the body. "Focus on identifying him, not irrelevant items," he said.

Arthur dug in his pocket until he found a handkerchief. Pretending to be interested in a mole by the dead man's ear, he waited until he was reasonably certain nobody was watching, then picked up a few shards of the glasslike stuff. Whatever it was, it was sharp—the edge sliced his finger, and he hissed as blood beaded up. He wrapped the shards carefully before replacing the handkerchief in his pocket.

"All right, time's up." The Chief Inspector was there. "Undertakers are here."

Arthur stood up and stepped back as an elderly gentleman and his young assistant came up the transept with a stretcher. "Maybe the post-mortem will reveal something," he said to Snell.

"Perhaps," said Snell. His eyes glittered.

They watched the undertakers struggle to get the body onto the stretcher— "He is heavier than I expected" he heard the assistant say —and strap it down, then cover it over, with Arthur, Kuiper and Snell following them as they took the body out and put it in the hearse. Watching them slide the body into the secret space below

18

where the coffin normally was carried on the day of the funeral made Arthur raise his eyebrows, he had never seen that before.

"Where's your Funeral ambulance lads?" asked Arthur.

The older Funeral director replied for them, "It's been a very busy few weeks with the cold, more than normal, very sad, all our vehicles are out tonight. We had to use the hearse this time, not our go-to under normal circumstances."

The Undertakers resumed securing the body in the hearse respectfully and turned away.

"I'm serious," Arthur said finally as the hearse rumbled to life and drove away. "How's a homeless man so important to this investigation?"

"He simply is," Snell replied. "And if you want to keep your job, you'll take this tip seriously, Stowe. Think of the kids."

For a moment he let himself imagine. If he broke this case, he wouldn't just keep his job. The solving of a case of this magnitude would come came with accolades and promotions and, more importantly, this would allow him to repair his reputation and lose that feeling of guilt over letting down his poor Dad, who would roll over in his grave if he knew how far his only son had fallen.

But the real world didn't work like that. And whenever anyone said *Think of the kids,* they always meant, *Think of me.* Snell, Missy, Missy's father… "I always think of the kids," he muttered.

They walked away from the cathedral. "Did you drive? I can have Kuiper drop you off somewhere," Snell said.

The day Arthur Stowe took a favour from Antonius Snell was the day he'd hand in his badge. "I'll take the bus," he said. "Gives me time to think."

Snell's nose wrinkled slightly at the word *bus.* "Suit yourself." He stuck out his hand, and Arthur shook against his will.

Then he frowned, looking past Snell, back at the cathedral. "What the hell is *that?*"

He'd seen the broken dome when he'd walked up. But he hadn't seen the… *thing* sticking out of it. It was bulky and oblong, with a back end that curved up and two strips like runners attached to the bottom.

19

"What?" Snell said. Arthur pointed. Snell's eyebrows raised in surprise, but he wasn't looking at the dome. He was looking at Arthur.

"Oh," he said at last. "That. Old Cessna. Flying illegally, probably. Saw them all the time in my Oxford days, even flew one. Horridly uncomfortable."

If that was a Cessna, Arthur would resign, right now. "Think that's how he got into the cathedral?" he asked sarcastically.

But Snell only clapped him on the back again. "Good instinct. See, Stowe, this is why I wanted *you*. Keep thinking, eh? And keep me updated." He tapped his temple, then turned and strode off. "And get a shave!" he called over his shoulder.

Kuiper shook his head and nodded to Arthur before following.

So, Antonius Snell wanted Arthur to believe that some unidentified homeless man had gotten his hands on a Cessna that clearly wasn't a Cessna, crashed it into St. Paul's, and fell to the floor without sustaining any of the usual fall injuries.

"Politicians," he said to no one in particular. They were always playing some kind of long game. Snell probably wanted answers. Maybe he was grasping at straws, as desperate as Arthur and Izzy were to find something. His job was on the line, after all.

Think of the kids. Arthur put Snell out of his mind and headed for a bus.

CHAPTER TWO

"Nasty business," Mr Hayne said as the hearse pulled away from St. Paul's. "Sorry to drag you out, Chris, but hospitals are full to busting this Christmas. I have never seen anything like it before, so we need to look after our guest back at ours until there is some room available at the hospital again."

"It's no problem, Mr Hayne," Chris said, folding his long brown fingers in front of him. And it really wasn't. He had nowhere to go and nothing to celebrate this year and, unlike some of the other undertakers, he didn't mind working alone at night. He didn't find anything particularly terrifying about the dead. "First time in St. Paul's, actually. What a sight."

"My youngest was married there." Mr Hayne chuckled. He was nearing seventy now, with thinning white hair and skinny limbs. His voice was strong as ever, though. "Cost me almost as much as a house."

"Yeah?" Chris never knew how to respond when Hayne started talking about money things. More than a few of his old school friends would have said, *Eat the rich.* They'd probably scoff at Chris, working for old money. Chris was just glad to have a steady job that could pay rent on his steady flat, to have a suit he could call his own, even if it was a mourning suit that spent more time with the dead than the living. Now that they were in the hearse and alone, he loosened his black tie a little. They drove in silence—Hayne abhorred modern Christmas music—and so for five minutes, the only sound was the mechanical whir of the windscreen wipers and the occasional shout of a partyer outside.

Hayne & Sons was in Rose Street, squished between a pub and an Italian place that Chris couldn't afford. The front was a lovely clean marble with columns carved in relief and gold lettering over the door, but Chris and Mr Hayne drove through a gate next to the front door and into the little courtyard that the undertaker shared with the pub. Chris waved to a bartender on his smoke break as they parked. Even at sixty-eight, Mr Hayne could hold the stretcher steady and guide Chris as he backed through the door to the mortuary and workshop.

Chris had always found the workshop to be cosy, in its own way. A long counter ran against one wall, equipped with a sink and shelves full of embalming materials. Another counter held an engraving machine. Much of the rest of the space was taken up by coffins in different lengths and styles all aligned on shelves, from simple cremation coffins to elaborate faux-marble. Chris and Mr Hayne set the body down on the metal embalming table in the middle of the room.

"Please tag him and complete the paperwork, Chris, won't you?" Hayne said, and though he was steady as ever, Chris could see the fatigue in his eyes. "I'll be upstairs. You all, right? And mind your shoes." He pointed. Chris had scuffed the side of his left shoe on a step at St. Paul's. Aside from that, his shoes were so polished he could have used them as a shaving mirror.

Chris smiled. "It'll be right as rain by morning," he said, and he meant it.

His mum wouldn't have liked him being an undertaker. She could be superstitious, and Chris could still hear her warm voice, telling him to be wary of the dead. But Chris liked the dead. They didn't cross to the other side of the road because he was a nineteen-year-old brown boy. They didn't tell him to bugger off back to where he came from. They didn't ask awkward questions like why he didn't have a girlfriend yet, or why did he live on his own. The dead were peaceful. And they listened to his jokes, even if they didn't laugh. They all had a story to tell, and he wished he could hear about them all. You got used to the quiet, the *plink* of water dripping from the tap into the stainless-steel sink, the creaking of the old building as it settled around you. And even if you didn't, some of the other undertakers had convinced Mr Hayne to let them play music from a countertop Bluetooth speaker while they worked.

Chris turned the speaker on, then shrugged out of his grey coat and hung it on a hook by the door. "I thought we'd have a silent night, eh? No pun intended." He pulled open a drawer and retrieved a toe tag. "Though if you can't laugh when you're dead, when can you laugh?"

John Doe did not reply.

The toe tag needed Doe's name, estimated height and weight, hair colour, eye colour and the case number provided by the police. Chris wrote it all down in a neat copperplate hand with the information he knew, weight being classed as heavy in his mind, pausing only to pry open one eyelid. "Brown-eyed blokes unite, eh, John?" he said aloud.

As he pulled off John Doe's boot, he spotted a spider scuttling over the toe. It was a little black thing, probably confused and scared. Well, Chris knew what that was like. He gently chased it into his hand before opening the back door and depositing it on the ground. "Be free, friend," he said as it scuttled away. Then he looked up, feeling suddenly self-conscious. A few paces away a bartender sat with a pint and a smoke, looking at him as though he'd released a soul out the back door. The smell of tobacco hung thick in the air.

"Happy Christmas," Chris said, trying not to cough. The barman mumbled something in return.

Back in the workshop, he pulled off Doe's sock and attached the toe tag. As his fingers touched the dead foot, a sudden jolt of heat shot from his arm, straight through his shoulder and down to his heart. Chris snatched his hand away. John Doe felt... alive. Chris stared at the chest, dark with blood and unmoving. He stared at the foot.

Maybe this job *was* starting to get to him.

He wasn't going to Mr Hayne about this, not unless he wanted the old man to think he was going mad. He needed this work. He took a steeling breath and touched the foot again.

This time he felt nothing out of the ordinary. Just the cold flesh of a dead man.

"Well, that's a relief. Though not for you, sorry, mate." Chris patted John Doe on the shoulder. Odd, though. His fingers still tingled with the shock of it, whatever it was.

There wasn't much question as to how he'd died, but Mr Haynes liked to have everything done properly and by the book, so Chris unbuttoned Doe's coat and went to fetch scissors so he could cut through the shirt. He put on some Christmas music. "You don't mind, do you? 'Tis the season, and all that."

He could have sworn he heard a sigh from behind him.

Keep it together, he chastised himself. He started to cut through John Doe's shirt. The scissors shirred and snipped neatly. The skin on his back prickled, and he found himself glancing back as though expecting to see something behind him. He shook his head and sang the last few bars of *Fairy Tale in New York* along with The Pogues. A lot of undertakers often told stories of unexplained experiences; he had not come across any to share. He should focus on the cheer of the season. Maybe when he got a break he'd see if there was any hot chocolate in the kitchen. He could sit and watch the snow and pretend he was a kid again.

The hairs on his arm rose. Feeling overwhelmed him and he whirled around, it was almost like the thin air behind him had been filled up with a presence —but he saw only the coldly lit back room. Coffins, table, countertop, the sound of the ticking clock on the wall. Nothing else

"Hello?" he said, feeling a little stupid. He patted John Doe's knee. "You know, I always wanted to know if ghosts were real. That would be an interesting Christmas present." Maybe when he let the spider out, he'd let something else in. The thought of the afterlife had always appealed to him, he wanted to believe so badly there was one. There had to be, or what was all this about? Sending people on their last journey was his gift and he wanted to know if it was all worthwhile.

He stared around the room a moment longer. Nothing materialized, and he shook his head to clear it. Ghosts or no, he had work to do. He turned back to the stretcher and joined Mariah Carey as she started on *All I want for Christmas.*

"For God's sake," said a voice that was definitely not in his imagination.

Chris spun and stumbled back into the stretcher. Someone *was* there. Right in front of him. A girl around his age. She was fairly tall, though that might have been the effect of her thick-soled Doc Martens. She wore black jeans and a black, corset-ish top with mesh sleeves that looked like it was struggling to keep what was in from getting out, a skirt, and a thick belt that looked like it ought to belong to a gothic plumber. Her tan, heart-shaped face was made up with dramatic dark lips and thick eyeliner, and her black hair sat in two buns on either side of her head. She was glaring straight past Chris, at the Bluetooth speaker. Then she looked down at the corpse.

Chris realized, at that moment, that he had *expectations* about ghosts. They should be bloody and staring and horrifying. Or they should be old-timey Victorians that walked through walls, ghostly knights charging right through him. They shouldn't look like the sort of goth girls that appear on album covers. They shouldn't smell faintly of cardamom and cloves.

And they shouldn't have the look she had in her eyes, that particular mix of bereavement and anger and fear that Chris saw all too often on the faces of relatives. The reality of death.

"You just had to do this to me," she said, quietly, as though she and the body were the only two things there. And something else sat in her wide, dark eyes. She looked almost afraid.

Chris cleared his throat. Even if this was a ghost, it felt as though he were intruding.

"And right before Christmas. Bloody good timing." She nudged the stretcher with her foot, like she wanted to kick something but knew better.

"Er. Sorry." Chris leaned over to catch her eye. Her eyes slid off him, like they didn't want to focus—then they snapped back. And they widened. "Are you a ghost?"

The surprise on her face was replaced by derision. Chris hastened to explain himself. "It's only, I'm not sure how you got in, the doors are locked, and I only opened the back door for a moment, which means maybe you walked through walls to get in here, which means, maybe…"

She stared at him, lips parted, for a moment. Then she raised a perfectly plucked eyebrow. "You can see me?"

Well, that sounded like something a ghost would say.

She pursed those lips, then reached into a compartment in her plumber's belt and pulled out a pack of silk cuts. She narrowed her eyes at him as she slid the cigarette between her lips. Her fingernails were painted in a harlequin pattern, black and red.

"No smoking inside. Sorry," Chris said. Did ghosts really smoke?

The girl rolled her eyes. Her other hand came up with a lighter and flicked twice before sparking a flame. She inhaled deeply and blew out a thin stream of grey.

Funny, though. Chris couldn't smell it. The tip glowed, but the only scent in the room was the chemical smell of formaldehyde and the scent she'd brought with her, warm spice.

"If you can see me, it must mean something," she murmured. Her eyes went back to the corpse. "What're you trying to tell me? Was I supposed to come here? Was I supposed to find him?" She gestured with the cigarette.

"Er, Chris," said Chris, and closed his mouth before he could let out another *sorry.*

"What?"

"I'm Chris." He stuck out his hand. Could ghosts shake hands? Her eyes flickered down, and her lip curled slightly. Chris tried not to feel insulted. People rarely wanted to shake hands with an undertaker, but he wouldn't have thought the dead felt the same way. He coughed and went over to the sink to wash. *Play it cool.* This goth girl was so different to anyone he had ever met, and he had a strange tingly feeling in his stomach even if she was probably dead.

"So, are you here to summon him to the afterlife or something? Talk him out of his body, that sort of thing? Ghost to ghost?"

She stared at him a moment longer. Then she snorted. "He's not dead. And neither am I."

Chris looked at John Doe. What was left of his shirt was soaked in red, some of it so dark it was practically black. He looked at the unmoving chest. "Beg pardon?"

"I'll grant you it doesn't look good." She went up to the stretcher and found an inner pocket on the corpse's coat. Patted it down. Moved to another. How did she know where these pockets were? "I'm actually not sure when it last looked worse. But *dead* is a very strong word for the state he's in now."

"It… is?"

"Yes. Dead would mean all is lost. Dead would mean I'm absolutely one hundred per cent screwed. But right now, I'd say I'm at a steady seventy-five percent, and if I can find the bones and the key…" She moved to John Doe's other side.

"Please stop grave robbing," Chris said weakly.

She ignored him. "Where're his personal effects?"

Her hand slid into a pocket deftly sewn into the lining of Doe's coat. Her frown of concentration cleared to a triumphant smile. "Got it." She pulled out a flat stone disc and set it on the stretcher. "Well. At least I've got the key. Though how I'm supposed to get the sleigh going if I can't find the deer…" She tapped the disc on her hand and looked at Chris critically.

Chris had the feeling he'd lost control of the situation. Scratch that, he'd never had control in the first place. But if Mr Haynes could see this, Chris would be out of a job before he could say, 'Happy Christmas.'

"All right, okay," he said. The girl looked at him, nonplussed. "Let's start again. You're alive, are you? This area's for employees only, so if you're here to collect personal effects you'll have to identify the body and prove your relation." He held out a hand for the disc.

She scoffed. "Who's going to take it away from me? You?" One side of her mouth curved up, as though the thought of it amused her.

"If I have to," Chris said defensively. He'd never been the biggest bloke in his year, but he was good enough. And hauling bodies around built muscle like you wouldn't believe. "This man's an ongoing part of a police investigation. This belongs to the police." He took a deep breath. "And if you can't identify this man, then I think you should leave."

Her fingers closed around the disc. "You want identification? Fine. He's my Dad."

Chris' heart softened. He put a hand on her arm, like he'd seen

Mr Haynes do many times. It was solid enough and sent a warm shiver through his veins. Another point in the *living* column. "I'm sorry," he said.

She shrugged his arm off. "For what? I told you, he's not dead."

Well, denial was one of the stages of grief. "Can you tell me your dad's name?"

She tapped ash onto the floor, where it melted away like snow. "Nicholas of Patara. You lot call him St. Nick or Father Christmas."

Chris blinked. "Sorry?" She *was* dead, surely. Or she was on something.

The girl stubbed the cigarette out on the top of the stretcher, then tucked the remains behind one small ear. Then she eased one hand under the dead man's back and pulled him up until he sagged forward. She acted as though he weighed no more than a kitten as she manhandled him off the stretcher and over her shoulder. Then she turned "Watch his head, won't you?" she said, and walked through the door.

Chris stared slack-jawed as the door swung back and forth. Never in his life had he been able to lift a man, much less a man topping out at over six feet. Much less a *dead* man topping out at over six feet.

He came to his senses as he heard her boots thud on the stone courtyard. She couldn't waltz into his mortuary and take his corpse. The police would be back for it, and he didn't care to face the firestorm of losing an entire dead man.

He grabbed his jacket and ran for the door. His phone was in his jacket pocket; he'd stop her first, then he'd have to figure out how to get Doe back into the mortuary without calling Mr Haynes and explaining his massive cock-up. He should've escorted her out first thing, but *no,* he was too obsessed with the idea of a ghost to think. What if the dead man wasn't even her father?

He pushed through the door as she disappeared around the side of the gate. The cold shocked him to gasping. Pulling his coat on as he ran, slipping in the light dusting of snow, Chris shouted after her as the strains of *Last Christmas* blared from the pub's speakers. "Stop! Ghost Girl! Stop in the name of George Michael!"

CHAPTER THREE

Chris careened onto King Street and looked around wildly. There she was—down the road a way, striding with purpose. She deftly skirted the crowds that had spilled out of the pubs to either side, sliding into the road when a girl draped in tinsel backed up to the curb, laughing.

"Stop," he shouted again. The girl walked on. How was she carrying a whole dead body so easily? Did the dead have superhuman strength? Had to admire her for that, even if she was currently engaged in a crime. He tried again. "Stop her! Stop that girl!"

A few people turned to look at him, then in the direction he pointed. Then they returned to their drinks. One gave him half a shrug in sympathy as he skidded past. "Nice suit, mate," someone laughed.

She turned a corner and Chris sped up. He'd always been rubbish at running and a stitch was rapidly developing in his side. But what he lacked in athletic prowess, he made up for in stubbornness. He rounded the corner in time to see her slip between two groups of sparkling, tipsy revellers and open the gate to a churchyard. He could add breaking and entering to her record. Did she think she was supposed to bury the man herself?

Chris squeezed between the groups. "Sorry, 'scuse me." No one paid him any mind, not even when he jostled someone's arm and sloshed sour-smelling beer. He tried the gate of the churchyard—unlocked—and followed her in. "Sorry," he said again, this time to the graves on either side of the path, fearing he was disturbing their sleep. His feet crunched a new path in the snow. "Hope you're having a lovely night—don't mean to disturb—"

"Enough already. Do you ever *stop* talking?" said the girl.

Chris forced himself to jog a few more steps until he could grab the edge of her sleeve and confirm it was solid. She tore it away from him. "Come on, keep up."

"Stop," he gasped.

She threw an incredulous look over her shoulder. "No."

Chris slowed to a walk. He was feeling less in control and more like a lost puppy. "You can't just take someone out of the mortuary," he tried to explain. "There're procedures and papers to sign, and you need coffins, and you need to prove you're his next of kin—"

The girl shifted the dead man to her other shoulder. Chris watched, open-mouthed. "He's still not dead, so I'll see he's not buried alive, thanks."

"Sorry. Excuse me. Which one of us is the undertaker here?"

"You apologize too much," she told him.

She went through the gate at the back of the church and out to Covent Garden. The market was strung with boughs of pine and holly and illumined with fairy lights and huge baubles the size of chandeliers. Glass icicles knocked together gently like wind chimes above one market hall entrance. An enormous Christmas Tree strung with red ribbon and glass baubles stood in one corner. The air smelled like spiced wine and warm mince pies. The men here wore fine suits, and the women wore velvety Christmas dresses trimmed with fake fur. They sipped their mulled wine as they watched a street performer juggle Christmas ornaments.

Chris tugged on the sleeve of the nearest man. "Excuse me, sorry, could I get some help?" he said. "Only this lady's trying to steal my corpse—"

Could've phrased that better. It didn't seem to matter, though, for the man made no indication that he'd heard Chris or even felt his hand.

"Give it up. No one can see me. No one can hear me." The girl had turned around and now stood facing him, one hand on her hip.

"Okay. Are you pissed, or are you taking the piss?" Chris said.

She cocked her head and gave him an unimpressed look. Then she cupped her hand around her mouth and shouted, "Hey everyone! Look at me! I stole my dead dad from the undertakers!"

The quiet roar of conversation didn't even change. Nobody looked at her. Nobody broke away from their conversation. Either she'd hired out the entirety of Covent Garden to play a very elaborate joke, or…

"So, you *are* a ghost," Chris said.

In reply, the girl flicked one dark lock of hair behind her ear and turned toward a small clump of partiers. They held cigarettes in one hand and drinks in the other. One boy who was sporting mistletoe on his head in the hopes of a Christmas kiss, held an unlit cigarette. As he chatted, the girl planted a kiss on his lips, plucked the cigarette from between his fingers, and stuck it in her own mouth. He looked down at his hand a moment later, frowning in confusion, then at his feet.

"Can ghosts smoke?" she asked.

"Well, I'm no expert on the afterlife." The best Chris could do was hope there was one.

"Anyway, if no one can see you or hear you, that sort of tells me all I need to know." Chris felt slightly annoyed about the kiss she had given out but could not unentangle that emotion straight away.

"No one can see or hear you," she replied, and puffed a strand of hair out of her face. The cloud of her breath mingled with the cigarette smoke. "Does that make you a ghost?"

Chris patted himself down, feeling for solid flesh beneath his mourning suit. "'Course I'm not a ghost. I'd have felt it if I died." Wouldn't he have felt it if he died?

"You're not dead. Like I'm not dead. Like *he's* not dead." She hefted the body on her shoulder. "He is getting heavy, though, so let's go."

"This is impossible," Chris said.

She shrugged. "That sounds like a you problem." Then she turned and walked into the market.

It *was* impossible. Chris was an ordinary bloke with an ordinary life. His parents had been ordinary people who sent him to an ordinary London school. Never mind that things like this didn't happen. They especially didn't happen to *him*.

"Look, I have no idea what's going on," he admitted, trotting to catch up with her again. He raised his voice to be heard over the bubble of a thousand different little conversations in the market hall. "In fact, I only know one thing: a strange girl stole a body in my care, and I can't let you walk away with it. No matter whose daughter you say you are."

"Hm." She sighed a stream of cigarette smoke. "Guess you'll have to come with me, then."

Chris couldn't remember the last time a pretty girl had told him something like that. Probably never. The rational part of his mind nudged him. He should call the police. He should return to his duties at the mortuary.

Then again, with no corpse there were no duties. And he didn't fancy explaining to Mr Hayne how he'd lost a man who weighed at least sixteen-stone.

Also, nothing interesting ever happened to him. Nothing *good* interesting.

She stopped in the middle of the market. People flowed around her like water, unaware that they were even making space. Over the loudspeakers a live acapella group began *Silent Night*. She took a deep breath, closed her eyes for a moment. The tip of the cigarette flared. Then she nodded. "It's this way," she said, and set off.

"I'm Chris, by the way," Chris said, trotting to catch up to her again.

"That's nice."

"Only, maybe I could know your name? So that I can stop saying, 'Hey you' and so on. If, you know, I need to get your attention."

She sighed, and looked sidelong at him, all dark eyes and thick eyeliner and long lashes. "You can call me Winter," she said.

"Is that your real name?" Chris asked before he thought better of it.

"It's what you can call me." Her voice brooked no argument. The warmth of the market was welcome after the run through the snow, but now Chris was feeling overheated in his coat.

He snagged a free mince pie sample from a plate. "So, you're

32

Father Christmas's daughter?" He wondered if there was a term for such a delusion. "How does that work out? Isn't he ridiculously old or something?" The pie was sweet and warm, the crust flaky.

"Almost two thousand years," Winter replied. "But for Myths like us, age has always been a bit… negotiable. A lot of it is about how people *expect* us to look."

Chris nearly choked on his mince pie. "Sorry—" He pounded on his chest to dislodge a stray crumb from his throat.

"You say sorry too much."

"—but who on earth expects Father Christmas's daughter to look like a Turkish Goth Girl?"

"Well, I look Turkish because I am Turkish. As is my dad. And I'm a Goth Girl because I like the make-up. And it irritates Mum. You know how it is." She kicked an empty plastic cup down the aisle.

Chris felt a pang at that. He didn't know how it was. But now was not the time for grief, so he listened to the carolers as they started in on *Hark the Herald Angels Sing* and he thought of all the good things he could still enjoy in this world.

"That must be mad, though. Being the daughter of someone like Father Christmas." He was by no means convinced this was real, but he might as well play along. "Do you live at the North Pole? Do you help him pack gifts each year? Do you ever get to drive his sleigh?"

"No, no, and no, though not for lack of wanting. The sleigh's the only good thing about that life." They passed the stage and Winter held up one angry middle finger as she marched by, waving it like a pennant until they were out on the piazza. "Honestly. I hate this Christmas stuff." She rubbed a velvet ribbon between her fingers. "And it's just like Dad to create some kind of drama right before Christmas."

Chris shivered as a breeze wormed under his coat, reminding him that he'd forgotten his scarf. They made for Russell Street. "That's good for you, isn't it? If you hate Christmas. Maybe Christmas will be cancelled this year."

"Yeah, well, that's the problem. If Christmas gets cancelled, it *might* kill Dad." Winter grimaced slightly, then shifted her father to her other shoulder again.

"Do you need a hand?" Chris asked.

She shot him another look, this one darkly amused. Snowflakes settled on her hair, sparkling in the Christmas lights of Covent Garden. "Like you could help me, pretty boy."

He flushed. He couldn't remember the last time someone had called him pretty, either.

"So, er, what's your plan, exactly? Other than body snatching."

"Well, we've got to revive him. You must be able to see me because you're special somehow—you're not another Myth, are you? —so you can keep close until we've sorted it all out. It shouldn't be too difficult."

Special somehow. Chris doubted it. He was, in all things, average: average in academics, average in sports, and hopefully a decent human being. After the fire there hadn't been a hope in hell for university education, so he'd nabbed the first job he could find— and he was decent at that, too. Until now, anyway.

They walked along the A4, and he watched the double-deckers and black cabs crawl past, spooked by the snow. It was falling faster, now, and thicker, clumping together and sticking to the sidewalk. It dampened the noise of motors and parties. Chris smiled. He'd always liked a White Christmas. The clouds hung low and pale. Couples clung to each other as they walked past on their way to a nightcap after the theatre or home to their cosy beds.

"You really don't like it at all?" he said. "The mulled wine? The pies? The trees and the lights? The good cheer and happy kids?"

"I don't like kids," Winter said, and that was that.

The walk was a good half-hour, and she stopped two more times to switch the body over to her other shoulder. They walked down Fleet Street and Ludgate Hill. Finally, Winter stopped and looked up. Chris followed her lead.

"You know, I've only been in St. Paul's for the first time today," he remarked.

"There's a first time for everything," she replied.

"What, now? With that?" He gestured to the body.

The square was covered in crime tape, and two men from the

34

Met leaned against the statue in the middle of the square, chatting. People scurried past beneath umbrellas and thick coats, ready to revel somewhere warm.

"Well, actually…" Winter craned her head as she studied the church. "I think we want to get up *there*." She pointed straight at the roof.

Chris laughed. "Yeah. Good luck with that." Then he crossed his arms. Should've stopped to grab his gloves, too. His fingers were freezing. "Listen, Winter, it's been lovely to get to know you, I really appreciate the chat and I think you've made my night," —he felt heat in his cheeks when he said that — "but seriously, a job is a job, and mine is to take Mr Nick there back to our mortuary, and make sure he's well looked after." Though how he was going to get the body back was a mystery to Chris. Well, one step at a time, and step one was getting the crazy girl to let go of the body.

"You talk a lot, but you don't listen very well. I've already told you, he's not dead and he's coming with me. And I'm not sure how you think you can stop me." Winter spared him an irritated glance before going back to her study of St. Paul's.

"I probably can't, all by myself," Chris admitted. "But I bet *they'd* be willing to help."

He pointed. She followed his finger and snorted. "The police? That's the best you can do? They can't even see me. How are you going to get them to believe I'm here?"

"I'll find a way," Chris muttered. He was starting to feel embarrassed. But he didn't like to give up on things, and there had to be some way to get their attention.

Winter had gone back to ignoring him. A line appeared between her brows, and she moved her mouth in silent calculation. Then she sighed and tossed the remains of her cigarette on the ground. "Well, it's a bit of a gamble, but we ought to be fine. Hold tight."

"What—?" Chris said. Then she grabbed his hand.

He had time to marvel at how her fingers were warm, warm as a night by the fire. And then he was falling.

35

CHAPTER FOUR

Arthur returned to the cold, bright, sterile-smelling Lewisham Metropolitan Police station shortly before midnight. He needed a sit-down and a cup of tea, and he wanted a quiet drink. Snow had sunk through a hole in his shoe and now his socks were soaked. Soon, he told himself as he trudged through the large room dotted with desks. He'd log evidence, make Izzy go home, then maybe sleep on the couch in the break room to avoid going home himself and remembering all the places he'd gone wrong in life.

His plan went awry the moment he passed Izzy's desk. She was scowling at her computer as though it had personally wronged her, but she paused her silent war with it to glare at him. "They're here. Where've you been?"

"Bloody Midnight Mass. Where do you think?" he grumbled. Then he ran a hand down his face, smoothing his expression. Izzy must be referring to Geordie Jones' family. "We get anything else from the clothes?"

"Not yet. They'll go for a full analysis tomorrow, but we won't get anything back before Christmas." Her expression softened. Izzy was a classic knockout, with wavy blonde hair and big blue eyes. Most of the time she was scowling, as though she thought no one would take her seriously if she didn't. Arthur had been working on getting her to relax. "Look, thanks for the help. You didn't have to."

"It's nice to have someone who owes me," Arthur replied.

The truth was, he did have to. He had to keep his partner optimistic. He had to keep her thinking they could do this—solve the big crimes, the crimes against kids and innocents. Because once she suspected it was pointless, she'd fall. As he had. He set off down the hall toward the interview rooms, shoes squeaking on the linoleum floor.

Mrs Jones sat in an interview room with a young girl. Geordie's sister, Arthur remembered. Last time he'd seen her, she'd been a thin, quiet kid. Now she was a teen with a choppy do and too much eye makeup.

He retrieved the evidence and poured two cups of tea. As he shouldered the door open, he said, "Sorry for the wait, Mrs Jones."

Mrs Jones didn't answer. Her brown hair was dull and lanky. Her face, once plump with middle age and happiness, was thin and sallow. She kept her eyes on the table and fiddled with a bracelet on her wrist. She had a cup of tea in front of her already, full but cold. Arthur pushed the second one across the table. She acknowledged it with a weak, obligated smile.

"Now, we've got a few items here. They do match your description of the clothes Geordie was wearing when he disappeared last September, but we'd like you to take a look. Is that all right?" He took a sip of tea. Hot and bitter and bloody awful.

Her chin dipped almost imperceptibly. Arthur knew that look. She was barely holding it together. She was afraid to meet his eye, to speak, in case it somehow made everything more real.

"Er, if you like I could get you a Liaison —"

"Let's see it." Geordie's sister, Mel, pulled the fresh tea over and helped herself to the mound of sugar on a little paper plate in the middle of the table. She took three sugars and dumped them in, one after the other, then attacked her cup with a wooden stirrer. Her lip curled as she worked.

"Right." Arthur cleared his throat and put the evidence down. The clothing had been sealed in plastic bags, neatly labelled. "They need to stay in the bags, of course, but perhaps you can tell us—"

"Geordie always labelled his trousers, did you look?" Mel said. She at least wasn't afraid to look at him. The hatred in her eyes was enough to make him scoot his chair back an inch or so.

He gathered himself. It was his job to be professional, not theirs. He was all too aware of the stubble on his chin. He doubted he could explain it as being too dedicated to the case to shave. "Most of the identifying marks have been washed away. We have determined that these were white shorts that students at Horrick

Secondary were instructed to use in Sports. They were found along with this." He nudged the second bag forward. "You did say he was wearing a yellow T-shirt the day he disappeared?"

Mrs Jones looked at the tee shirt. Her hands trembled. Her eyes filled, then overflowed. She bowed her head as the sobs came.

In the movies, the lead detective put a gentle hand over the mum's hand and swore to do everything he could to find the bastards. The mum cried a few perfect tears, then the scene cut to action. Not here. Mrs Jones fought to breathe. Mel put a hand on her back and the tea against her mouth. "Here, Mum. Here, Mum." She glared at Arthur like this was all his fault.

"We will, of course, be doing a full forensic report when the labs reopen," he said.

Mrs Jones gulped air. "It's his. I know it's his. I know it."

"It's okay, Mum." Mel looked at him like she was trying to set him on fire.

"We, er, do have someone who can speak with you."

"We're good," Mel spat.

He felt himself growing hot under her rage. "Is there anything else you remember? Anything he might have said, a change in his routine, a new friend he made?"

Mel shoved the evidence bags back across the table. Her bulky hoodie made it hard to see, but he caught a glimpse of a thin wrist. Her cheekbones were sharp, too, and her cheeks hollow. Hollow like she'd been skipping meals. Christ, no wonder she hated him. What had men in positions of authority ever done for her? Times had never been easy for families like the Joneses, who relied on council housing and meal programs for their kids. Mrs Jones probably didn't have any heat in her building, either. And now, as they prepared themselves for a cold winter and a dismal Christmas, some useless bobby called them down to the station to give them the worst possible news. Happy bloody Christmas.

"We told you what we knew when he disappeared. You couldn't do anything about it then, how are you going to do it now? There's blokes on TikTok who're doing better than you."

She slammed her cup down so hard that the paper bottom

crumpled, and beige tea sloshed over the table. "Come on, Mum," she snarled, grabbing Mrs Jones by the arm. She hauled her mum up bodily. Mrs Jones' coat was frayed at the cuff and bottom and hung loose on her frame.

Mrs Jones stopped at the door long enough to swallow and say, "Thank you," before Mel pulled her through.

Arthur watched the door slam behind them. Then he picked up the evidence bags. "Another Stowe success," he muttered, and went to find some kitchen roll to clean up the tea.

Families were in pieces. There was no evidence. It was easier to say the kids had disappeared off the face of the earth than it was to point to where they might be. They hadn't found a single body. The logical thing to assume was that the kids were being trafficked, but he was dumbfounded as to how.

"I see you brought your particular touch to that one," said his boss as he left the interview room. Commander Montague was a mere five years older than Arthur but had been on the up and up since the beginning of his career. He'd broken some of London's baddest while Arthur was fighting to bring justice to the small-town criminals of Colchester before it became a City. "Don't you think Izzy would have been a better choice?"

Montague also was the kind of bloke who thought that Izzy would have a soft touch because Izzy was a woman. "It was mostly a formality, anyway."

"See the latest TikTok theory? It involves cannibalism." Montague shook his head.

That was another problem. Everyone thought Arthur was so bad at his job that they had to do it for him. The Social Media Detectives, as he called them, had tramped through private fields and construction sites, broken into the victims' schools at night, and trespassed on crime scenes in their attempts to blow the case wide open. More than once they'd wrecked something that might have been decent evidence. "I think I'll skip the TikTok today, sir."

"I'm surprised you didn't go back home after the call. You're not on shift now. Izzy's going for that promotion, it's no shock she's putting in the hours. But this is the first time you've let work get in the way of a stiff drink." Montague folded his arms. "Snell told me you hadn't shaved."

He was baiting Arthur. And it was working. Arthur felt his hackles rise and tasted sour anger in his throat. And deep in the pit of his stomach, he felt a twinge of shame. Because if Montague hadn't insisted he come, he'd be too drunk to see straight by now.

He needed to stay professional. He needed to keep his job. "I've got some evidence to log, sir." He pulled the handkerchief out of his pocket. "Not sure why Snell called me over— take a look." He pulled out his phone.

Montague looked at the photos, frowning. "St. Nick get plastered and try to lead a sermon?" he said.

"Snell's convinced he's connected to the kidnappings," Arthur said.

Montague grunted. "Maybe *he's* been looking at too many TikToks."

"And look at this, sir." Arthur swiped to a photo of the outside of the church.

Montague whistled low. "What happened there? Lightning strike?"

Arthur pointed to the odd shape protruding from the roof. "Snell said it was a Cessna. You've flown, sir, does that look like a Cessna to you?"

Montague squinted at the photo. Then he shook his head. "I don't see anything. Just the dome," he said.

Arthur studied the photo. It was impossible to see what, exactly, had crashed into the dome. But there was unmistakably *something*. Maybe a traffic camera had the angle he needed. Or a security camera from one of the buildings across the street—though he doubted he'd be able to access it before Christmas, either. *What time of year d'you call this?*

He let Montague wander off to Izzy's desk, probably to shower her with similar criticisms. Montague was the kind of boss who felt that too much praise led to complacency. Arthur wanted a drink. And his bed. But he still smarted from his Commander's earlier comment. He was no lazy bastard, and while he might not be the sharpest detective, he did his work and he paid attention. He thought of the kids, and of the people like Mrs Jones who needed answers, and he kept on trying.

He sat at his desk with a fresh cup of tea. Someone had put an Elf-on-the-Shelf on his monitor; he tossed it in the bin. He logged in and went in search of his mystery object.

The traffic cams were pointed at the ground, of course. He wasn't going to get far with those. The road shone with snowmelt, and wind gusted snow across his screen.

Then someone walked across it.

No, that was wrong. *Two* someones walked across it, and they were carrying a third someone. Someone in a Father Christmas suit with a dark stain on its back.

Arthur leaned in until his nose nearly touched the screen.

It was *definitely* his victim—or if not his victim, someone extremely similar, who'd been murdered in extremely similar circumstances. *Please don't tell me we have a serial killer who targets Father Christmas,* he thought. The corpse was being carried by what looked like a young woman, though Arthur could only see the back of her. If it was a man, he was quite convincing in a dress, wig, and boots. Following behind was a skinny lad, tan skin, dark hair—

"Hang on a minute," muttered Arthur. The kid turned to watch a black cab cross the intersection, and all doubt vanished from Arthur's mind. Traffic cams didn't have the best resolution, but he recognized the sharp nose and the mourning suit. The young undertaker.

Arthur fumbled for his mobile. He had to make a couple of calls first, but he finally got Officer Waylan's number. When Waylan answered grumpily, Arthur cut straight to the chase: "I've got two suspects on traffic cam outside St. Paul's, headed your way. One of them's carrying the victim. The John Doe from earlier tonight."

"Who is this?" Wayland demanded.

"It's Stowe. Can you see them?"

There was a long pause. Then Waylan said, "Bloody Hell," to whoever was on the other end with him. "Nobody's here, mate. You looking at the right time?"

"There's not that much of a lag. And they're carrying a full-on dead man, they shouldn't be running a marathon."

"Hang on a mo." Arthur heard the *crunch* of Waylan's boots on snow as he walked. Arthur tapped his fingers on the desk. Finally, Waylan said, "I hope you don't think this is funny."

"It's no joke," Arthur insisted. "I saw them, plain as day."

"Well, I don't see them. And if you're too drunk to see reality, then you should've called in instead of wasting time."

The line clicked. Arthur clenched his fist and, with much effort, resisted punching his desk.

Too drunk to see reality. What a laugh. He was sober enough to drive, now. And he would.

"Headed home?" Izzy asked as he passed her desk.

"Headed out. Got a hunch," he replied.

"Hey." He stopped and looked back. She smiled at him, a little sadly. She'd be a brilliant interrogator when she learned how to use that smile. "Thanks for handling the Joneses tonight. It sounded rough."

"It was nothing," he said, giving her a brief smile in return. Let Izzy Blair think she could save the world for a few more years.

He took a Met car, easing his way along the slick streets, watching London celebrate. People had had a hard year between the rampant inflation, the cuts to schools and the NHS, the rising fees for everything from electricity to university education. And it was important to forget your troubles at Christmas time. If you didn't forget, you'd wallow.

His mobile pinged as he pulled up to St. Paul's. Speaking of wallowing. It was Missy, with an update. *Broken arm. Not too bad, needs cast for 6 wks.*

He stared at the text. He even tapped out a reply. *Can I call? Sounds like trouble. Happy Christmas.* Then he closed his app without pressing *send.*

Think of the children. His children didn't need a loser drunk of a father. And there might actually be someone in London who could use him.

He got out of the car. Wind flurried little drifts of snow over his shoes. His sock would be wet all bloody night at this rate. He found the footprints at the edge of the road. Snow was collecting in them, but he could still track them up to the front of St. Paul's, a dozen feet or so from where Waylan stared at him with open hostility. Two pairs. One a woman's boot, the other a man's.

And then… they stopped. As though the body and the undertaker and the woman had vanished. Arthur looked up. Then he looked down.

A solitary cigarette end lay between the woman's boots in the snow. Arthur fished out a tissue and wrapped it up. You never knew. Then he called over to Waylan. "You didn't see anyone? Standing right here?"

"Go home, Stowe," Waylan called back coldly.

Arthur made a circuit of the church. Snow creaked under his feet. The world was falling to silence as people gave up on the night or moved their parties inside. A street or two over a car door slammed.

He found nothing else of note on the ground around St. Paul's, but kept his eye on the roof as well. The dome was still broken, but the object that had crashed into it was gone. Curiouser and curiouser.

His mobile rang again. Snell. *He pays you,* Arthur reminded himself, and put on his nice voice. "How can I help you tonight, Minister?"

"Art! You find anything on your John Doe?"

Arthur was back where he'd started. He tapped the toe of his shoe against the suspicious footprint. Something told him to play these cards close to his chest. "I'm following some leads." Why Snell thought he'd be able to identify the Doe near midnight on Little Christmas Eve…

"Look, I've got government ministers breathing down my neck. They want good news for Christmas. Good news. Do you think you can give it to me?"

"I'm certainly doing my best, sir," Arthur replied. Which he couldn't if Snell wouldn't let him get on with it. "Did you remove

43

the, er, Cessna?"

"What Cessna? What are you talking about?"

Arthur opened his mouth. Then he closed it again. Antonius Snell had lied to him, and forgotten he'd lied.

"Sorry sir," he managed. "Mixing up case facts. I'll just focus on Doe, shall I?"

"Do that. I want results, Art. I want you to be a hero by Christmas." Arthur heard Snell chortling in his smoky voice as he hung up.

Hero by Christmas. Wouldn't that be wonderful? Arthur stared up at the dome, at the wound gaping on its white façade. How had two misfits and a corpse simply disappeared?

CHAPTER FIVE

Chris hit lead-lined tile. His feet slid out from under him. Before him was a sheer drop and 250 feet of air. The city stretched before him, marble and glass and steel and Christmas lights all the way down to the black garland of the Thames. While his brain was catching up on the *What? Why? How?* his arms flailed until his fingers caught something and gripped tight. His shoes slid against the slippery surface. His stomach plunged.

"Oops." A hand clasped around his and Chris found himself being hauled up by his right arm. "I might have misjudged the distance. Just a tad. You're all right, aren't you?" He thumped down on something hard and blessedly solid.

"Fine," wheezed Chris. He massaged his shoulder, eyes shut tight, remembering the look of nothing between his feet and the earth far, far below. His heart galloped. He forced himself to slow down—deep breath in, deep breath out—the way he'd done when he was younger and missing his parents too much to think.

When his hands stopped shaking, he gathered the courage to open his eyes again. Ahead, the city of London spread out before him like a quilt of light and distant sound. Snatches of song drifted up on the wind—*White Christmas, Carol of the Bells* and, because it was always playing somewhere in London, *Bohemian Rhapsody*. Off to his left was a long, dark roof and an illumined tower. He recognized the columns clustered toward the top, the golden pineapple that capped the tower. He looked down again. Beneath whatever he was sitting on, the roof sloped away steeply.

They were on the dome.

How were they on the dome of St. Paul's?

"We teleported," Winter explained as she caught his expression. "Short-distance teleportation, one of the powers I inherited from

Dad." The wind whipped her words away and her black hair blew across her face. She made a face and retied a ponytail.

She'd set him down on the bench of a sleigh. John Doe was on the opposite side, lolling as though he were dead drunk and not... dead. Snow collected in the folds of his coat. Even in the dim light of night, the sleigh gleamed red, as though the very essence of it could pierce the dark. Snow had settled on the edges and into the cracks, and it even seemed to glow faintly. The body of the sleigh was sleek. *The sports model,* Chris thought. Two wicked-looking gold runners curved up in front of him, edged with frost. At the front of the sleigh sat a console with a circle the size of his palm.

On the floor in front of him lay a long lead of leather. Chris picked it up. Saint Nicholas, sleigh, and reins. They had everything but the reindeer.

"So, you... teleport," he said weakly.

"Well, in addition to all this. How else do you think he gets inside houses? By the chimney? Mum would go mad at the dirt. Now stay in there and don't move too much. If you tilt the sleigh you might go through the dome. I've got to find something." She hopped over the side of the sleigh and walked away from him, balancing on the edge of the roof like she scaled church domes every day.

Chris leaned over the side of the sleigh, gently brushing a spider off the edge as he did so. The tile beneath them was shattered, and—was that more open air? He sat up straight again, tensing as the sleigh rocked a little. He breathed deep again until his heart stopped trying to claw its way out of his mouth.

"All right. All right." Chris tried to stand up; the sleigh tilted dangerously. He sat down again. "I'm hanging out on the top of St. Paul's, with St. Nick, who's dead, and St. Nick's daughter, and we might plummet to our deaths any minute. No big deal." He looked over at the body and patted its knee. "You know, one of my coworkers always jokes about faking his death so he can get out of Christmas dinner. This wouldn't be some kind of elaborate scheme, would it?"

"They've got to be around here somewhere." Winter's

mouth twisted and put her hands on her hips. Chris shivered. The temperature up here was no joke, and the wind had a way of winding down a man's jacket like a ribbon. She looked back at Chris. "Are they in there?"

"Um, what?"

"Bones. We're looking for some bones."

Chris leaned forward gingerly and peered into the corners of the sleigh. "I don't see anything remotely bone-looking. But I think I'm on board now with the whole 'St. Nick' thing. So sorry, but could you tell me a bit more about what's *actually* going on?"

"I suppose," Winter said. She sounded like she'd rather sit through five hours of the *Nutcracker.* She disappeared behind the side of the sleigh, then reappeared, the frown on her face more pronounced than ever. "Look, you know about Father Christmas. But did you ever hear about Krampus?"

Chris shrugged. "Sorry, no."

"Well, Krampus is like the anti-Father Christmas. He's the nightmare who comes for bad little girls and boys. Sticks them in his basket and takes them straight to Hell." She peered into a corner.

"Er. Okay." The wind was starting to draw tears. He drew his hands inside the sleeves of his coat before they could turn blue.

"You're not going to go all sceptical on me now, are you?" Winter tapped the edge of her father's sleigh and sighed, clouding the air around her. She shot him an appraising look.

"Sorry." It was a lot to get used to. He looked out at the city, at the headlights as small as pinpricks making their little way along roads that threaded through London like a spiderweb. Up here the whole place glittered like a tree strung with lights. The air tasted cleaner somehow, though perhaps that was the snow more than the height.

"Well, you could say that Krampus and my dad have never really got on. Their core purpose being at odds and all. They've been fighting for centuries. But it's been a long time since Krampus gained an upper hand like this."

She moved away from him and started searching again, making for the little pineapple at the top of the dome. "The real problem is timing. It's the 23rd, and if we can't revive him by midnight tomorrow, Christmas is off."

Off? "I don't get it," Chris called as she moved farther afield. Only kids thought Father Christmas actually *brought* presents. "Will people forget about Christmas or something?"

"It's more like the spirit of it. You've heard of the spirit of Christmas," she said. Chris nodded, even though she couldn't see. "Well, Dad doesn't go from house to house giving out candy canes and train sets. He gives hope and love and generosity, and the desire to care for others. Spirit. If he's gone, that's gone."

"Sounds brutal," Chris said. Next to him, Saint Nick—John Doe, whoever—slumped against the side of the sleigh. Chris patted him on the shoulder before he could think better of it.

"Hang on…" Winter headed around the cupola at the top of the dome. The wind whistled, then died down in time for Chris to hear a low growl.

"Watch out!" He stood up and the sleigh rocked, making his legs go wobbly and his heart pound.

"Oh, for goodness sake," came Winter's voice. A moment later, Chris heard a series of high yips. They sounded like… "And what are we supposed to do with you? Go on then, back to the sleigh. I found Dad."

Chris heard three more yips in quick succession, then the scrabble of claws on tile. He looked over the side of the sleigh again and spotted two long shapes trotting toward him, ears flapping wildly in the wind. Their little paws slipped on the tile, but amazingly they kept their balance as they galumphed up to the sleigh.

Sausage dogs?

The nearest one, a black with tan markings to either side of his jaw, stopped as he spotted Chris. A low growl rumbled from him. The other dog, a long haired red, trotted right up and put her paws on the edge of the sleigh, tongue lolling. Her eyes looked like she had eye liner on, he noticed.

"Are these… the reindeer?" he asked. The red dog yipped expectantly.

"Do they *look* like reindeer? Come on, Ottie." Winter scooped up the growling black dog in one arm. He squirmed and fixed Chris with a glare. "Rosie, stop begging and get in the sleigh." The red one hopped futilely until Chris took pity on her and picked her up. Her tail wagged her whole lower body, and she attacked the arms of his coat with dog kisses. She smelled like wet fur. Chris couldn't remember the last time he'd been this close to a dog. "Now. I can't find the deer, what's going on?" Ottie growled. "Yes, I know, but he's a friend. Sort of. We need him to start the sleigh."

Ottie started to squirm. His growl became angrier and more desperate. Chris put up his hands. "Whoa, mate. I didn't do this. I know it looks bad, but—"

"Quiet." Winter's voice sliced across the wind. She set the dog down, gently, and her hands went to the buttons on her long black coat. "Something's wrong." Her eyes darted from side to side. In the sleigh, both dogs' noses lifted into the air. Rosie began to yap loudly.

Winter pulled her coat off and tossed it in the sleigh. "Are you mad?" Chris hunched his shoulders. Then she turned, and he realized why she'd taken her coat off.

Two short axes were strapped to her back.

Just my luck, he thought as she pulled one free, then the other. *I start on a magical adventure and get knocked off by a serial killer five minutes in.* Her blades gleamed in the night.

"Start the sleigh," she said. Then she moved.

She swung her axe to the side, and where there had been air before, there was something else. Exactly *what* was a mystery to Chris—it was a shape of darkness, a shadow that stretched and bent the way shadows did in candlelight. But when Winter's blade sliced through it, a bit of the shadow fell to the roof, leaking black, like smoke. The creature shrieked. The air filled with a scent like hot iron.

"Start the sleigh," she shouted. She chopped off another long tentacle as it reached for the back of the sleigh.

"Me? How?" Chris said.

Rosie stood up and put one paw on the console, then looked at him. "The button on the dash: use it!" said Winter. Then she grunted and doubled over. A shadow limb had kicked her in the gut. She raised one axe in time to block a punch, then swung the other.

"Okay. Uh." *Focus on one thing at a time.* Chris examined the button. It was smooth, and painted with a square cross bisected by an X. It looked a little like a snowflake, or a star. Probably the point. He pressed the button. Nothing. "Do I need a key or something?"

Something grabbed him by the shoulder, and he yelled. A pitch-black, multi-fingered hand curled around his coat and started to pull him backwards. He smelled smoke and an acrid stink, like singed hair. Winter shouted something feral and angry, and the hand loosened and fell to the floor, flopping.

Chris chanced a look behind. Winter leapt from the sleigh, swinging her axes in bright arcs. The edges of her blades were glowing with a soft golden light. The shadow thing couldn't break through her guard. It stumbled as pieces fell from its body to the roof of the dome.

Then a second figure darted out from behind the cupola.

"Watch out!" he shouted. Too late. The shadow grabbed her by the leg and pulled. She went down hard on her back. As she sucked air through gritted teeth the first shadow slithered forward. One tendril caressed the side of her jaw while another pinned her arm. The shadow slipped between her teeth.

Her eyes widened in panic. She flailed, punched the creature with her free axe, then kicked down. She scrambled to her feet. "Come *on,* pretty boy," she growled, bringing her axes up.

Chris turned back to the dashboard. *Focus.* What was the next problem? "There's no key. What is this, the Tesla of sleighs?"

"Of course not." She cut the second shadow cleanly in half. "Musk's been on the naughty list for decades." She grunted as one of the shadows grabbed hold of her hair but made short work of it.

"Well, how am I supposed to start it?" Chris's voice rose in panic.

"Spirit of Christmas, remember? Think of the Spirit of Christmas."

"That is *extremely* unhelpful and unspecific!"

Three more shadow figures drew up from the dome.

"Yeah, well." Winter wiped her nose. Blood smeared across her face. "I'm kind of busy right now."

They attacked. Two grabbed for the body of St. Nick, while one went for her. Winter dispatched her assailant with an easy swing, then leapt onto the sleigh to protect her father. It tilted dangerously.

"*Chris,*" Winter said.

Spirit of Christmas. Chris took a deep breath. He loved Christmas. Watching people exchange gifts or snuggle up with their mugs of hot chocolate or look wonderingly at the snow. He remembered gathering around his mother's table with a slice of Christmas cake, seeing the love she put into everything she cooked.

Rosie's paw was still next to the button. She barked.

"You really think so?" He pressed it again.

He felt a pulling in his chest, an invisible magnet that kept his hand pressed to the ignition. Memories flashed by of him trying to learn to knit as a boy, sitting next to Mum on the couch. Of Dad teaching him to wrap Christmas presents badly, Of nights piled under every blanket in the house, reading by flashlight. Of the little excitement whenever he opened the next day on an advent calendar. Of inviting Mrs Andrianakis over for dinner the year her husband passed away.

The reins uncurled from the bottom of the sleigh. Rosie did three little hops, then managed to jump onto the dash. Ottie jumped after. They looked out over the top of the dome, then each other. Then back at Chris, as though they were talking about him. Then they jumped into thin air.

The air flashed. And now Chris was holding the reins in one hand, the other still pressed firmly to the ignition. Ahead of him the reins spooled out, leading to harnesses that hadn't been there before. Attached to the harnesses were Ottie and Rosie. One dog per side.

"You must be joking," Chris said.

They scrambled midair, little heads bobbing up and down. Their ears flopped. Chris could see Rosie's tongue flapping out of the side of her mouth.

The sleigh started to tilt up.

51

"Hold this." Winter stuck an axe in his hand. Chris fumbled to hold both the axe and the reins—the axe was heavy —as Winter braced one foot on the bench. She grappled for her second axe with a shadow that had to be at least nine feet tall. "No—you—don't—" she grunted.

The sleigh teetered at the broken edge of the dome. Everyone staggered. But somehow Winter turned that to her advantage, pulling the axe free and using it to punch the shadow off the sleigh. "Hurry *up*," she shouted.

The dogs strained. There was no way, Chris thought—but then the sleigh began to move. With a scream like two metal beams scraping together, they slid from the roof, and Chris was falling for the second time tonight.

They sped toward the ground. Wind whipped through his hair. Chris couldn't help it; he screamed. Winter screamed something rude, snatching her axe from Chris's hand as the shadow figures made a last desperate leap.

And then, they levelled out. The sleigh ran parallel to the ground, then tilted up, up, over the roofs of London and into the grey, snow-swirled sky.

Winter swung one more time, then straightened, chest heaving. He was acutely aware of the heaving chest. Chris tried not to stare.

Evidently, he wasn't doing a very good job. "What?" she said, narrowing her eyes at him.

"I, er. I just had the weirdest night of my life." He started to laugh. It surprised him, but it felt good. All that panic and fear needed an outlet somehow, and here it was in the crisp, cold air. "Am I really flying St. Nick's sleigh?"

"I told you you could do it." Winter sat next to her almost-dead father and pulled a cloth from her belt. She started cleaning her blades. "Ottie? Rosie? How are we doing up there?"

Ottie yapped something in reply, his small legs going as fast as they could as if he was running for his life or theirs, which he was of course. They shot over the Thames. Next to the ignition point, a space on the console illuminated, filling with lines and squares and little squiggly bends. A map. Sensible, he supposed.

Suddenly Something reared up out of the back of the sleigh. A gaping, black mouth with too many teeth and fingers. It scrambled for Saint Nicholas's shoulder. Chris yelled and ducked.

Winter snatched a knife from her belt and hurled it. It disappeared into the shadow figure's throat and the figure fell, trailing black smoke as it went, leaving behind the faint stench of brimstone.

Winter peered over the side of the sleigh. "Bollocks," she said. "I liked that knife."

Chris started to laugh again. Hysterically.

He was a decent bloke. He'd never been anything less, nor anything more. Yet here he was with St. Nick's goth daughter, fighting strange and enormously frightening creatures and flying a sleigh pulled by the two least aerodynamic miniature dachshunds in existence. How did decent, normal Chris's life get turned so upside-down in a couple of hours? This sort of thing didn't happen. Well, not to him.

"All right, all right. Have your mental breakdown elsewhere, if you please." Winter checked the other side of the sleigh for any remaining shadows, then pulled her coat on and sat down. She continued to clean her axes. Her hair had come loose from her ponytail again and danced in the wind. She looked beautiful, thought Chris. Heat returned to his cheeks.

"Sorry." He wiped at a streaming eye and considered the bench. He could squeeze in, but to do so felt quintessentially un-British. Also, he still wasn't completely convinced that Father Christmas was no corpse. "So, where are we going? Aside from away from those things."

"A course. Right." She stood up and tapped the map. When it didn't respond, she frowned and tapped again. Then she rolled her eyes. "You have to do it."

"Me?"

"Yes. Dad banned me from using the sleigh after I took it for a joyride in 1665 and I made the news, it seems, in Stralsund, Germany. Thank God Cameras were not around then. Dad was very, very angry. It won't obey me now, and I guess that goes *even* for the map." She kicked the console gently.

So that was why she needed him. Well, lucky him. "What's our course?"

"Turkey," she said. "Ever heard of Myra? We're going to Dad's grave."

CHAPTER SIX

It was gone midnight now, and Arthur had every right to go home. Or to the pub. Arthur knew what he wanted to do, and perhaps that was why he was at the Lewisham Met station. The Detective Inspector with nothing to prove had something to prove after all: that he wasn't a lush.

Of course, he could kill for a drink. Arthur sucked in his cheeks and pushed back his blond-ginger hair. He pulled out the *Save the Children* case file and went through it again, this time looking for signs of his three new suspects.

A goth girl, a homeless Father Christmas, and an undertaker. What connected the three of them, and what connected them to the missing kids? Aside from the fact that Antonius Snell insisted the homeless sod had something to do with it.

At some point, Izzy came over with a cup of PG Tips. She wore her trademark scowl as she set it down. "Don't think this is going to become a habit."

"I never asked you to," Arthur said. But he took it and added, "You're a peach."

She bent over the picture of the three new suspects. "Kidnapping? Assault? That kid looks like he belongs at a funeral."

"Tell me about it. It's corpse theft at the very least. But what would they be trying to do with the body?" Arthur took a sip of tea. It was fresh off the boil and scalded his tongue.

As he gulped from a day-old cup of water on his desk, Izzy stuck her thumbs in her belt. "Maybe they're taking it for a human sacrifice. Like you tried to convince us in the good old days." She laughed as though remembering good times.

Arthur did not laugh. After a few moments Izzy patted a blond curl back into place and said, "Well, I guess human sacrifices are supposed to be alive, anyway," and strode back to her desk.

Arthur picked up his tea again, sipping more cautiously this time. It was bitter enough to pucker a man's mouth. Izzy always over-brewed her tea. Human sacrifice... he supposed the goth girl might be connected to that? Better not air that theory, he could already hear the papers screaming discrimination.

He didn't want to bring the cult angle up again, anyway. He'd nearly been laughed off the force. There wasn't much evidence at that point, and he'd been thinking out loud. Black powder on a site that had turned out to be coal dust, and a cloven footprint too large to be a goat's. As it happened, the kid had been on a field trip to a coal mine, and the warehouse where they found his jacket had been used to hold livestock. Arthur had endured weeks of 'Hail Satan' and other hilarious ribbing, until the next case came in and it became clear they were dealing with a serial offender. The next time he found something that looked like a ritual object, he kept his observations to himself. All the same, he remembered the bones they'd bagged for evidence. Animal bones without a doubt.

He rubbed his itching eyes and went back to the photographs. Printouts upon printouts of footprints, fingerprints, fibres. All of it leading nowhere. Getting so old and so picked over that the best they could hope for was another kidnapping with a clue that could tie it all together. Good Lord, thought Arthur. No wonder people like Mel Jones hated him: he had to wish for another crime to solve the case.

At last, he found what he was looking for. He pulled the photograph free. It was of a carved stone, a ram's head with curved horns. It looked like obsidian in the photograph, but he remembered the odd way it had glinted in the light. Much like the shards he had in his handkerchief right now.

He'd investigated it on his own time. Talked to a museum curator and everything. And like every other lead in this God-forsaken case, he'd come up with nothing.

Were a few shards of stone really going to change anything? These kids were gone, he knew it in his bones. If not gone from this earth entirely, then gone from England, at least. There were too many bad men in this world who were willing to figure out how to do it. And too few good men to catch them or stop them.

And yet… if Arthur Stowe never cracked this case, it wouldn't be for want of trying. Doing his job had lost him his family already. What was a little more ridicule from his new colleagues? He wasn't like Izzy, trying to rise through the ranks. He wanted to solve this and get on with the next.

A plan formed in his mind. And, at last, he stood up, with somewhere to go other than the pub.

"You off?" Izzy said, stretching. She had a full cup of coffee before her, getting ready for a long night.

"Need some sleep," Arthur replied. "I've got a date at the British Museum tomorrow."

***

"So, your Dad took away the keys to the car?" Chris had given up and squeezed in on the bench after one too many sharp turns had left him off-balance. The sleigh was a red star low in the sky, making for the edge of England. The wind howled and drove snow around them in flurrying whorls, but some sort of bubble kept the wind from pinning Chris to his seat or stealing his voice. The snow stopped its frenzied dance as it entered the air around the sleigh and instead drifted downward, peaceful at last. They'd left the glow of London behind, and now lights twinkled like stars as they flew over snow-dusted villages. Rosie and Ottie loped up ahead, ears flapping.

"In my defence, I really needed it." Winter examined her nails. She was in the middle, shoved up against her Dad, and for that Chris was grateful. No shade to the old man, but there was a difference between dressing a body and cosying up to one. This close he could just catch her scent: cardamom and cloves. That tingling feeling started again.

"How did you know I'd be able to start it?" Chris said.

She shifted, looking guilty. "I didn't," she admitted finally, and her lips turned up in the first real smile he'd seen from her. It felt like sharing a secret. "But you could see us, even when I didn't want you to, and I figured that had to count for something. Still haven't figured that out, by the way. Did you take something off him?"

Chris shook his head. But he thought of the weird hooking feeling when he'd touched the body's toe, the jolt of heat and the sudden certainty that the man wasn't dead after all. Maybe he *had* taken something off Father Christmas. Something intangible.

"He probably *selected* you for some reason." Winter shrugged and looked out over the sleigh. She ran her hand along a chip in the paint.

"I hate to point it out to you, but bodies don't pick their undertakers," Chris told her.

She gave him a sidelong, appraising look from under her lashes. "You'd be surprised at what a Myth can do." She fell silent, and for a few moments they watched the land speed beneath them. Earth gave way to the deep blackness of waves, and Chris' stomach jolted, half with excitement and half with fear. He'd never been out of the country before, and now he was crossing the English Channel. He didn't even have a passport.

"Well, my name *is* Christmas," Chris said at last. "Maybe that's got something to do with it."

Winter snorted. "Pull the other one."

"I mean it." He dug around in his coat—yes, there it was, at least he'd not left his wallet in London. Imagine getting stranded in Turkey with no money and no ID. He pulled out his driver's license.

Winter squinted at it. "What the hell."

"I told you." He replaced it and leaned back, feeling smug. "My Mum really liked Christmas, and I was born on the 24th, and that was that."

"That's… awful." She looked out at the snow with wide eyes. "I thought Winter Noelle was bad."

There was something warming about her sympathy. Like drinking the perfect cup of tea whilst holding a biscuit in the other hand. Chris found himself smiling at her. "It's all right. I don't mind my name. But you see why I go by Chris."

Winter shuddered. "What'd your Mum name everyone else in the family? Father's Day? Guy Fawkes Night?"

"My sister was named Saba."

The silence that followed this was absolute. Even the wind had died down a little. Loneliness tolled in him like a bell. He coughed, trying to break the silence and dislodge the lump in his throat without making the incredibly cool girl next to him cotton on. Funny how grief worked. It had been five years since the fire roared through the apartment block, which hadn't been inspected and wasn't up to code. Chris had been out working. His father, mother and sister had been trapped inside.

He'd learned to live with it, because he couldn't do anything else. But every so often the grief hit, and he didn't know what to do besides weather the storm and hope it quickly passed.

He sucked air through his teeth until they hurt, and he concentrated on finding something else to talk about. Finally, he managed, "I, er, I've never heard of Myra. Is that where you were born?"

Winter nodded. She leaned over her father's chest and poked his cheek.

"And were you born with all your superpowers?" She shot him a quizzical look. "You know. Killing things, teleporting, being invisible on command. Whatever else you can do."

"I was born with invisibility." She slouched back against her seat. Her tone had turned sullen. "That's it. Everything else I've worked for. Or I got it when I hit puberty." She stuck a hand in her pocket. "I'm going to smoke."

She didn't ask if he minded. She didn't apologize. She did whatever she liked, and Chris had the feeling that if he told her he didn't like it, she'd tell him to hop out of the sleigh and figure it all out on the way down.

He liked it. It was sort of cool.

"So, what else do you do?" Her face clouded over, and he hastened to correct himself. "Sorry. Probably an insensitive question You don't have to tell me, or—"

"You apologize too much." She leaned over her Dad's body and flicked ash off the side of the sleigh. "I can also manipulate time. Not a lot. I can't go back in time and stop wars or anything. I can do maybe a couple of minutes. Enough to teleport into someone's house and dole out that good old Christmas spirit, then get out again."

Two minutes. The right two minutes could make a hell of a difference, Chris thought. "That's amazing," he said.

"Is it?" She cocked one perfectly plucked eyebrow at him. "Imagine being able to time travel, and all you're supposed to do with it is visit five houses on the same row at the same time. What a waste." She sucked on her cigarette like it owed her something.

Chris hated silence, but Winter seemed to live by it. They sat awkwardly, legs pressed together, listening to the wind creak and the odd plane drone. He was painfully conscious of the touch of her against him. The snow stopped somewhere over France and the sky cleared to a cold blue-black.

"Hang on," Chris said as they came up on the tail of a Boeing 777. "Are we passing that plane?"

"My father picked you for your observational skills, I see." Winter had finished her cigarette and now she dug around in her coat until she found a compact. She flipped it open and started touching up her eyeliner.

"Sorry. Sorry, but there is *no way* that those"—Chris pointed at Ottie and Rosie, gamely galumphing— "are faster than *that*." Rosie growled. "No offense, Rosie."

"It's the sleigh more than anything. It needs something to pull, but once it gets going it gets going. What do you expect from a man who has to fly everywhere in the world in one night?"

She had a point there. Chris waved to the pilot, who couldn't see him anyway, and enjoyed the view of a fluffy cloud as it passed in front of the moon.

They passed over a pale shoreline and onto waters that gleamed like onyx. "The Mediterranean," Winter said. "We'll be there soon."

Myra didn't exist anymore, she explained to him as they skirted Italy and headed for Greece. But Demre sat where Myra had been, and the Church of Saint Nicholas was still there.

Ottie and Rosie angled them toward a cluster of lights against the coast. The air stank of salt and fish and petrol. The lights grew, and soon they could hear the sounds of a city: cars honking, people shouting, music playing. Someone's bass thudded, jarring Chris' blood.

They descended far more gently than they had when taking off from St. Paul's, but Chris' stomach still jolted unpleasantly when he looked toward the ground. He focused on his knees instead and resisted the urge to take Winter's hand for support. She'd probably chop it off, anyway. They landed with a gentle bump, and Chris sighed in relief as he looked up.

They were in a car park. "Oh," he said.

"What did you expect? Come on." Winter hopped out and heaved on the body.

It was colder than Chris expected. He'd always pictured himself in Turkey in shorts and a Hawaiian shirt. He was supposed to take his Mum back when he got a good job; save up some money, get a passport, bring her home to see her sister and old friends. Instead— well. He popped the collar of his coat and followed Winter as she made for a dark cluster of shapes in front of them. Rosie and Ottie trotted after them. Their harnesses had disappeared as easily as they'd materialized.

The shapes turned out to be an old church. It looked half ruin, half museum. A low rectangular modern entrance led to a mishmash of brick domes that hadn't been in style for over a thousand years. Weeds sprouted at the base of the walls, nature trying gamely to win the war against civilization. The wall had crumbled on one side, leaving a jagged edge like a broken tooth that shone dimly in the moonlight.

Winter strode up to the entrance and, as she had done in London, she only had to touch the door and it opened for her. "That's another neat trick," Chris said. His voice bounced off the walls.

She went in without answering.

They came into a courtyard first, a wide square paved with neat grey stones and strewn with the remains of fluted pillars and the nub of a fountain long run dry. Chris turned on his mobile's torch. He was relieved to see he still had battery. Grass sprouted between the paving stones. He could see the columns of an ambulatory, still standing, and a darkness beyond so thick it looked solid.

"Turn that off," Winter said. "Can't take the chance of anyone seeing us. Ottie!" Ottie lowered his leg from the side of a fallen pillar, looking embarrassed. *But he hadn't been for ages! And where was his treat, anyways? Ungrateful humans*, he thought.

Chris lowered the torch but didn't turn it off. He still needed to see where he was going, after all.

Winter led him through one of two arches and into a hallway. Their shoes thudded like a hammer on nails. Chris couldn't help himself. He turned his torch to the walls, revealing painted scenes from centuries past. Apostles and angels and haloed men with books dressed in robes of blue and red and adorned with gold. Chris had never been to Sunday school, but he marvelled at the way the paint shimmered and shone.

"Honestly, turn that off." Winter sounded proper annoyed now. "Don't you know the light damages the paint?"

"Sorry." Chris turned the torch back toward the floor. It was enough to see by, at any rate—enough to see Winter walk straight past what looked remarkably like an ornate tomb. "Hold up. Isn't that it?"

"That's the decoy. Come on." She kept going. With one regretful glance at the shadow-wreathed tomb, Chris followed.

They came out into the main hall of the church. Beneath Chris' feet, the flagstones were decorated with little mosaic wave patterns in chips of stone no larger than his fingernail. He tried to step carefully. The ceiling arched above them in plain red brick, but the walls held more painted saints.

A rope divided the top third of the hall, cutting it off from visitors. Winter stepped easily over the rope and made her way between two rows of columns, towards a wide set of benches built amphitheatre-style against the wall. There was an arch beneath the seats to either side, and within that, darkness. Chris stepped over the ropes to follow her, silently apologizing to the caretakers, archaeologists, and St. Nicholas himself.

Winter knelt down below one arch and rolled her dad off her

shoulder. Chris winced as his head *tacked* against the floor. "Here we are." She stood up and shook out her coat, looking pleased with herself. "The real spot's in there. Well, the real fake spot."

"The what?" Chris was getting confused.

"He never died, did he? So, the grave was never really a grave, anyway. But he stashed a few things in here for safekeeping, and that's what we're going to collect. You can come in and hold the torch high. I'll need to use both my hands."

For what? Chris thought. He raised the torch nervously and bent double to follow her in.

Winter ran her hands over the stones until her fingers found a small recess. The recessed stone looked hardly large enough for a man, and especially the man currently lying on the floor of the church. But Winter worked her fingernail around a certain brick and pried it up, grumbling all the while. "Just got my nails done, and a touch-up's not going to save them now, *honestly...*"

"I can do it," Chris offered.

"You probably can't. No offence."

Winter pried the brick up and rummaged around in the hole beneath it. She reached further. Then further. She leaned forward until her arm was stuck in the hole up to her shoulder. "Bollocks." She shook her head at Chris. "It's not there."

"What're we looking for?" Chris' gut dropped unpleasantly. Winter, who'd fought off shadow figures and teleported to the top of St. Paul's, who'd sat on the sleigh as it plummeted as though it were a rather boring amusement park ride—Winter looked afraid.

"His resurrection kit," she said.

"That sounds like a handy thing to have."

"It's not funny, *Christmas*. Did I mention we have to get him up and going again by midnight tomorrow? What are we supposed to do if we can't find the kit?"

Chris' shoulders came up in defence. "Well, you brought me along for this ride, so—"

"It was a rhetorical question."

They both froze. From the hall behind them, there had come a very audible clunk.

"Piss," hissed Winter. "Piss bollocks *shit*. Move." She shoved him, then shoved past him as Chris flattened himself as best he could against the side of the arch. She scrambled out of the dark like an ungainly spider, tugging her coat off as she went. Her boots scraped on the wall and she kicked a pebble, creating a patter that went all the way down to the front. Well, as long as they weren't relying on stealth.

Apparently, they weren't. Winter jerked her axes from their sheaths and held them up. Rosie and Ottie flanked her, growling. "Come out, coward," she called.

"Dear me. Jumping to conclusions, darling? I suppose it's nice you haven't changed, though. It makes me feel like not *too* much time has passed since your last visit."

The voice was the last sort of voice Chris had expected to hear in an old church at three in the morning Turkish time. It sounded old, world-weary but kind. It sounded a lot like his old neighbor Mrs Andrianakis.

The growls turned to excited yips. Rosie did a little circular dance of joy.

"Oh, no." Winter's voice and face were full of dread. She lowered her axes and stared as a figure came up the way, moving slowly but surely. The dogs took off. Chris raised the torch.

The woman was dressed in a sensible blue skirt, grey shirt and coat, with a paisley scarf wrapped around her head for the cold. The wrinkles on her face told the story of a lifetime—a lot of laughter, a fair bit of frowning. Chris recognized her warm brown eyes, her sharp chin, her slim nose. He looked between Winter and the woman, waiting for someone to say it.

"*Oh no?* It must be fifty years since I saw you last, and the best you can do is *oh no?*" The woman put her arms out. "How about a hug for your dear old mum?"

CHAPTER SEVEN

"Hi, Mum," Winter sighed and sheathed her axes. Rosie rushed over and threw herself against the old woman's skirts.

The woman crossed her arms. "Hi? Fifty years, and the best you can do is 'Hi'?" She turned to Chris. "If you had not seen your poor mother in fifty years, would you start with 'Hi?'"

"Er," Chris said. He liked to think his situation was a tad different.

Fortunately for him, Winter's mother was more interested in talking than in listening. "Did I truly raise my daughter to be no better than this?"

"Apparently," Winter muttered. Beneath her make-up, two bright red spots were spreading on her cheeks.

The woman picked Rosie up. Rosie went wild, covering everything she could reach with long-tongued kisses. "Oh, you," she cooed. "Your big sister's driving Mummy up the wall, she is. Coming home with Daddy in a right state, won't even introduce me to her boyfriend—"

"He's not—*God,* Mum, this is why I never come round." Winter threw her head back and swiped a strand of hair out of her eyes. Chris was rather glad she didn't have the axes handy anymore, she looked half-tempted to chuck them at a pillar.

"Sorry, I'm Chris. The driver." He came forward and stuck his hand out.

The woman shifted Rosie so that she could shake Chris's hand. Rosie lay on her back like a baby, gazing up adoringly. "I'm Zarina. So, my husband still has his child locks on?"

"I'm afraid so." Chris smiled.

Winter looked ready to breathe fire. "What are you doing here, Mum? I thought you were staying up North."

"Well, I'm here for the same reason as you, aren't I? You think I wouldn't feel it when my own husband is on the brink of death? Honestly, Winter. Just because you're his mythological heir doesn't make you the only one who can suss it all out."

"I'm not his mythological heir," Winter muttered. She crouched down to scratch Ottie between the ears. Chris suspected it was only because she didn't know what else to do.

"Saying no doesn't make it so," Zarina quipped, and Winter rolled her eyes. "Now, it's frightfully dark in here, and I forgot my spectacles, and if we go right over the road we can drink tea and have a little chat. What say you?"

"Mum, we don't have time for a catch-up over tea," Winter said.

"What else are you going to do? The resurrection kit's gone. Do you know where to get another one?"

Winter worried her lower lip between her teeth. Then she said, "You know it's gone?"

"Of course, darling. I looked for it first thing. Honestly. Do all children think their mother's such simpletons?" Zarina turned and started to walk away. "Lucky for you, I know where to find what you'll need. And I'll tell you over tea. Are you hungry? I've got lamb and rice in the refrigerator. Why don't I make us all some cake?"

"*No cake,*" Winter seethed. Ottie, who was trotting after her mum, stopped to throw her a reproachful glance over his shoulder. Winter puffed up her cheeks and sighed. "I can't believe this. Blackmailed into having dinner."

"It's only tea." Chris offered his hand and she pulled herself up, stretching her shoulders and scuffing at the floor with her boots until dust obscured their footprints. "And it's your mum."

"Say that again after you've spent a few hours with her." She picked up Father Christmas again, and off they went.

Zarina—or was her name Mrs Christmas?, Chris wondered—took them out of the church, where real life assaulted him and reminded him where and when he was. Someone was roasting mouth-watering meat, undercut by the fish-and-seaweed smell of

Demre, while someone else blasted dance music from an apartment nearby. Two men argued loudly on the corner, and Chris picked out a few words before they crossed the road and the voices faded from hearing.

The little building across from the church was the St. Nicholas Museum. Zarina unlocked a door Chris was fairly certain no one else could see and ushered them into a cosy one-bedroom flat. She sat them at a tiny wooden table, then bustled into the kitchen to put on some water. "I hope you like it in the Turkish style," she said. "I don't hold with the barbaric stuff the English call proper tea."

"Do you have coffee?" Winter said.

"You know I don't." Zarina sounded fondly irritated, as though they'd had this argument many times before. She opened the refrigerator and began to pull out Tupperware, tutting all the while.

While Zarina banged in the kitchen, Chris looked around. The place was fairly simple, and more modern than he'd expect for a mythical being that was nearly two thousand years old. Behind their table was a living room, which held a dark red couch and a television. An oval mirror on the wall next to the table provided Winter with the perfect spot to touch up her dark blue lipstick. Against one wall sat a bookcase, full of books on folklore and Christmas traditions. He spotted a couple of John Grishams in the mix. The walls were butter-yellow, trimmed with white.

"What?" said Winter. He looked over. She slid her lipstick back into her pocket. "You're frowning."

"I... think I expected something else from the house of Father Christmas," Chris admitted.

"Like a mansion in the Arctic Circle full of reindeer and elves?" Chris flushed, and Winter snorted. "This is why I hate Christmas. All the assumptions. My dad was from Patara, you know. He's not some random white guy."

"Oh, don't let her bully you." Zarina was back with a plate of steaming rice and cubed lamb. She handed it to Chris. "We do have a lovely house in the Arctic circle. And we have reindeer. And I wouldn't say we *have* the elves, but they're a type of Little Myth, and they've been housing with us lately." She gave him a brief,

67

motherly smile, brown eyes crinkling. "They haven't got on well with the industrialization of Scandinavia. And drones scare them, poor things. Eat up."

Chris took a bite. The lamb was flavored with sumac, and beautifully juicy.

"No food for me," Winter said.

Zarina snorted. "Look at you. You need at least five meals in you before you leave. I'll make you an egg."

"*No.*"

She went back into the kitchen. Chris looked at Winter. "What?"

"Your mum's lovely," he said.

"To guests," Winter muttered. "And don't let her fool you about the elves. They're *really* annoying. Like, you don't know frustration until you've had to share the sleigh with a Norwegian nisse."

"Sounds rough." Chris couldn't help but grin—the thought of Winter sitting black-clad and surly in the sleigh while little elves distributed presents was almost too much.

He got two helpings of lamb and rice and cucumber salad, and Winter, after much badgering from her mother, ate a single scrambled egg. Then Zarina brought out three tulip-shaped glasses on a tray and poured a gorgeous deep amber tea into each. She topped them off with water, then passed around a sugar bowl and a plate of almond biscuits.

The glass had the same pattern as the ignition on the sleigh, Chris noticed. That was his last thought before he picked it up.

He knelt on the ground, on legs that weren't his, swathed in robes he'd never worn in his life. Hands that were too large to be his hands held a heavy book open, and a voice that was too deep to be his voice rumbled as he chanted from it. His heart filled with feeling, with love and hope and happiness, until he thought it would burst apart and leave nothing but the essence of a man, all light and spirit.

The scene shifted. He stood on the street, negotiating with a lascivious Roman at a stall with two thin girls. Coin changed hands and the girls stepped forward. He clung to the looks on their faces, the desperation and fear, and the certainty that if he did not help them, they were doomed. His heart filled with anger.

The scene shifted again. A small, dirty house in front of him with an open window. A heavy purse in his hand. He stole up to the window and heaved the purse through, smiling as he heard the clack of coins smacking against the desk. A purse full of gold would make a fine dowry for the maiden within, who had no money for herself. His heart filled with satisfaction.

Shift. Rain lashed at his face and bare arms. The sea rolled around him, and he gripped the tiller with all his strength. They were bound for the Holy Land. Sailors hung on and prayed for their lives. But he knew he wasn't finished yet. He had so much to do. He had so much to give. His heart filled with determination.

Shift. He lay in bed, sweating and delirious. Someone clasped his hand. He looked over at her. Winter. No—she looked like Winter, but not quite the same. Zarina. A younger Zarina, whose hair was untouched by grey, whose face was screwed up in misery. His heart filled with sadness.

Behind her, through the window, he saw a light, growing brighter and brighter—

Shift. He was somewhere cold, dark. The very air weighed on his lungs. He tried to sit up and knocked his head on something hard.

A tomb. He was in a tomb.

The knowledge hit him with certainty, but the fear did not come with it. His hands sought the lid of the coffin and pushed. Light sliced across his vision. The coffin lid crashed to the ground, cracking with a sound like the earth breaking open.

He had died, he knew. Yet he was not dead. He still had so much work to do. His heart filled with hope.

He pulled himself from the tomb and went in search of Zarina.

***

Chris blinked. He was slouched in his chair, head against the wall. He must have nodded off. Terribly embarrassing to do something like that in company. "Sorry." He tried to sit up. Only then did he notice Winter was holding his hand.

Her brown eyes were filled with worry. Then red blazed up her cheeks as she realized he was awake. She dropped his hand. "What happened?" She busied herself with taking cookies and sugar cubes.

"Sorry, love." Zarina sipped her tea and smiled at him over the rim. "You must understand, you're the first boy our Winter's brought home."

"*Mum.*"

Zarina continued unperturbed. "I wanted to get a good handle on you. What did you see?"

"I saw… you," he realized. "And also him. Father Christmas. I think."

"Tell me," Zarina said.

He did. She listened and held up a slender finger when Winter started to interrupt. When he was done, she nodded. "Do take some tea, dear. I promise it won't happen again. And help yourself to the biscuits."

He was thirsty, he realized suddenly. He took three biscuits and a large swallow of tea. The biscuits crumbled in his mouth. The tea tasted faintly of rose.

"And you saw nothing else?" When he shook his head, she *tsked*. "Interesting. Well, it might explain why you can see us when others can't. Nicholas may have tasked you with being a sort of emergency mythological heir, since certain young ladies in the room want nothing to do with it." She arched an eyebrow at her daughter.

"Dad's not dead, so Chris is no heir," Winter said, glaring at Chris as though he suggested it. He shrugged. "And neither am I."

Zarina ignored her and focused on Chris. "What you saw is the story of my husband. He was dedicated to helping others, especially those who could not help themselves. He was filled with such fire…" She shook her head, smiling as though remembering something from long ago. "I think it's what made him a saint, in the end. And it's certainly what made him a Myth. Well, that and the comet."

70

"A comet?" Chris said.

"Yeah. A comet struck right when Dad died," Winter said. "It's what's responsible for all of—" she waved a hand. "This."

"That's not entirely true. If your father hadn't become the Myth, someone else would have. People are always looking for a good story, and they'll find one to embellish just about any way they can."

"Did the comet also create the other one? The anti-Christmas?" Chris asked.

"Krampus," Winter corrected him, and she filled her mum in on their fight and flight in the sleigh between bites of biscuit.

Zarina's face clouded over. She poured him some more tea, which he took with a suspicious nod. "Krampus came later, another story turned to Myth. He never seemed that powerful before, but now..." She sighed and looked over at the couch, where Nicholas lay sprawled. "There's no doubt this is Krampus' work. He has a unique obsession with your father, which I don't suppose is surprising since they share such polar opposites of the spirit of Christmas and want their own versions to win. And, of course, he stands for everything Nicholas does not. Fear, anger, selfishness. He wants to gain power through fearful obedience."

She stood up and went over to the couch where Rosie lay curled next to Nicholas. Zarina unbuttoned Nicholas's coat and probed at the wound beneath. Her nose wrinkled. "Get me a cloth and a bowl of water," she said.

Winter fetched it, and Zarina dabbed at the entry point until the skin was more or less clean. Blood still leaked sluggishly from the wound, refusing to coagulate. And three dark tendrils snaked away from it, spreading over Nicholas's chest.

"He was worried about Krampus," Zarina said. "Said something about a scheme to capture children and harvest fear. And fear is, sadly, easy to spread and hard to fight. If Krampus can keep your father out of the way, he can do a lot of damage in a very short time."

"So, we need that resurrection kit," Winter said.

"Hang on. What do you mean about captured children?" said Chris.

"I don't know much. But I do know he was out on an emergency flight tonight. If I had to guess, I'd say he found one of the children. Or more. One of his special powers is that he can locate any human in the world. Only Krampus seems to have found a way to hide these ones."

Chris took another biscuit. Ottie snuffled between his feet for the crumbs. "That sounds like a great power to have. Really useful."

"Winter can do it too," Zarina said.

"No, I can't," said Winter. She shifted, uncomfortable, then sighed and unclipped the harness that held her axes. She took off her belt, too, folding it all up and putting it on the couch. "I can only locate people I've met before. Mum thinks I'm not trying hard enough."

"I *know* you're not trying hard enough," Zarina said sweetly. "I'm your mother, don't tell me what you can and can't do."

That strange lightness, the same fire he'd felt in the vision of Nicholas, was curling inside him now. Trying to grow. Trying to reach out. "What if we can do it? What if we can find the kids?"

Winter shook her head at him in warning. But he knew this was the right thing to do. In many ways, it was the only thing to do. "It was important to your father, wasn't it? And your mum says you can find them—"

"Yeah, thanks for that, Mum. Maybe you shouldn't listen to her. Maybe you should listen to me when I tell you I *can't.*"

"It is difficult," said Zarina. Her face was kind but serious now. "But I will help you."

"Don't you want to try? For your dad, at least?" Chris said.

"I want to *resurrect* my dad. The kid stuff is his job. It's what he's good at. Not me." Winter's eyes were wider now. She sounded close to panic.

Zarina put a hand on her daughter's shoulder. She opened her mouth, thought for a moment, then said, "No matter what, your father would be proud of you for trying."

Winter stared down at the body on the couch. Her eyebrows drew together, and her mouth turned down. "That's what I'm afraid of."

She sat at the table again, and Chris and Zarina took up chairs to either side of her. Zarina offered her hand, and Winter took it. Gripped it hard, Chris noticed. For all her sighing and grumbling, she was afraid, and she wanted her Mum's support.

"Focus," Zarina said gently. Winter closed her eyes and breathed slowly. The line between her eyebrows became more pronounced. Zarina closed her eyes, too, breathing deep and even.

Chris wasn't sure what to do, so he took another biscuit. The crunch sounded like a crash in the sudden quiet of the room, so he put it on his plate and folded his hands. The electric kettle clicked in the kitchen.

For many long moments, there was silence. Then Winter exhaled. "Nothing," she said. She sounded frustrated.

"Maybe you can't concentrate. Maybe you need another egg—"

"*Mum,*" Winter grated. A muscle worked in her jaw. "Let's try again."

She closed her eyes. Chris waited. A vein throbbed in her temple. Her scowl became fiercer, and her knuckles whitened where her fingers clasped her mother's. "It's no use," she said, eyes still shut tight.

"Hey," said Chris gently, surprising himself. He put a hand on her shoulder. "It's all right. It's going to be all right—"

Memory came to him, as if it had been pulled from the back of his mind. Running through the snow, howling with laughter. Snowballs pelting around him. Rare pocket money jingling like bells. Winter sucked in a breath and stiffened. Rosie and Ottie sat up. Ottie started to howl.

The light in the room shifted and dimmed. At first, Chris thought someone had turned off the lamp. But all the light was sucking into the mirror above the table, which had turned pitch black.

Winter and Zarina opened their eyes. Winter's were wide with wonder.

The picture in the mirror began to resolve, but the lighting was still dim. Yet they could make out the shape of a head, cradled in two hands. A child's head.

"He's far away," Zarina murmured.

"London," Winter replied. "I recognize the feel of London."

"Focus on that feeling," Zarina ordered. "Can you get more specific? Can you find out *where* in London?"

Chris could swear he heard a dripping noise. And sniffling. It echoed in the space. Wherever they were, it was somewhere big.

The child looked up. His brown curls were matted, his blue eyes red. They bulged with fear, and he scrambled back, away from the frame. Black oozed over the picture, and he disappeared from sight. The connection snapped.

The black wasn't finished with them yet. It dripped like warm tar, overflowing the edges of the mirror and gliding down the gold frame. Winter hissed. Zarina shot to her feet as the black solidified and merged, becoming a long finger. She seized the top of the mirror and brought it down from the wall. It smashed to the floor, scattering glass. Ottie leapt onto Chris' lap, barking furiously.

Zarina's mouth was a thin pale line as she stomped down on the mirror again and again. The rug under her foot smoked wherever the shadow figure had touched it. When all remnants of the figure had disappeared, she put her hands on her hips and sighed. "Well. That's a shame." She bent down and wrapped the mirror in the rug. "Be a love, won't you Chris, and fetch my bin bags from under the sink. It'll all have to go, I'm afraid. Lovely mirror. But needs must."

Winter shoved her hands into her dark hair. Her mouth worked and she was breathing hard through her nose. She started to pace.

"Calm down, love, you'll walk a hole in my floor," Zarina said as Chris rummaged under the sink. "Have some tea."

"This is exactly why I didn't want to do it. I'm no good. Now we have no clue where the kid is, *and* Krampus spotted us. What if he comes here when we're gone?"

Zarina flapped a hand. "Please. His dark elves got lucky, that's all. Once I dispose of their entry point, they'll be hard-pressed to find another. Your father and I worked a lot of protections into our safe houses over the years."

"I just..." Winter stopped. She flung herself on the couch, sending Rosie flying. Rosie scrambled to regain her dignity and sought out Winter's lap. "I can't do this. I can't be him. I keep failing. I've always failed." She drew one knee up and rested her forehead against it. Her hand tangled in Rosie's ears.

Zarina hefted the broken mirror and smoking rug into the bin bag, then went over to the sofa and sat next to Winter. "Winter, my love. Feet off the sofa, we're not animals." Winter flopped back.

"Being a Myth is in your blood. As are your powers. And you've failed no one. Perhaps we didn't get all the information we'd hoped, but we know something we didn't know before. And that counts for something."

Winter spoke to the ceiling. "But now Krampus has information too, doesn't he? He knows we know about the kids. And he'll make a move. So, the best plan, the fastest plan, is to find a way to get Dad back."

Zarina put a hand on Winter's shoulder. "Your father never intended to live forever, you know." Winter tensed. "But I think you're right. Bringing your father back is the fastest way to stop this plan here and now. Fortunately, you only need one thing from his resurrection kit to really bring him back, though I'm sure he'd appreciate the paracetamol for the headache. Unfortunately, the thing you need is protected from people like us."

Winter looked over at her. Her nose wrinkled. "So why are you smiling like that?"

"Because fortunately, I know how to get it." Zarina probed at her husband's chest. "Listen carefully. Your father was killed by a knife made from the Apollonius meteorite. The meteorite that fell the night he died. You'll need its sister-knife."

"Which is where?" Winter asked.

"The British Museum." Zarina arched an eyebrow. "Where else?"

CHAPTER EIGHT

The British Museum. Chris had been twice, on school trips. "Sounds fun."

Winter curled her lip. "Yeah. Fun. Well, at least I'll be stealing something from the colonisers, for a change. Thanks for the tea, Mum. We'll take it from here."

"Not yet." Zarina was amused but firm. "The British Museum isn't a random house or park. You can't ignore locks. Myths have worked there, and they've put in security that will stop even our kind. You're going to have to get a special key, a key that will open the case without anyone noticing you're opening the case. And for that, you'll need to visit a friend of mine."

She got to her feet and went over to the television. It sat above a little wood cabinet, and the wood groaned and squeaked as she coaxed a drawer open. She picked up a metal box and flipped the lid. Her fingers *snicked* against index cards as she flipped through them.

"My mum must be the last person in existence who uses a Rolodex," Winter said.

"Mrs Pavuka uses one too," Zarina said.

"Mum, you know I hate Mrs Pavuka."

Zarina only smiled.

Chris took out the broken mirror, slinging it into a big bin around the back of the museum. Glass slid, tinkling, into the cracks of the skip, but when he peered he saw no trace of the tarry shadows that Zarina had called dark elves. He snorted the sweet-rot scent of the bin out of his nose and went out toward the street, shivering a little. He'd forgotten to put his coat back on.

He was grateful that he could still see the door to the apartment, and he went back in without incident. Zarina sat at the little table with an index card between two fingers and her tea in her other hand.

"You're going to the house of Iain Ross. He knows more about Myths than most Myths. He'll understand your predicament. He might even be able to help you with other things. Like your powers, Winter."

Winter was strapping on her axes. "My powers work fine," she muttered. She rubbed her eye. Makeup smudged in a crescent over her cheek. She looked exhausted. Chris, used to the night shift and high on the thrill of being in another country for the first time in his life, hadn't crashed yet. But it was only a matter of time.

Zarina looked back and forth between them. "And where do you think you're going?"

"To London. To your friend. It's nearly Christmas."

"And you'll do what? Knock on his door at three in the morning?" Zarina's lips pursed at the look on her daughter's face. "Don't you dare, Winter Noelle. Besides, all of you are tired. Ottie and Rosie aren't meant to pull the sleigh like that, and Chris will fall out if you make him travel all the way back to London now. You'll stay here and go to London after breakfast."

"Mum." Winter gestured at Nicholas. "We're on the clock."

"Trust me, you're *not* going to get into the British Museum before it opens. I'll make up the couch for you, Chris."

Chris eyed the bleeding Father Christmas. "I'm fine on the floor," he said.

Zarina clicked her tongue. "Boys. We'll move him, darling, don't be a stick. Winter, you can share the bed with me. Chris, there are linens in the wardrobe next to the door."

Chris fetched the linens and a blanket while they rolled Nicholas off the couch and pulled it out into a bed. Zarina rummaged until she found two spare toothbrushes. "Good night," he said as Zarina went into her bedroom.

"Good night, dear," Zarina said. She sounded fond. Chris had always been good with mums. Had something to do with being decent, he supposed.

Winter made to follow.

"Winter?" he said.

She paused at the door. She'd borrowed one of her mum's shirts to sleep in and pulled her hair into a messy braid. The whole thing made her look softer somehow. He forgot what he'd wanted to say. "Is your middle name really Noelle?" he blurted.

"Shut up, Christmas."

She shook her head and went in. As the door clicked shut, he heard Zarina say, "Whatever happened to the reindeer?"

"No clue," Winter replied.

Ottie had followed Zarina and Winter into the bedroom. Rosie sat on the made-up couch bed, looking soulfully at him. He patted her on the head and her tail thumped. Her hair was silky-soft. "So, you aren't a secret reindeer," he said.

She cocked her head and gave him a look that said, *Of course not.*

Chris lay down on crisp linens that smelled faintly of roses. He thought it would be impossible to sleep while a man who was mostly corpse lay on the floor at the end of his bed. He was wrong. His thoughts swirled like snow, confused and scattered, and it wasn't long before he sank into oblivion.

***

They flew back across the Mediterranean early the next morning, squeezed in three to the bench again. Winter had insisted on bringing her father along. "We might not have moments to spare, to fly back to Turkey," she'd said. Now she stared at the map as it took them closer and closer to Iain Ross. Up ahead Rosie and Ottie trotted, tongues lolling. Ottie had given Winter a dirty look this morning, though, when she'd told him to stand in front of the sleigh.

"Yes, you have to go," Zarina had told him firmly. He whined. "But I don't expect them to keep themselves out of trouble. You know what she's like, always needs looking after." Then she'd shaken her head. "Make sure you listen to the dogs, dear."

Winter groaned. "The dogs don't give good advice." Rosie yipped. "No, you don't."

"I mean it," Zarina said.

Now Winter's voice cut across his thoughts. "You look sick. Are you going to be sick?"

His attention snapped back to her. "Hm?"

"Only, if you're going to be sick, lean way over the side. Dad's already going to be stroppy that I smoked in here."

"I'm not going to be sick," he assured her. "Sorry. I was thinking about something."

She shook her head and leaned back. "You say sorry too much."

Breakfast had been pleasant. Chris was used to Weetabix and PG Tips, not eggs and bread and olives and hummus. He'd chatted with Zarina while Winter drank three cups of tea in quick succession, then disappeared into the bathroom to wash the raccoon look from her eyes and reapply her makeup.

"It's a bit mad, isn't it?" he'd said, looking at the closed bathroom door.

"What is?" Zarina looked amused as she popped an olive in her mouth.

"There's this whole... world, I guess. That I never saw. Then last night, I suddenly got in the middle of it. And in a few days, I'll be out again."

"Hm." Zarina washed the olive down with a long drink of tea. "I wouldn't be so sure about that." She set the cup down and leaned over the table. Her eyes searched his face, but for what, he couldn't guess. "There's something that ties you to my husband. To his story, his myth. You like people, don't you Chris?"

"Who doesn't?" he said.

Zarina laughed. "You've met my daughter. But there's more to it than that. Can you think of any person you don't like? Anyone in the whole world?"

Chris considered. "Putin?"

"Anyone you've met personally."

Chris took the time to consider this as he tucked away two eggs and helped himself to some sharp, salty cheese. "I guess not," he said around bites.

"I didn't think so. You have a goodness in you, Chris, a

goodness that wants to get out. You want to believe the best in everyone. You want to give everyone the chance to be as good as you are, and you want to give them that chance again and again. It's a rare thing."

Chris felt heat up to the tips of his ears. "I'm just trying to be a decent person," he said, looking down.

"Keep going, Chris." He wouldn't look at her, but her hand sneaked across the table and squeezed his in a motherly fashion. Her almond scent wafted across the table with it. "Keep being as decent as you can. You have no idea how important it is."

Now, as they crossed over France and skimmed dismal clouds, Chris wondered. Winter could kill dark elves with at least two kinds of weapon. Being a decent bloke wouldn't have saved his life then.

The snow began again as they crossed the English channel, dancing around the sleigh with less frenzy than when they'd left. "We might get a white Christmas," Chris said, and stuck out his tongue until a cold flake landed on it. "I love a white Christmas."

"Of course, you do." Winter leaned over the map. "We're almost there."

Iain Ross lived in an elegant stuccoed terraced house in Kensington. Rosie and Ottie touched down in the middle of the street outside a tall white façade lined with half-columns, sitting pristine behind a neat, wrought iron fence. The minuscule garden was neatly kept. A Christmas star wreath hung on the door.

They headed up the drive. Chris was glad to be wearing his mourning suit, even if it was wrinkled beyond belief. Winter, on the other hand, looked like she'd come fresh off a rave in Soho. At least no one could see her, right?

"And we're sure he's expecting us?" he said. He hoped Winter didn't pick up on his nervous tones. Then again, why shouldn't he be nervous? Two brown kids looking less than their best, hanging out in a posh neighbourhood in London? That was begging for some nosy neighbour to call the Police.

"Mum said she'd call." Winter tilted her chin up and adopted an imperious look. Then she knocked with three sharp raps.

The door creaked and drifted open.

Chris and Winter exchanged glances.

"This is bad, right?" Chris said.

"Statistical likelihood is high." Winter unbuttoned her coat and slid her arms behind her back, loosening her axes. "Stay behind me, just in case."

Chris didn't need to be told twice. He took one last look behind him at the clear street before stepping after Winter, into the dark of the hallway.

The door shut behind them. "Bollocks," said Winter into the pitch black. Then every light in the world seemed to come on at once.

Chris threw one arm up to shade his eyes. It was a white-bright light, like the heart of a fire, like beach sand on the brightest day of the year. No matter which way he turned, the light was there.

"My apologies," said a deep, weathered voice. "I understand the light's a bit intense."

"Turn it off," Winter growled through gritted teeth.

"I'm afraid I can't do that. It's part of the house's security system, you see. To keep our darkest creepy-crawly associates outside of the residence, where they belong. You, on the other hand, *can* do something about it."

He could? They could? Chris tried to lower his arm, but he could barely see past his feet. The floorboards were a lovely dark wood, and they gleamed with polish. "Did my mother ring you?" Winter called. "Zarina Myra?"

"Indeed, she did. If she is your mother, and this isn't some trick. But if you can demonstrate the mythological powers of your family, it will be much easier to trust you."

"Yeah, light was never my specialty," Winter muttered.

"What do we do?" Chris said.

"*We* don't do anything. *I* try to get us out of this mess. Trust my mum to turn the end of Christmas as we know it into a teachable moment for me. Ugh."

Chris waited. Winter shuffled along the floor, but other than a few sighs and a couple of swears, nothing much changed. At least, not at first. But as he waited, he became slowly aware of a growing feeling in him. That same hooking heat he'd felt when he'd touched Nicholas and the ignition on the sleigh. He was starting to recognize it, and now it felt as though it were calling to him. What if he called back?

He reached out. He could barely keep his eyes open. The light flared. He stumbled back as blackness dotted his vision. "*Shite,*" said Winter. "What was that?"

"Very good," said the voice. "That was a start."

"Er, how do I make it tone down a bit?" he asked.

"The light recognizes you. When you ask, it will obey."

Okay? Okay. Chris took a deep breath. This time he kept his eyes shut tight, but when he extended his hand he imagined the light dimming, dimming to something the size of a candle flame in his palm.

The blaze against his eyelids diminished. "Chris," said Winter wonderingly.

Chris opened his eyes. The unutterable brightness had left the room, and only a small orb of light sat on his open hand.

"How did you do that?" Winter asked.

"You can pass it along, too," the voice told him. "Give it a try."

Chris tipped the orb into Winter's palm, careful as if it were a newborn kitten. She held it up wonderingly. Light slicked off her cheekbones. She breathed deep, and it expanded. She exhaled, and it diminished. Chris tugged, and a little bubble of light popped free of the orb and drifted over to him.

"Could I always do this?" he said.

"*I* couldn't." A troubled look crossed her face like a shadow.

Now that they had tamed the light, they looked around. They stood in a narrow hallway. A stair to their right ran up to the first and second floors. A dark blue door at the end of the hall was shut tight and, Chris suspected, locked. There was an identical door to their left. Right in front of the stairs stood a tall and wide curio cabinet, its glass shelves lined with all sorts: Egyptian statuettes, inlaid boxes, ancient Chinese teapots. A three-foot bird skeleton. The collection of a museum buff.

"Now, Winter, my dear. This is a task for you. Look to the curio cabinet." They looked. "There's something alive in there. Bring it up for me, won't you?"

"Alive?" Winter's lip curled doubtfully. "What is it, mould?"

"Certainly not." He sounded offended.

Her eyes widened and she crossed her arms, sending the light in her hand scattering. "It's not a spider, is it? Because I don't do spiders."

The voice chuckled. It sounded like ripping paper. "No, indeed, and I don't blame you. No spiders, no spiders. Take a look."

Winter opened the cabinet with care. "What's your thing with spiders?" Chris asked.

"Nothing." She stood on tiptoe to examine the top shelf, then moved down, shaking her head as she ticked off items.

"They get a bad rap, really. They eat mosquitos, which are some of the worst things for disease—"

"Shut it," said Winter. Had she put on extra makeup this morning or was she looking unusually pale?

She bent down and examined every item in the curio cabinet, down to an ancient chess piece that had probably cost Iain Ross more than Chris made in a year. She peered inside the Ostrich egg before declaring, "There's nothing alive in here, mate."

"No?"

"Best you've got is this bird." She tapped the beak. The bird in question had a hooked bill, a round cranium and a neck as long as Chris's arm. Its skeletal wings were folded in over its chest.

"Is she not alive?" The voice sounded pleasantly surprised.

Winter, on the other hand, was gearing up for her breathing-fire look. "Come on, old man. We don't have time for games."

"I assure you, this is no game. Your father carried reindeer bones in his pocket and could bring them to life at a moment's notice. Can you not do the same?"

Winter's jaw clenched. "This is *so* Mum's doing," she muttered.

"Let's talk through it together," said Chris. She gave him a dirty look, but he ignored it. He was starting to think that Winter had a very limited stable of expressions. "Focus on one thing at a time. What would your Dad do? Did he ever tell you about it?"

"He tried." Winter bit her lip. "A long time ago, he tried." She ran a finger down the bird's curved beak. "He said that some bones clung to life. They kept a part of it within themselves. And our job was to coax it out. To remind them why life is joyful."

"And why is life joyful?" Chris asked. He thought of years past, of running home with a new school drawing for Mum, of making flower crowns and paper chains. He thought of getting builder's tea for a pound and watching his sister ice skate in the park. So many of the moments after were sheer pain, but that was only because of the joy that had come before.

"Life's not joyful. It's short. And sometimes meaningless. And sometimes brutal. And no matter where you're born, you never do everything you wanted to do, and you always die with some big dream unfulfilled. If I were going to coax a dead thing back, I'd tell it that it gets another chance. It can maybe do all those things it never got to do. Try one more time."

There was a rattle of bones.

Winter and Chris both stared at the skeleton. "Try it again," said Chris. Winter adopted a look of great concentration. Her nostrils flared, and she put her hand flat on the bird's skull.

It shivered. Then it rustled, with a sound like a dozen stones falling down a stair. Then it settled. Her mouth turned down.

"You can do it. I know you can." Chris put an encouraging hand on her shoulder.

Sensation flashed through him, warmth and light and comfort. The bird's beak tilted. Winter gasped and pulled her hand away. It cocked its head at her, fixing her with one round hole where its eye ought to be. Then it hopped down from the cabinet. Its talons clicked on the floor.

"What just happened?" Winter said. Her mouth was half open in surprise.

"You brought it back to life." Chris grinned. She'd really done it.

"Dad's never looked like that. His were always more... fleshy." They turned as the bird bobbed back and forth, bending its long neck to peck at specks of dust on the lacquered wood. Some hundreds of years in one dusty box or another was bound to make it hungry.

"You said it yourself, you're not your dad." She was amazing. Incredible. Intimidatingly powerful.

Winter crouched and reached out a hand. The bird came over and nudged her fingers with its beak. "What's her name?" Winter asked.

"Diedre," said Iain Ross. "Diedre the dodo."

Winter stood and beckoned to Diedre. "Ready to go upstairs then, girl?" she said.

"We're not quite finished," Iain said. "Young man, I have to confess something. You have me utterly flummoxed. I thought I knew every Myth and Little Myth on Earth. But in God's name, who are *you*?"

Chris looked up at the ceiling, as though he could see Iain Ross looking down on him. "Er, Chris."

"*Chris?*" Iain sounded incredulous.

"Yeah. Chris Demer." Chris glanced at Winter. She made a *get a move on* motion with her hands. "We're losing time," she whispered.

"I'm not a Myth of any kind, if that helps."

There was a pause. Then, "Indeed, it does not." Iain sounded amused. "Are you so certain that you're not somehow mythological?"

Chris looked at the dodo bird, clacking around like a sack of pebbles. She was a cute sack of pebbles, in an odd sort of way. Really worked with Winter's look. "Yup. I'm completely normal."

Iain chuckled dryly. "Now in that, I know you are mistaken. This trial is for you. So, *Chris*"—he said it delicately, as if to add *if that really is your name*—"I want you to give Diedre her feathers. Can you do that?"

Chris glanced at Winter. She was scowling, as usual, and gave a little shrug. *Losing time.* "I don't think so," he said honestly.

"What would you do, if you wanted to give her feathers?" Iain asked over the loudspeaker.

Chris crouched and held out his hand as Winter had done.

Diedre came over easily enough. The peck she gave his palm wasn't as pinching as he'd expected and, once she realized that he neither was nor had food, she rubbed her beak on him. She smelled a bit musty. He hoped that was from a decade or two in the curio cabinet, and not from some element of decay. He scratched her skull. It wasn't nearly as satisfying as scratching Rosie behind the ears. *Feathers,* he thought, and tried to focus as he'd pushed Winter to do. How were dodos supposed to look? He drew a finger down her neck, as if he could will feathers into existence in his wake.

Diedre clacked her beak, looking between him and Winter. "I don't think it's doing much."

Iain's voice was slow, considering. "No… and yet you undoubtedly had a hand in Diedre's creation. What… what if you took Winter's hand?"

Winter leaned against the wall. She looked like she needed a cigarette. "Did my mum put you up to this?"

Iain's laugh crackled in the speakers. "I have a little hunch about your friend. Indulge me, won't you? Then you can come up."

Winter heaved a sigh. Then she came over and crouched next to Diedre. She offered her hand, palm out. Chris gently rested his fingers against hers.

He felt it immediately, and by the way she stiffened, so did she. A little *zip* of energy that travelled from his fingers and made the hair rise all along his arms. Memory assaulted him once more: reading stories to Saba under the blanket, helping his Mum as she tried to make a Christmas pudding for the neighbours two floors down.

For a moment, Diedre felt velvet-soft.

"I did *not* like that," Winter said. Chris tried to scrub a blush out of his cheeks. He hadn't minded.

"I… I think I need to try again," he said.

"Fine." She rolled her eyes to the ceiling and grabbed his hand.

The *zip* shot through him again, flowing through his other arm and into the bird. This time, though, he tried to ignore the memories that came with it and followed that thread back, toward Winter. He started to pull. Power unravelled, flooding his body and flowing out into Diedre. A soft flush of downy feathers rippled into existence over her skeleton. She squawked. Chris drew in a sharp breath. The feathers quickened in hue, turning grey and blue. Her eye socket filled and the tip of her beak blackened. Yellow skin washed over her feet.

"Ow. *Ow.*" Winter pulled on her hand.

"Let go," Iain Ross said, quickly and seriously.

Chris let go. The feathers dropped from Diedre's body to create a cloud of fluff on the floor. She was a skeleton again.

"Are you all right?" Chris wanted to take her by the shoulder. But what if he put her in pain again?

Winter leaned back and eyed him warily as she massaged her chest. "I think I'll be." She looked at the loudspeaker in the corner. "So, what is that? The power of electrocution? I'm all buzzy, and my ribs hurt."

"Come up, and I will tell you," Iain said.

Diedre pecked—a little sadly, Chris thought—at her feathers. But Winter said, "Come on, you," and the dodo hopped up the stairs. Winter followed, and Chris trailed behind, confused. Had he suddenly become dangerous?

The first floor was a grand open-plan kitchen and sitting area with a blue sofa and two leather armchairs, floored with the same dark wood as the hall downstairs. Wide glass windows looked out onto the snow-dusted roofs of Kensington. Against every wall was a bookcase, and every bookcase was stuffed. Stacks of books shared space with a variety of curious objects: reptile skeletons, carved heads, pieces of parchment and papyrus carefully kept behind glass.

In one of the armchairs sat a slim, elderly man with a few strands of brown in his white hair. His eyes sparkled behind a pair of reading glasses, and he was dressed in a crisp collared shirt and sweater, and fine dark trousers that wouldn't have looked out of place at a wedding. Chris was starting to feel like a second-rate magician in his abused suit.

"Welcome," said Iain Ross. "Do help yourselves to some tea. My knee's acting up, I'm afraid, but cups are above the dishwasher and the tea shelf is in the next cabinet over. I highly recommend the Souchong."

Chris hoped that was another word for English Breakfast. He went over to the kitchen, all black marble and oak countertops, and found three cups and the Souchong, which was neatly labelled. At first, he was afraid that a cup would shatter under his touch, but as he pulled everything down the ritual of it began to soothe him.

As he made three cups, Iain started to talk to Winter. "I was sorry to hear about your father. I've known him for a good while, at least in human years."

"How do you know about us?" Winter sounded curious.

"Humans who become aware of Myths usually do so through contact: either direct contact with a Myth who chooses to be seen, or indirect contact—a meaningful object to their story, a bit of their blood, et cetera. I met your father because I became the curator for a very particular series of objects at the British Museum. The very same series I believe you're looking for now." He raised an eyebrow.

Winter leaned forward and put a hand on her belt, as though she were considering drawing her knives. "The Apollonion knife. Give it."

"I'm afraid I can't. The knife's in the British Museum, and I am here. I hope you see the problem."

Winter's fingers started to drum a tattoo on her sides. "Yeah," she said. She sounded calm, but Chris spotted the twitching of her jaw and retreated to a spot on the couch far away from her. "I do see the problem. Some old white men stole *my dad's* stuff, and now it's time to give it back."

Iain regarded her for a moment with a hooded expression. Then he laughed. "Your mother warned me you don't mess about," he said, and reached out to take a cup from Chris. Chris tried to angle it so that their fingers wouldn't touch. "Don't worry about that," said Iain, and patted him on the wrist. "I don't think you can activate this power by accident. I'll tell you all about it in a moment, but for now I need to convince young Miss Myra that we're on the same side." He took a sip of tea and smiled at Winter.

Winter looked like she very much doubted him, but she took her tea too.

"When I was first entrusted with care of the kit, he paid me a visit. I don't think he realized I'd be able to see him. 'What're you doing here?' I asked him. He must've jumped three feet." Iain chuckled.

"He let you keep it?" Winter said.

"Believe it or not, the British Museum is one of the safest places on the planet, especially from less savoury Myths. I had no intention of leaving my post, so I made a deal with Nick. I told him I'd keep it safe, with the agreement that should he need it during my lifetime, I would hand it over and handle the fallout." He looked at the bookcase next to him. "Chris, my friend. On the top shelf, there is a box. Get it for me, won't you?"

The box was smooth and plain, made of a dark wood and polished until it glowed. Chris handed it to Iain and the old man opened it up. He picked up a little stub of iron. "The key to the exhibition case," he said, and held it out.

Winter plucked it from his fingers. "That's it?"

"Oftentimes, the best magic isn't flashy. Subtlety is an art, and one earned wisely," Iain told her. She sat back, sipped her tea, and frowned at the key in her hand.

"I have a question," Chris said.

Iain inclined his head.

"I saw Father—er, Nicholas—before I ever touched anything of his. He was a dead body at a crime scene. Everyone could see him, actually."

"It may be that he chose to become visible in his final moments of consciousness," Iain said. "Or it could be that Myths become visible when they die. I've never seen it happen before, so I'm afraid I cannot say. But you could see Winter…"

"Maybe because I'd already touched Nick by then," Chris said.

"Perhaps. But that doesn't explain your powers."

"My power to…" he glanced at Winter. She rubbed the spot over her heart as if remembering. "My power to kill people?"

"Zarina told me you powered and drove the sleigh. That takes some power of belief, and some, shall we call it… Christmas spirit. And now, you brought Diedre back to life."

"Well, *Winter* brought Diedre back to life…" Chris said as Winter snorted.

"Winter had the ability. But it seems you have the *power.*" Iain tapped his lips with his finger and regarded Chris critically. "When you put your hand on her shoulder, Diedre started to move. And when the two of you joined forces, Diedre started to become *complete.*"

Diedre, busy pecking at the bottom of a potted plant, looked up at the mention of her name.

"But it felt awful," Winter said. "I thought my heart would squeeze right out."

"Yes…" Iain frowned. "I need a battery and a light bulb. Fetch them for me, lad?"

Chris followed his directions and found a watch battery in a kitchen drawer. Iain couldn't remember where his housekeeper kept the bulbs so, in the end, Chris turned off the kitchen light and carefully unscrewed a little spotlight from over the kitchen table. "Hold the battery in one hand and the bulb in the other," Iain told him when he was back on the couch. "Now make the light glow."

Chris sat, feeling a right fool. He looked at the battery, then at the light bulb. And he thought, *Okay, on.*

And it was as though the lightbulb heard him. It flickered on with an electric hum. The battery grew hot in his hand, and he dropped it in surprise. The light bulb brightened a second or two longer before dimming again.

Iain Ross' eyes were bright. He pushed his half-moon glasses up his nose. "You are a conduit, if I had to make an educated guess. You make things stronger. Powers, belief, even feelings, I'd wager…" He petered off and took a sip of tea, though his eyes never left Chris. Chris felt like an item in a collection. It was off-putting. He drank some of his own tea to distract himself. Not English Breakfast, this, but not bad. It had a delicate, flowery scent, and a clear taste that didn't need milk.

They sat in silence for a few moments. At last, though, Chris had to put the cup down. He had a question, and Iain Ross seemed the most likely person to have the answer. "Why me?" he asked. "I could never do all this before. Why me, and why now?"

Iain glanced at Winter. His eyes no longer twinkled behind his spectacles. They were somber, thoughtful. "There is one possibility," he said. He spoke as though he were picking his words carefully out of a lineup. "In some cases, when a Myth is in crisis and there is no heir, it's said that a human is drawn in. Nicholas of Myra became a Myth because he was needed as a force for good in this world. And perhaps, now that he's dying, perhaps *you* are needed as that force for good."

"He's not replacing my dad," Winter said in short, clipped tones. She glared at Iain, then at Chris. "And Dad's not dying."

Chris put his hands up. There was a stain on his suit cuff, he saw with chagrin. "I agree. I'm not some force for good. I'm doing my best, sure, but—"

"That's the ticket, Chris," said Iain, and he smiled. He had a nice smile, Chris thought. The perfect smile to bestow on grandchildren. "A lot of people say they're doing their best. But I think you're one of the few people who *is* doing his best, with all he has, every day." He took a sip of tea and cleared his throat. "You'd best face facts, my young friends. No matter the reason, Chris is coming into powers. If necessary, he *will* become Father Christmas. Right now, he's a conduit, and that's a major power in itself. You can boost the power of other Myths, but you will also be able to access a Myth's powers for yourself, as you did with Diedre. You could even use Winter or myself as a battery."

Winter leaned back and crossed her arms protectively. Iain laughed at her scowl. "Don't worry, Winter. We won't be doing that today. It's quite dangerous if unsupervised. You can easily drain a person, Chris. Never use another human as your battery, and *especially* never yourself. Everyone thinks it's a good idea at the time. Then suddenly you're dealing with new mythological heirs and unplanned bodies that need disposal."

Chris tucked his hands under his thighs.

Iain leaned back. "I am an old man, so you will forgive me if I don't have the energy to conduct further lessons. However, if all goes well, you'll have your father back by noon, Winter, and he can continue in my stead. Please, finish your tea. At ten, the Museum will open for a special Do with a bunch of rotter politicians. That's the best time to slip in, I'd say."

Winter checked the large clock that hung above the mantle. "That's two hours away."

"Well, you can always check in with Mrs Pavuka," Iain said. "I heard she got her hands on an Apollonius knife."

"Absolutely not," Winter said shortly.

Iain's lips twitched. "I hardly blame you. But aside from Mrs Pavuka, I only know of one place with a relic that can revive your father. And until it opens, you are quite welcome to sit and indulge yourselves with my fine tea selection."

"It's a good idea," Chris said, putting a little tea on his saucer and setting it down for Diedre. Her beak clacked as she investigated it. "We can make a plan."

"I already have a plan." Winter's arms wrapped around her like a hug, touching the axe handles on her back. "Head in, get the relic, head out."

"And what about security?" Chris said.

Winter laughed. "I've never had a problem with security in my life. And now that I have this…" she held up the little iron key, then tucked it in her pocket. "We'll be fine."

CHAPTER NINE

Arthur Stowe took a big sip of scalding coffee and tried not to sputter. He stood outside the British Museum itself, holding his takeaway cup for warmth and wishing he'd woken early enough for a shower and shave.

He'd overslept, and then he'd blearily called Mr Borson, the curator of ancient Anatolian art and artefacts at the British Museum. Borson had been one of the few people to take Arthur seriously when he'd been investigating the cult angle. He'd worried Borson would be irritated by his phone call Christmas Eve, but the fellow was only too happy to invite him down to the office for a chat.

"It's quite a serious case, isn't it?" he'd said. "Awful stuff. Can't be too proactive. Besides, there's a horrid party scheduled for today, MPs coming to congratulate themselves and demand to touch the Rosetta Stone and such. Consulting the police sounds like a grand excuse to avoid them all."

As Arthur watched a black car spit out the Minister of State for Transport and his girlfriend, both fresh and sparkling like a newly frosted morning, he wondered idly: did *anyone* like politicians?

"Detective Inspector!" Arthur turned to see Mr Borson trotting down the steps, dressed in a black and periwinkle three-piece suit and surprisingly lively for a man who'd been on the brink of retirement for twenty years. His grip was firm as they shook hands, and his eyes and voice were both clear. Even his hair was a dark, even brown, though Arthur suspected chemical assistance for that. "Pleasure to meet you again. Though, of course, I wish it were under different circumstances."

Arthur nodded. He chucked the last of his over-bitter coffee into a rubbish bin near the security tent and followed Borson inside, nodding to a scowling guard as he passed. He didn't exactly fit the dress code with his plainclothes coat and burgeoning beard.

The white-on-white atrium sported a small Christmas tree near the entrance and a thick band of green around the library in the centre. People stood in small clusters, the men in their dark suits, the women bursts of colour in their morning dresses. They held mimosas and little canape plates filled with fragrant brunch sausages and mince pies. Their footsteps clapped on the floor, and their conversation doubled and mixed into an unintelligible cacophony underscored by Handel's *Messiah*. Their smiles were wide and false. Lord, even politicians didn't like politicians.

"I see right away why you made the connection," Mr Borson was saying. "The shards—you did bring the shards, didn't you? — are almost certainly the same material as the Anatolian Ram you called me about last year. Or was it the year before?"

"And you said there's another artifact? Made from the same stone?" Arthur said.

"Without testing, I can promise you nothing," Borson warned. "But the look is quite unique. It's made from meteorite, you see. The geologists can get more specific, but I can tell you that comets have often had a special significance in religious and spiritual superstition."

Arthur let Borson talk as they crossed the atrium and headed through the Egyptian section. He went on for a bit about the history of the knife and how it came to the Museum, then flashed a keycard at a closed door. It unlocked with a click.

"Recently we've had some minister who wants to look at it all the time," Borson said. He sounded grumpy. "Going on and on about heritage and preservation, using it as an example of Britain's ancient material culture, as though we found it at Sutton Hoo or some such." He snorted. Arthur only understood about sixty percent of Borson's words, but he narrowed his eyes. Which minister, exactly, was interested in this object?

Borson's office held a fine old teak desk, a leather chair, and a computer that looked as though it had been bought in the eighties. Stacks of books, papers and notepads covered every inch. A bookcase behind the desk had more of the same. As they entered,

Arthur shut the door behind them while Borson started to clear space on his desk. He picked up a small figurine of a lady, arms crossed over her bare chest. A triangle carved into her lower half denoted hips and thighs.

"Fertility statue. Isn't she beautiful?" he beamed. Arthur nodded. "She has a large supporting role in my current research. But let's have a look at what you brought, shall we? Who knows? I might get a paper out of it." He set the statue carefully on the shelf behind him.

Arthur removed the handkerchief from his pocket and handed it over. Borson took it into his steady open palm and nudged a stack of books with his other hand until he could set the handkerchief down on his desk.

He stared for a few long moments at the shards. Then he opened a drawer in his desk and fetched out a magnifying glass. "Remarkable," he said. "All these jagged edges; it must have struck something with tremendous force."

"It did fall from a great height," Arthur said.

"Well, the geologists might say something different when they come back from holiday. But there's no doubt in *my* mind it's the same stone. You see these little pieces, here? Like shards of mica?" Arthur bent over. Borson ran a finger delicately along one glimmering edge. "They're dead ringers for the ceremonial knife."

Ceremonial knife. And a stabbing victim stolen from the mortuary. "Can I see that knife?" Arthur said.

"Naturally. It's on display. I hope we won't have to lend it out for the investigation, you understand how fragile these things are." Borson's eye was glued to the magnifying glass. "It's one of three recorded ceremonial knives from a dig in Myra in 1929. One knife's in a private collection, some little old lady who won't give it up. One went missing in the fifties... I wonder if we've found it now." He poked the shards again.

"They're sharp," Arthur warned him.

"Amazing, isn't it?" Borson turned over his hand and showed off a scar that ran straight across his palm like a second lifeline. "I got this handling what I suspect is the sister knife. Almost two thousand years in the ground, and they—"

A high-pitched wail cut them off. Borson closed his hand reflexively. His blue eyes widened. "Dear me."

"What is it?" Arthur asked, though he was pretty sure he knew already.

"It's a security alarm. Someone has tried to access an artefact."

Why couldn't these academics just say *burglary?*

Arthur looked at the shards. He looked at Borson. It could be a coincidence. Then again, a good detective never assumed coincidence. "Where's the knife?" he said. "What exhibit? Can you show me?"

Borson went pale and shot to his feet. "This way," he said.

They pelted up a staircase. Borson could run fast when he was worried about his precious artefacts, Arthur had to give him that. Human sounds receded around them as the ministers and their plus ones filed out of the museum, no doubt grumbling at their ruined morning. And then only the siren was left, grating against Bach.

At the top of the stairs, they came into a gallery lit by a few safety bulbs. They raced through rooms featuring friezes, vases, and statues. As they entered a room with an azure lion frieze on the wall, they stopped. The double doors before them were closed, and security guards stood to either side.

The first thing Arthur noticed about them were their eyes. Was it because the rooms were poorly lit? Or was it more that those eyes were black all the way through, as though their pupils had expanded too far? He found himself reaching for his truncheon.

One guard fixed Mr Borson with his too-dark stare. His expression was haughty and cruel. "All right, sir? We've a bit of a security issue at the moment. Please go down to the atrium and step outside."

Borson gestured. "My colleague is with the London Metropolitan Police. You will allow him through."

"Can't do that, sir." The other guard smiled briefly, flashing teeth that looked too sharp to be human. A shiver made its way down Arthur's spine. "Blackout protocol. No one in, no one out until the targets have been neutralized."

Borson drew himself up to his full height, which was still half a head shorter than the beefy guards. "I've been working here longer than you've been alive, and I'll have you know there's no such thing as a blackout protocol."

The guards exchanged amused glances. Something in their collars seemed to shift. Muscles? The very shadows? "Times change, sir," said the first one.

The door behind him moved a fraction. It was closed and guarded, Arthur realized, but it wasn't locked.

He took a deep breath. He stepped back, trying to look nonchalant. "Really, I'd love to help. But I'd hate to get in the way of your hardworking security." He nodded to them, as one professional to the other.

Then he ran at them.

They were too surprised to do anything other than shout. Fingers brushed the back of his coat, but Arthur's instincts were right: the door wasn't locked, and he crashed through, hoping he hadn't destroyed something priceless as he dove to the floor.

Something whizzed over his head. Arthur covered it and looked up in time to see a figure swirling away from him. She held something in her hand. An axe.

I can't believe this is how I die, he thought, and curled up in the foetal position.

"Oh, get out of the way," said a very annoyed young woman's voice.

He looked up. She'd leaned over him to swing her axe. In the other she held a lamp of some kind.

"Wait a second," he realized as he took in her dark dress and dark hair.

She wasn't paying him any mind. She held the lamp aloft and the light intensified. "Hurry up, Chris."

"Look, I'm sorry, but this is extremely fiddly," said another voice. "Are you sure we just insert the key?"

"I'm going to break the glass."

"Don't you *dare*, Winter, this is a *museum.*" Arthur could see him now that the other figure—Winter, he guessed—had moved away. It was undoubtedly the young undertaker.

"We wouldn't have to do things my way if you hadn't triggered the alarms," Winter growled. "I have *never* had a problem taking from museums before."

"You, you…" the undertaker sputtered. "You steal from museums?"

"And what's more, I put whatever I take back. Where it *belongs*," Winter said.

Arthur had heard enough. He clambered to his feet. His shoe nudged something dark and sludgy on the floor. It looked as though there were no other guards in here, living or dead. The ones outside must be on the payroll. He wondered idly why they hadn't come in after him. "I love hearing a confession. You're under arrest," he told Winter, and pulled out his father's truncheon. It was no axe, but it was better than nothing.

A strange red glow began to fill the room.

The girl backed up and held her lamp high. Her face drew tight. Behind her, the boy held up his hand. Light appeared in it, too. What the hell kind of lamp was that?

"He's here," Winter said.

The boy turned as though protecting the case. Behind him, Arthur spotted the knife, glimmering red and green and opalescent.

He raised his truncheon. "All right, you two. Drop the weapons, come quietly. There's no way you're getting out of here. Not this time."

The girl's eyes flicked to his. "Wait. You can see us?"

The undertaker gestured wildly. "I thought no one could see you. How can no one see you until the *one worst time*—"

The shadows sprung up.

Arthur had no other explanation for it. They shifted in the light and recoiled as Winter held her lamp out, but one wriggled from behind the door and grabbed her wrist, forcing her arm down and dimming the light. She yelled and swung her axe again. The shadow split in half and thrashed violently. It retreated. Then two more sprouted in its place.

What?

"I need my other axe. Hold the light," Winter called, and pulled the second axe free. The light disappeared from her hand as though it had never been there.

Arthur had no time to wonder, for the girl moved. She lunged and hooked her axe blade around a wriggling tendril not two feet from Arthur, then brought it in to chop with her other axe. Then she swung around in time to come down on a shadow that had appeared around the corner of a display. The axe glanced off the glass with a *clang* and Arthur hissed involuntarily.

He was used to handling belligerent drunks, not well-trained medieval reenactors. He squared his shoulders and held the truncheon up. "What're the odds you'll come quietly?"

She looked at him and a shadow thing took advantage of her distraction to snake one limb around her throat. She kicked fiercely against a mass behind her until its hold broke, then turned around and punched with her axe. The blade came away glowing, little rivulets like sunlight running down its burnished gunmetal surface.

She turned back and gave him a once-over. Good Lord, the younger generation didn't skimp on their disdain. "With you? Nowhere. Now stay out of the way."

"Uh, Winter?" Chris called. He held his light out in front of him, concentrating. It flickered and it took Arthur a moment to see why: a shadow had wrapped up his arm and was trying to slither into his ear. He pulled at it futilely.

Arthur was lost on a lot of things, but there was one thing he knew: he wanted these two down at the station, and he wanted them alive. He didn't know what these shadow things were, and he wanted them out of the picture. So, for now, he was on the kids' side.

"Hold still," Winter said.

She drew back her arm. At the same time a shadow reared up behind her. As she released, Arthur sprang. He clubbed the shadow thing on its head, half expecting his truncheon to pass through it like air. But it didn't—it connected with a soft *schlop* and sank halfway in. It felt like hitting jelly.

Winter's axe left her hand. It made one and a half rotations in

99

the air, passed neatly through the gap between Chris's arm and his ear, and crashed into the glass, severing the shadow along the way. There was a great crash and Chris flew to the side. "What the *hell*?" he yelled.

"Get the knife. Now," she snapped.

Something hit Arthur from behind and he went down.

A soft and viscous tendril wrapped around his neck. It felt like tar with a mission of vengeance. Arthur struggled and flipped himself around. He tried to jab his attacker's throat. His fingers pierced a black void where a neck should be.

Then his skin started to burn.

Everywhere the shadow creature touched him seared like fire. Blisters formed and broke on his neck. He gurgled and tasted blood in the back of his throat.

On second thoughts, he was ready to die by the axe.

Light erupted in his vision. At first Arthur thought it was that tunnel people were always going on about. Then he heard a hiss of pain, and the fingers withdrew from his neck. He was no longer pinned down. A body moved into view, and he recognized the shabby suit of the undertaker.

The undertaker knelt and offered Arthur a hand. Arthur wasn't too proud to take it. "Let's get you up, mate," the undertaker said, and hauled Arthur to his feet. Arthur staggered.

He looked around. The shadows were gone. Only the girl, Winter, stood in the room, one axe in her hand and the other embedded above a massive stone tablet. She was staring at the case, stricken. The knife was gone. The sirens had stopped singing and the place was eerily silent by comparison.

"Tell me you have it," she said, in a voice all the more dangerous in its softness.

"Winter, he needed help," the undertaker began.

"Tell. Me. You. Have. It."

"I wasn't going to let him die."

"You *idiot!*" She wrenched the axe from the wall, spraying more glass as she pulled it out of the case. It scattered over the floor with a sound like wind chimes. She kicked a chunk of glass at the wall. "Do you have any idea how many people will suffer? All because you had to save one?"

"I'm sorry. But he was right here, and I couldn't do it." The undertaker shook his head, resolute.

Arthur's hands were trembling. He went for his handcuffs. "All right, kids. It's been a wild ride, but we're going to go down to the station together and sort this out. I have a few questions for you. There are guards at the entrance, there's nowhere to run."

Winter glared at him. Arthur had faced down enough criminal gazes in his lifetime to remain unfazed. Then she said to her companion, "This isn't over." She sheathed her axes.

Then she held up her hands. Her very empty hands.

Light flared, brighter than a flashbomb.

Arthur swore and clapped his hands over his eyes. In front of him he heard footsteps slapping on the stone tile, the echoes of her dimming voice as she yelled at the undertaker. He blinked furiously, but by the time the spots in his vision cleared, they were long gone.

The door behind him burst open. Borson was there, flanked by security guards. Real security guards, Arthur saw immediately, with normal eyes and normal teeth and no odd shadows lurking in the corners of their uniforms.

"They wouldn't let me through," Borson said. "And then they simply...left. Said the threat was gone. What happened?" He recoiled in horror. "My *God,* man. What happened to your neck?"

Arthur touched the skin on his neck gingerly. It throbbed and felt hot to the touch, like a third-degree sunburn. He smelled charred hair.

"I want the security footage for this room," he said. "I want it now."

There were stairs ahead of them, but Arthur doubted Winter and the undertaker had bothered to use them. As they headed down, they began to hear noise again. The partygoers were back. "They didn't all get cleared off?" he said.

Borson's expression was troubled. "The alarm stopped, so there was little reason to keep them out. I'm sure it has nothing to do with the Prime Minister's presence." He looked like he'd been asked to eat a long-dead mouse.

Borson took the lead once they were at the bottom of the stairs. "Security's this way." He led them into the atrium.

Arthur felt the pressure of dozens of eyes. He was the scruffiest looking thing here, and that was before he'd gotten into a fight with the spawn of Satan. He straightened up and set his best scowl on. Nothing for it. Let a few bigwigs see what a working man gets up to on Christmas Eve. He glared at the crowd.

Then he saw Antonius Snell.

His gut twisted with an instinct he knew all too well. He broke away from Borson and the flock of guards and made his way over to the minister. He ignored Borson's somewhat panicked, "Detective!" and the widening eyes of the political snakes around him.

Snell looked none too happy to see him. He exchanged glances with Kuiper, then offered a grudging hand to shake. "Arthur," he said in his polished, smoky voice. "I thought you'd be taking the day off with a pint. Or perhaps working on our shared case."

Arthur ignored the dig about the pint. He barely heard anything. He was staring at Snell. "What're you doing here?" he asked, and only realized how rude it sounded after he'd said it.

Snell laughed, short and crisp and angry. "I was invited, old chap. Not sure you can say the same."

A horrible suspicion grew in Arthur. And a temptation. A temptation to shove Snell against the wall and search his pockets. Would he find the knife?

Certainly not. Snell was right; he'd been invited to this. Besides, even if he'd orchestrated the theft of the knife, he'd never be so foolish as to hide it on his person in the direct aftermath. All that would get Arthur was a huge scene and the sack before New Year's.

He was suddenly aware of Snell's gaze on his throat. Snell regarded him coldly. "Do think of the children, Stowe. Clock is ticking."

He turned. Kuiper's eyes lingered a little too long on his neck, but then they snapped to his face, and he gave Arthur a quick apologetic nod. Then he followed his boss. People turned away then, too polite to keep staring at Arthur like some circus act. But Arthur stayed rooted to the spot, watching Snell. Perhaps his eyes were playing tricks on him. Perhaps he saw shadows in everything. But he could swear that two dark shapes curved away from Antonius Snell's brow. And from beneath Snell's suit jacket, something shadowy curved like a tail.

***

The security cameras were blank. Of course. They'd shorted out or some such nonsense. "How can they *all* have had technical difficulties? Our backups have backups." Borson leaned on the security desk, glaring at the guard.

"It's not her fault," Arthur said wearily, earning a small, terrified, grateful look from the guard as she cowered in her chair. "I don't know whose fault it is, but it's not hers."

The alarm had gone off at ten twenty-nine. The cameras had shorted at ten twenty-eight. There was no evidence that the goth girl and the undertaker had ever been in the museum.

Arthur had never believed in God, or the Devil, or ghosts, or anything he couldn't see with his own eyes. He'd believed in love for a little while, but Missy's dad made short work of that. If he'd heard some ridiculous story about shadow things and magic knives, he'd have wondered what was in his last drink. But now he'd seen it all for himself.

What the hell was he supposed to think?

He didn't have much to go on. But he did have names. Winter for the girl, Chris for the boy. And while he was in town, he might as well pay a little visit to *Hayne & Sons*.

CHAPTER TEN

Winter and Chris ran up the stairs, through a gallery of Japanese artefacts and out a fire exit. The snowstorm had grown fiercer while they were inside. Snowflakes stung Chris's face and he pulled up the collar of his coat. The world was a wall of gray around them.

Winter hopped onto the railing and balanced like a circus performer. She gripped the wall and hauled herself up, then turned to offer Chris a hand. "Well?" she demanded when he didn't take it.

"Er." Chris scrambled up on the railing. "This makes me a tad nervous."

"That sounds like a you problem." Winter took his hand and squeezed hard.

Don't look down. Chris clung to her and crawled up, feeling like a four-legged spider trying to tap dance over a wall. She heaved, and he finally flopped onto the roof of the Museum.

They'd parked the sleigh on the atrium. St. Nicholas still lolled inside it. In the gloomy daylight it was red as blood. Rosie and Ottie had taken refuge under the dash in a blanket provided by Zarina. Ottie's head poked over the side, and he began to bark madly as they approached. The glass roof was slick underfoot. It squeaked beneath Chris's shoes.

"It's only us," Winter said, and kicked at a little snowdrift. "Only us, *nothing* else." She shot Chris a furious look. "I can't *believe* you. What part of 'get the knife' did you not understand?"

"I'm sorry, but they were going to kill him," Chris said. "That's—that's not on."

"What if those kids are going to die now? Was it better to save some arsehole pig than any of them? Than *all* of them?"

Unease and guilt cramped his stomach. "Look, what would your dad have done?"

Winter spun toward him, hands curling into fists. The wind whipped her hair across her face. "He'd have done both. Somehow. But I'm *not* Dad and that's not what I can do!"

She stomped up to the sleigh and climbed in. "All right, you two. You get on with Diedre?"

Diedre had made herself a nest out of a plaid scarf. Rosie looked mortally offended in her blanket. As soon as Chris got into the sleigh, she climbed up into his lap.

She was trembling. He opened his coat so she could crawl inside. "You cold, girl?" He brought forth a bit of light, hoping it might give them some heat as well. If he'd been better at handling it, he might have been able to fight the shadows. He might have been able to get the knife.

Rosie heaved a little dachshund sigh.

"She's tired," Winter said. She patted her knees and Ottie hopped up too, looking at the clucking Diedre resentfully. "They both are. If we'd gotten the knife, we could've brought Dad back and found out what happened to the real reindeer. As it is, we're stuck." She sounded bitter.

"I'm sorry," Chris tried again.

"Stop apologizing!" she half shouted, startling Ollie. Two red spots appeared on her cheeks and her brown eyes flashed. "You don't wish you'd done anything differently, so you're not sorry anyway." Her glower was a challenge.

"I'm sorry we couldn't do it all," Chris told her gently. She was grieving, he told himself. Like the families that came to the mortuary. "I was sorry the light failed us. I wish I'd been better at it."

Winter sighed and dropped her gaze. She found her pack of cigarettes and rattled the box before pulling one out. "Don't look at me like that," she told Ollie as she stuck one in her mouth. Chris looked out over London as she lit it, the haphazard squares of houses and courtyards, snow-dusted trees, and steel skyscrapers.

"I don't know how much good it would have done," she admitted when she'd taken a couple of drags and calmed down. "They were strong. Stronger than I've ever fought before. I

105

don't know if it's because he's got a lot of kids, or if it's because Christmas is tomorrow, or if it's the general... everything about Britain right now." She waved a hand. Chris understood. Heating and food shortages, skyrocketing prices, staffing issues in schools and hospitals mingled with high unemployment... a lot of people were afraid. Even if they stuck to the old adage and carried on, worry permeated the air over Britain.

"Krampus wasn't even around," Winter said. "Even Dad can't manipulate creatures out of light that he can't see. And if this is what they're like..."

"We'll do all right. We'll manage." He had no idea why he said it. It flew contrary to everything they'd experienced so far. But he couldn't let Winter wallow. And somehow... he did believe. They had a plan. Sure, it hit a snag, but all plans did.

"We?" Winter turned to look at him frankly. Her brown irises were ringed with black, he noticed. There was a freckle in one. And for once, she didn't seem hostile or impatient. Her fingers tugged at the sleeve of her coat and she looked down, as though suddenly embarrassed.

"Look... I didn't give you much choice, I realize that. Sort of walked in and told you to help out."

"Actually, you told me to leave you alone first." Chris felt the corners of his mouth pull up.

Winter had a deep furrow between her brows. "You don't have to do this, is what I'm saying. It's my fight, for my dad. I shouldn't have expected you to suddenly know how to handle it, and I don't expect you to risk your life for it. Just so you know. You don't— have to."

Except maybe he was some kind of mythological heir, Chris thought. He might be too wrapped up to quit. And even if he wasn't... was he ready to give up this power he'd just discovered? The power to make light and fight the darkness? The power to make others stronger?"

He grinned. "You're not getting rid of me that easily. I said we'll manage, and I meant *we'll* manage." He tussled Rosie's silky ears and looked out over the city, a frown furrowing his brow.

"Maybe we've lost the one relic, but didn't Mr Ross say there was another one?"

Winter's eyes narrowed and she looked back up at him. "We're not going to see Mrs Pavuka." She patted Ottie's head. "Anyway, even if we did want to see her, we can't go anywhere. Ottie and Rosie are tapped out."

"Think Diedre could help out?" Chris was half joking. But Diedre cocked her dodo head at him, as though the idea merited some consideration.

"We want big animals," Winter contemplated her cigarette smoke as it mingled with the snow. The smell was harsh, and surprisingly pungent. "That's why Dad got caribou. They're strong, and they can be tamed."

"So, we should go get some big animals," Chris said.

"From where?" Winter snorted.

"The Zoo?"

"Haven't got time to tame anything we might pick up from the zoo." Winter picked at a bit of fluff on her coat. "Though I like the idea of lions pulling the sleigh."

"You didn't have to tame Diedre," Chris pointed out.

"She was already dead, wasn't she?"

Chris leaned on the edge of the sleigh and put his chin in his hand. Already dead…

He thought of a school trip he'd taken, long ago. A place with a grand hall and thousands of skeletons behind glass. He remembered staring open-mouthed at dinosaur teeth the size of swords, at a bird's egg too large to carry. He found himself smiling. "I've got an idea," he said.

Winter turned toward him. Her eyes widened in alarm and the cigarette dropped from her mouth. She leapt to her feet, sending Ottie to the ground, and whipped forward, pulling a knife from nowhere. Her arm grazed the top of his head. Chris dropped to the bottom of the sleigh, clutching Rosie in his coat. He turned in time to see another dark elf wrap its long shadow-hand around Winter's wrist.

So much for being free and clear.

107

"You're going to have to help us for a little while longer," he murmured to Rosie and Ottie, who stood growling in the bottom of the sleigh. "Think you can? Think you can get Diedre to help?"

Rosie looked at him. Then her little chin jerked, like a nod. She hopped three times and jumped on the dash. From there she got down, with Ottie close behind. Chris picked up Diedre, marvelling at her lightness, and placed her carefully on the atrium roof. "Go join Ottie," he said. She trotted up to stand between the dogs.

Something grabbed his ankle. He stomped down, hard, as he smelled singeing cotton. This suit was never going to recover. He put one hand over the ignition and used the other to conjure the brightest light he could think of, and the shadow retreated, hissing. He could feel the strain of effort dragging on his exhausted limbs. As the sleigh rumbled to life and the harness winked into existence, he focused. They didn't have to go far. They didn't have to go far.

Rosie and Ottie started to run. Diedre clacked after them. Their tongues hung from their open mouths. "It's only a couple of minutes," Chris promised as he checked the map.

They lifted off the roof of the British Museum. Winter shoved one shadow free, then chopped another straight in half. "Hangers-on," she said, coming up to stand beside Chris. She leaned over the side of the sleigh. "I think we... Shite."

Chris looked down. Tottenham Court Road was empty except for the stray bus or taxi still trying to best the weather. Fairy lights strung along the shops glittered and winked. And one by one, they were going out.

Shadows roiled up the road, heedless of traffic that moved around them without knowing it moved around them. As they pressed forward the garland decorations withered, the wreaths sprouted mold. The lights flickered and died.

"How far can they follow us?" Chris said.

"The question's not how far they can follow." Winter looked ahead. Rosie and Ottie stumbled as they cleared the museum roof. The sleigh dipped dangerously. "The question's how far *we* can make it."

They cut through Mayfair, flying over blue-lit streets adorned with Christmas stars and blaring Michael Bublé. Chris looked behind him in time to see the river of shadows turn a corner and flow over the asphalt. The sleigh jerked. "A little farther," he pleaded. Ottie howled piteously.

They sailed over the winter wonderland of Hyde Park, spotting the Ferris wheel and the tiny huts of the Christmas market. Bublé turned into Tchaikovsky. Chris caught sight of a pale octagonal tower. The Victoria & Albert. "Almost there," he urged the dogs.

The sleigh dropped a good foot in the sky.

"They're too tired," Winter braced herself. "We're going to crash."

"There!" Chris pointed. "We're setting down there. You can make it, girls! You can make it, Ottie!"

Diedre strained at her lead. Rosie and Ottie tried to match her, but the sleigh was losing altitude fast. They swerved around the columned tower, skidded over the roof of the V&A, and barely made the bump across the road. The snow-capped double tower of the Natural History Museum loomed like a fairy-tale palace, and as they flew past they barely avoided crashing into the wall.

The sleigh skidded to a stop between two gables behind the double tower. The leads disappeared and Rosie and Ottie flopped on their sides, panting. Diedre nudged Ottie with her hooked beak but got nothing more than a whimper.

Chris hopped out to collect them. Winter stood up and looked around. "What are we doing here?" she said.

He returned with a dog under each arm. "We're getting some reindeer," he said. "Or something." He turned to Diedre. "You're on sleigh duty," he said. Diedre made a strange cooing that he assumed was the song of her people, then squatted over Zarina's blanket as though it were a nest.

They tromped over the roof until they found an access door that Winter opened with her magical ability that still made Chris look in awe. Chris conjured a light for the stair while Winter drew an axe. "You never know what's waiting for you," she said.

Nothing waited for them. They crept down into a dark and dry and dusty-smelling place that turned out to be an attic under the gable, stacked with furniture and old signs. The shadows here were refreshingly unmoving. "Freezing in here," Chris said. Rosie sneezed. The sound bounced off the sloping ceiling.

A door at the end of the attic space led to another stair. Winter went first, holding her axe ready, and Chris followed. Chris held his light and hoped that Winter's ability to bypass security would work without trouble here.

They came out into a small room filled with bones. Fragments no longer than Chris' middle finger, from species he'd never heard of, millions of years old. He put the dogs down at last and they promptly went off to sniff every corner.

"Creepy," said Winter, holding up her own light. "I like it."

"Pretty cool that you can make your own skeleton army, then," Chris replied.

"I brought back one bird, let's not get ahead of ourselves." Winter moved on.

They went through rooms full of beetles and iridescent butterflies, ancient, browning mammoth tusks, and fish fossils in stone. When they came out into the upper gallery, Winter stopped.

The gallery was long, paved with brick and lined with arches that looked out over the enormous front hall. When Chris increased his light, with effort, he spotted the famous blue whale hanging in the middle and wreathed in darkness. Hope, her name was. They could use a little of that right now. Chris put his hand on a fluted column adorned with stone monkeys, beetles, and sloths. The whole place was eerily silent except for the faint scratch of Ottie's and Rosie's claws on the floor, the squeak of Chris' and Winter's shoes.

"This one." Winter stood before a saber-toothed tiger. The fossil stood on a plinth, smaller than Chris had imagined, arranged in the act of stalking some invisible prey. A thin rope separated the specimen from the public. She reached across the rope now—Chris found himself wincing on principle— and touched the top of the cat's head. She closed her eyes and concentrated.

Chris waited for a few long moments. Then Winter opened her eyes. "Nothing," she said, voice thick with disappointment.

"Here." He took her hand.

She whipped it away. "What are you doing?"

"I'm a conduit, remember?" He held his hand out, palm up. "Just like Diedre. Er, the first time. Not with the feathers."

She hesitated, then placed her fingers over his. He tried to ignore the tingle that travelled all the way up his arm and over the rest of his body. He tried not to think about how cool and smooth her fingers were. He tried not to think about how cool *she* was, the coolest person he'd ever met. Instead, he thought of the way snow looked as it fell past his window, the way his mum's tea tasted when he was sick.

"I can't even… feel it," she said. "It's been dead for so long."

Chris imagined his power flowing into her. He thought of it like the light he could create —except instead of concentrating on making the light, he imagined pushing it through his body and into hers.

She inhaled sharply and touched the creature again. There was a sound like two rusty hinges grating together, and the thing's head turned toward them.

The tiger yawned.

Winter's smile was as bright as any light Chris could conjure. "Incredible," she said.

"God, I hope he's friendly," Chris said.

Ottie stood on two hind legs to sniff at the tiger. The tiger lowered its head obediently. A shiver of light ran down its saber teeth. Ottie looked at it, then looked at Winter. Then he dropped down to all fours and headed off, snuffling.

"Well, if Ottie says he's fine…" Winter's eyes sparkled. She tucked a strand of hair behind her ear and stroked the tiger on the top of its skull.

Rosie barked from the darkness. They followed the sound of her voice to a tortoise with a shell the size of a small bed. "Really?" Winter sounded doubtful. Rosie glared. "All right, all right." Winter pressed her hand to the tortoise's shell, and Chris let his power flow. The tortoise shot off her perch and made her way down the hall as fast as she could. Which was surprisingly fast, Chris realized as she disappeared into the gloomy gallery.

"What got under her arse?" Winter asked.

They heard a *clickety-clack* behind them, and something growled. Chris smelled smoke.

It's the tiger, he thought, even as he saw the tiger on the other side of Winter. Rosie barked again. Together they turned. Chris conjured a light and held it high.

A horn loomed out of the dark, much bigger than it looked when the rhino was flesh and blood. Its yellowing skull lowered in challenge. Shadow leaked from its eye sockets, like ink spilled in water. They twined and stretched like fingers, brushing against his trouser leg. The cloth scorched beneath them.

"Run," said Winter.

They jerked apart as the rhinoceros lunged, then turned and fled. The saber-tooth swiped at it and bounded after them. It overtook them easily but slipped on the smooth floor, bones shrieking. Chris scooped up Rosie as he pelted past her. "Ottie!" he yelled as they rounded the corner. Behind them, the rhino smashed into a brick pillar. "Ottie, where are you?"

They heard a pattering, like a waterfall on stone, like someone dropping a whole bag of pebbles on the floor. "Krampus can animate them," Winter gasped. "He can use the dark elves to animate them all at once, I did not turn them!"

Chris grabbed Winter's hand. "Touch everything you can," he called over the rising din. She flung out her hand and he pushed with everything he had, sparing only enough energy for a light to see where they were going. Pain lanced through his chest. *Never use yourself as a power source,* Iain Ross's voice warned him. They flashed past dinosaurs, a woolly mammoth, and some kind of deer the size of a people carrier. Creatures Chris couldn't even name reared to life at her touch. They joined the flood, shoving the shadow-filled fossils aside, buying Chris and Winter precious seconds.

"I told you you could do this," he grated.

"That's great." Off to the left, Ottie barked frantically. Winter swung Chris ahead and he slid over the floor. A claw slashed at where he'd been. "We'll celebrate later."

They passed a grand staircase teeming with shadow-filled bones trying to get up the stairs. Ottie's bark turned high-pitched and frightened. Rosie wriggled free of Chris and took off for her brother, leading them around another corner.

Ottie had been backed against the railing. His tail was down, his teeth bared in a snarl. Rabbits and cats and little creatures surrounded him, bleeding smoke. Rosie barreled through them all, no one was harming Ottie on her watch. Vertebrae and toe bones tumbled over the floor. Rosie skidded around and stood beside him. Her lips pulled back and she growled, furious.

Winter dropped Chris' hand and swung her axe. Bones sailed through the air, *plinking* off the walls or disappearing into the main gallery, chattering like angry teeth as they landed. Chris forced his way through to Rosie. Winter took up on Ottie's other side.

"Okay, ideas man," she said. "Now what?"

She swung her axe in a wide arc. It kept the beasts at bay for now, but growls rumbled in their throats, and chirps echoed down the gallery. Something in the crowd snarled.

"Maybe you could touch them and turn them back," Chris said.

"And lose my fingers? No, thank you."

"Okay." He bent down, slowly. Something tried to slink toward him but backed off as Winter's axe came round. "I do have an idea. He picked up Ottie and plopped him in Winter's arm. He held on to Rosie himself. Then he climbed, very carefully, onto the railing along the gallery. *Don't look down.*

Winter, ever the experienced acrobat, hopped up beside him. The emboldened shadow-animals drew closer. "What are we doing?"

"Don't hate me," said Chris, and grabbed her arm. "Just jump." And he did.

They hit the blue whale where her neck met her head. Chris smacked his head so hard on the bone that his teeth cut into his cheek, flooding his mouth with a metallic taste. Winter shrieked beside him. He flailed and grabbed on to the nearest thing he could manage. Rosie clung to his shoulder, whining.

"Change her!" he shouted. *"Change her!"* And he gripped

Winter's hand so tight he could no longer feel where his skin ended and hers began. Agony bit into his chest, so sharp he thought for a moment that Winter's axe had slipped.

A deep rumble-like baritone whale song filled the hall.

The skeleton began to shake. Chris held on with everything he had, gasping through the pain, praying that Winter and Rosie and Ottie could hold on, too. Above them, cables snapped like gunshots. The blue whale's body undulated in the air.

They began to move.

Hope the Whale crashed through the ceiling of the museum like she was breaching. Glass sprayed into the grey air. Chris' fingers were turning white, but he didn't let go; he squeezed his eyes shut and breathed through the pain as they scraped past a skylight and left the Natural History Museum in shambles.

Winter rolled off as soon as she was on the roof. Chris gingerly opened his eyes. Glass had cut through her coat and dress, leaving blood to drip down one arm onto the snow. She still held Ottie tight. And she looked up at the blue whale with naked astonishment.

"I did *that?*" she whispered.

Adrenaline surged through Chris. Even though it wasn't remotely funny, he started laughing. It hurt to laugh. It hurt like a heart attack. "Yeah. You did." Let her compare herself to her dad *now.*

Rosie growled softly. "Yeah," Winter said, forcing her eyes away from the skeletal whale. Hope drifted gently in the air, waiting. "You're right. They'll be coming after us." She staggered for the sleigh. "Start her up, genius boy."

Chris followed her, still grinning. Genius boy. Pretty boy. For someone as permanently dour as Winter, she gave nice compliments.

It was a peculiar magic of the sleigh that harnesses could appear from midair and somehow arrange to fit both sausage dogs and the largest animal on the planet. Chris half-tumbled onto the seat and propped his forehead on the dash, fingers pressed to the ignition. Winter sat next to her dad and started pulling glass out of her coat.

Hope's tail undulated and they soared up into the clouds. Rosie and Ottie nosed at Diedre, rustling her featherless wings in her blanket nest, then flopped down next to her when she didn't take the hint and move. "Job well done, you two," Chris said.

Ottie put his head on his paws and fixed Chris with a look that said, *I still don't trust you, but I'll tolerate you.* "Thanks, mate," Chris replied.

Winter checked her father, then the sleigh. "I think we're free this time," she said.

"Free and clear." Chris leaned back.

"You look horrible." Winter propped her arms on her knees. "What'd you do to yourself?"

"I'm fine." Adrenaline made him laugh, even if his chest pulsed with pain.

"It was too much, wasn't it?" Her eyes were serious, her mouth turned down. "You pulled too much power from yourself."

He mustered up a shrug. It was colder now. He wished he had a blanket like Diedre did. "I'm still here, aren't I?"

Winter shook her head firmly. "Don't fall into that trap. Do that, and you'll be fine until you're dead. No more conduiting, okay?"

"What if we really need to?"

"I said *no more.*"

"You know, you remind me of your mum when you do that—"

"Ugh." Winter flapped a hand and looked out over the city. She was flushed from the excitement, too. Her hair hung half out of its ponytails.

"How's your arm?" Chris said, afraid she'd catch him looking and it'd be awkward.

"Fine." She pulled off her coat and rolled up her net sleeve. "The loss of my axe hurts more than the arm. I can't believe you made me drop it," she grumbled. "And *don't* say sorry."

Chris settled for smiling in a sort of apologetic way.

Winter found a bit of gauze in her gothic plumber's belt and started to wrap her arm. "Looks like you escaped unscathed, aside from the magic business. And now we've got a working sleigh, so things could be worse. But we still have no knife. So, we're not *exactly* free and clear."

"Mr Ross did mention Mrs Pavuka," Chris said.

Winter paused to glare at him. "For the *last time*—"

"Have you got any other options?" Chris checked his watch. It was a miracle the face hadn't broken in all the excitement. "We've got thirteen hours before your Dad's lost forever."

"Mrs Pavuka won't help me. She hates me. She's hated me for ages. Also… I'm afraid of spiders." Winter sat back and crossed her arms, turning pink.

"What do spiders have to do with any of it?" Chris said.

She huffed like he'd asked her what clouds have to do with snow. "It's exhausting, you not knowing anything."

"I do know that the British Museum break-in will have hit the news. I know that we don't have time to search every museum in London for a relic like the knife, and I know that detective could see you, even though he shouldn't. And I know you can find people you've met before. So, I'll make you a deal. You locate this Mrs Pavuka, and when we find her, I'll do the talking. All right?"

"She's still not going to help. When I said she hates me, I really meant it."

"With your sunny disposition? How could anyone?"

"Oh, shut it." She stuck her feet on the dash and closed her eyes. "All right, you've got a deal. But only because I don't know what else to do. And don't say I didn't warn you."

The sleigh made a wide turn to avoid a passenger plane and headed east. Its occupants relaxed, unaware of the scrap of shadow that clung to the underside.

CHAPTER ELEVEN

A familiar figure stood up as Arthur entered Lewisham station. Arthur stared for a moment, uncomprehending, before his brain kicked in. Kuiper. Kuiper was the man's name.

"I'm sorry about this," Kuiper said as they shook hands. "Really am. He insisted on coming down, but I thought I'd stay out here to warn you."

"Bloody politicians," Arthur muttered. "No offence."

"Stowe," barked Commander Montague as Arthur tried to sit down at his desk. "My office."

Snell sat in the chair opposite Montague's desk, legs crossed. He still wore the fine morning suit he'd sported at the British Museum. He looked as composed as ever, in contrast to Arthur's increasing shabbiness. He had a faint cigar smell about him. "Surprised to see me, Stowe?" His pale eyes gleamed. He was shredding what looked like a holly leaf in his fingers.

Thankfully, no. "Always a pleasure."

"I wish I could say the same. What sort of time are you wasting? I handed you a gold-plated tip and you made a scene at the British Museum? You humiliated the Met and gave this project a bad name."

Arthur watched him carefully, looking for the telltale shadows he'd seen at the Museum. But Snell was, it seemed, just a man. A greedy, slithering snake of a man, though really that was an insult to snakes.

"There are budget cuts coming, Stowe. There are journalists salivating at the idea that this project would fail. That *I* would fail." Snell leaned forward. "Is that what you want? Because if I fail, I'll want your head. The utter incompetence of the Met will not be tolerated. Not when there are children involved."

He sounded like he'd practised that bit in front of a mirror. Getting ready to deflect the blame for the cameras, no doubt.

"I was following a lead, sir," Arthur said, opting to speak with Montague and do his best to ignore Snell. "And I believe that the break-in at the Museum is directly related to that lead—"

"I know what you think." Montague's voice was full of contempt. A vein at his temple throbbed and his moustache twitched with rage. "You're obsessed with a theory we've already debunked. You're living in the past, Stowe. You were when I hired you, and you never got your head out of your arse. So here it is: get me results by tomorrow or pack up your desk and go home."

Arthur reeled back. He and Montague had their differences, yes, but to get this kind of ultimatum?

"Tomorrow's Christmas, sir," he blurted.

"And?" Montague fixed him with a steely glare. "You got somewhere more important to be?"

**

Arthur stopped at Izzy's desk on the way back to his own. She was typing as though her computer had committed three different felonies and must be punished. "Montague talk to you?"

She didn't look up. "Yes."

"You all right?"

"No." Her tone was ice-cold.

He hesitated. "Look, Montague won't sack you. You're moving up. You've got promise. I'm an old man who washed up here with nowhere else to go."

Izzy finally looked up at him. Her mouth was a grim line and her blue eyes sparkled with fury. "You're an old man who ignores his partner and indiscriminately chases leads, you mean."

Arthur opened his mouth. Then he closed it again. "I told you I was going to the Museum," he managed.

"You didn't say why. You didn't have me come." She thumped the desk, and a couple of others looked up from their computers. "Why are you being so secretive about this? You work late last

118

night, come in early this morning, and now I find out you've been driving all over central London?"

"I haven't been driving all over central London. I've only been to the Museum. And the undertaker's," Arthur added.

Izzy swelled. "You did *what?*" she growled.

Arthur leaned over the desk. "Look, I'm sorry. I am. But something's not adding up, and I'm certain it's got to do with *him.*" He jerked his head toward Montague's office.

"What, the commissioner?" Izzy's lip curled.

"No. Snell. Look, he was the one who put us on this angle. And he was at the Museum, too. And the thing that went missing, the artefact—it's made from the same stone as whatever killed our John Doe."

The disdain on her face flickered. "You get some kind of forensics on that?"

"No, but I know. I *know.*" Izzy rolled her eyes. "You know that gut feeling."

She crossed her arms. "Yeah. My gut feeling's telling me that if I keep standing behind you, I'll get sacked when you do. So go back to your desk, and let me solve the case, and remember that the least you can do when you stuff up is not drag me down with you."

Arthur stopped. Part of him wanted to make a clever retort, but she was right. Best he could do was look after her.

All the same, looking after her also meant putting her on the right track. "One piece of advice? Those kids aren't child traffickers. They just aren't."

Izzy frowned at him. "What kids?"

The kids who'd stolen John Doe's body. The kids no one but Arthur was able to see.

That wasn't quite true. Mr Hayne of *Hayne & Sons* knew exactly who Arthur was talking about. "Chris Demper," he'd said over a cup of strong tea. "A treasure of an employee."

Chris had been working with *Hayne & Sons* for about a year. Hayne had never had trouble with him—"Not one sick day, not one minute late to work." He was amenable, happy, hardworking, and he'd never stolen so much as a pen from his workplace.

Arthur had tried to describe the girl, Winter, but Haynes had looked at him blankly until he switched back to Chris.

He'd finagled Chris' address out of Hayne, at least. He'd planned on collecting Izzy and going for a look. But something told him he wouldn't find anything anyway.

Snell was working him over. He didn't know how, but he knew it was happening. And if Snell gave the order, Montague would sack him. Montague had been dancing to Snell's tune for years now, why would he stop?

Why should he stop? The kidnapped children were long gone, and sooner or later the Met wouldn't be able to deny it anymore. And Montague could keep his job by passing the blame. Why not pass it to an officer who'd never achieved anything? Who never *would* achieve anything?

The world wasn't set up for good guys to win.

"You need anything?" Izzy asked pointedly.

I need to resign. "Nah." Arthur went back to his desk. The file lay open and half scattered across his keyboard. He sighed and started to tidy it up.

This stank like the business in Colchester.

Arthur had never wanted to be a big city detective. The London Met held little appeal for him. By the time he'd finished his training, he'd already proposed to Missy, and she wanted a smaller town life. Wanted to stay near her father, a rich widower who hated Arthur and thought his Missy should have tried harder to nab a millionaire. Missy'd always said that Arthur could bring her father round. It was one of the rare things she was wrong about.

The case that had ruined him started small. Monetary discrepancies in a minor fraud situation. Then the crooked accountant Arthur arrested had offered to make a deal, information in exchange for a reduced sentence. Arthur had followed his tip and kept following the money all the way up to the Town Council. And the more he dug, the more he found.

But justice didn't exist, and the world wasn't set up for good guys to win. Arthur didn't close the case in the courtroom, or with a big confession. Money flowed, bribes were made, and the case never went anywhere at all. And suddenly he was transferred to London, the scapegoat, demoted to walking the beat until he made his way up again the hard way and now still a laughingstock to his peers, behind on his mortgage, and wondering how the kids were going to get new school uniforms. And then Missy's father showed up at the pub one night and laid it all out, reasonable as anything. *Man to man,* he'd said. *No need to get her involved.*

Arthur could leave them be, and the old man would buy off the house and provide an allowance. Missy and the boys could live comfortably. Or Arthur could stay, and the house would be repossessed, and they'd all be homeless by Christmas.

Arthur had chosen to leave. And hell, maybe that was his way. He'd leave again this time for Dover or Edinburgh or somewhere far from all his failures, and he'd start over again, and the *Save the Children* campaign would be added to the list of things he mulled over with his sweet stout.

He closed the file.

That brought him back to himself. Something was off, he realized. The heft of it wasn't what it had been.

"Izzy?" He looked over to where Izzy's curly head was bent over her keyboard again. She didn't acknowledge him. "You take anything out of here?"

She shook her head.

He opened the file and looked through it. Things were missing. Photographs, mostly. Photos Arthur had seen yesterday. What sort of idiot took photos out without putting them back?

No matter. There were digital copies of everything. Arthur logged on to the Police National Database and started to poke around. It was dull work, and truly, how likely was it to save his arse? But he found the *Save the Children* project and started flipping through the files.

Why would someone take the photographs away? To what purpose? And why would they bother?

An hour or so in, a shadow fell over his desk. Arthur looked up.

"I'm going to the undertaker's," Izzy said. "Doing an interview."

"I already went. You want my notes?" Arthur said.

"I'll collect my own," she said coldly. "Don't run off on some scheme while I'm gone."

That hurt, Arthur realized as she stalked out of the building. She didn't even trust him to interview a witness.

He pored over the photos again. What exactly was he looking for?

His colleagues ignored him when they went to lunch. Fine by him. He didn't need a break until he had answers.

It still took him another hour to find one.

He almost missed it, lulled into a sort of meditative mindlessness by the repetitive work. His brain took a few scrolls to register what he'd seen. Then he zoomed back up.

Shazi Hashem. Third-year student who won a prize at a science fair for building a robot. The photo had been taken perhaps six months before she went missing. The girl in the photo was gap-toothed and dressed all in purple, grinning from ear to ear. In one hand she held the robotic dog that won her a prize. And shaking her other hand was the previous Minister for Education, Antonius Snell.

Arthur had never seen this photo before. Of course, physical evidence got lost, it happened. But why had all the photographs disappeared today, and how much of a coincidence was it that Snell was in the station?

You're trying to hide something, Arthur thought. *I don't know what, but I know you are.* And he was going to find out if it was the last thing he did at the London Metropolitan Police.

CHAPTER TWELVE

The sleigh drifted through the snowy skies of London, pulled by the skeleton of a blue whale.

Chris stuck his arms inside his jacket and sat back as Hope took them down at the edge of Victoria Park. The ground was a mishmash of footprints in the snow, with a few game grasses poking their heads up. It was only a ten minute walk to Mrs Pavuka's place from here, and a good place for Hope to wait.

Chris clambered out and patted a fin that was bigger than his bed. "Thanks," he said. Hope opened her great jaws and gently clacked the bones together.

Winter stroked the tail contemplatively. She cut a striking figure—black hair blowing in the wind, black coat, black tights against white snow against yellowing bone. Chris went over to her. "It's not the usual Yuletide look, but it's more impressive than a reindeer."

She smiled a quick, sudden smile, as though surprised by the compliment. Then she looked back at her dad, immobile in the sleigh. "Hope he gets the chance to see it," she said.

They set off. Neither of them noticed the shadow that followed.

They crossed Victoria Park Road and headed up a little street lined with terraced houses. Though cold had sapped most of the scent from the air, Chris picked up the stink of rotting garbage, the sort of slimy smell that clung to everything. The city hadn't bothered to clean off the roads here yet and a few neighbours were out with their shovels, doing the good deed of clearing off everyone's pavement. No decorations hung outside; electricity was too dear, and the council wasn't paying for any sort of Christmas cheer. Instead of carols, they got the occasional grunted *morning* and the slide of snow shovels.

As they walked, Winter's demeanor changed. She breathed hard through her nose, and several times she seemed on the brink of saying something. She finally stopped on the edge of the pavement, looking out across the slushy street. She bounced on her toes as though getting up the courage to go—then stopped.

After the third time, Chris said, "What'd you do to make Mrs Pavuka hate you, anyway?"

Red blazed up to Winter's ears. "Nothing any sane person wouldn't have done."

"It'd be nice to know. In case it helps us with her," Chris said.

Winter worked her jaw and glared at him. "She's the Christmas Spider, all right?"

"The what now?"

"The Christmas Spider. It's a legend. A Little Myth that sort of got tangled up with my dad. You just... need to be ready. She's freaky, especially when she drops the human act. And she did that one day when Dad and I were visiting, and I totally panicked, and I stepped on this really rare Malaysian spider. And trust me, you do *not* get over having a thousand crawlies rushing angrily towards you while you still got spider guts splatted on your shoes."

"Okay. Okay. I won't step on any spiders. And I won't panic, I promise. And if you start to panic, I'll help you."

"Don't make promises you can't keep." Winter's shoulders hunched. She put her hand over the pocket holding her cigarettes, but she didn't take one out.

Mrs Pavuka lived in a line of beige brick flats with bright blue garages. Chris and Winter scanned the door telephone until they found a U. Pavuka on the first floor. "Here." Chris pressed the buzzer.

A spider crawled contemplatively up the wall. Winter took a sharp step back. "This is a bad idea," she muttered.

"It's the only idea we've got," Chris reminded her.

The intercom crackled. "Who is it?" demanded a shrill voice in a sharp Slavic accent.

"Um, excuse me—sorry, Ma'am. And Happy Christmas."

"No carol singers." Mrs Pavuka hung up.

Chris buzzed again. Then again. He was preparing for a third time when the intercom cut to life. "Go away," she snapped.

"We're here about Father Christmas," he said quickly.

There was a pause. "No one here by that name," she said.

Winter threw her head back and sighed. "Mrs Pavuka?" She softened her voice, made it sweeter. Chris was pretty sure it was nerves. "This is Winter. Winter Myra. We're here about my dad."

"I *told* you not to come back on my property," Mrs Pavuka snarled.

Winter stepped back again. Three more spiders had crawled down the wall, each larger than the other. "That was years ago," she said, louder. "Look, I'm—I'm really sorry. And I wouldn't have come if it weren't really important. But Dad needs help, and we think you're the only one who can do it."

"Please. The fate of Christmas is at stake," Chris said. Then he shook his head. He'd just said *the fate of Christmas is at stake,* and he'd meant it.

"I know what's at stake, child. Don't patronize me." Her breath rasped over the intercom for a couple of moments. Then she said, "Boy. You may come in. Girl. You may stay."

"Suits me," muttered Winter.

The door unlocked. Chris pulled it open and paused with one foot over the threshold. "I go in, I get the knife, I get out. Deal?" he said.

"Don't make her angry," Winter said. "You do *not* want the problems."

"Got it." He went in.

"Eight-legged problems," he heard Winter mutter as the door clicked shut.

He ascended a linoleum stair that smelled like cigarettes and dirt and old people. The wooden bannister was worn smooth by years of use and rattled loosely against the wall. It was a dozen short steps up to Mrs Pavuka's door, a cheap particle board thing that was already slightly ajar. Chris knocked anyway. It echoed hollowly. He pushed it gently, half ducking as he went inside.

He'd been worried about the state of the flat, but the door

opened onto a neat hallway with a blue rug in front of the door and a distinct lack of webs. "Put your shoes by the door, there's a love," said a voice from the other room. Chris slid his shoes off.

The hallway was bare, aside from a bookshelf filled with books in Cyrillic script. The top of the bookshelf was covered in lace doilies, and in the centre of each doily was a spider. Glass ones, Chris realized after a moment. They were motionless in bright yellows and blues and reds, rearing or investigating or crouching. The whole place smelled fresh, somehow. Like a pine forest.

Chris went through the nearest doorway and found himself in a dark sitting room. Heavy curtains obscured what little light made it through the dirty windows, and the single lamp did a poor job of illuminating the room. Shelves along the walls held the usual Granny décor—plates, figurines, the odd book, and a lot of crocheted lace. Unlike most grannies, though, every single thing was about spiders. The plates had spider patterns. The lace was spiderwebs. And the figurines were all spiders, ranging from the size of Chris' little fingernail to the size of a cat. And while he didn't see any living specimens, webs ran from shelf to shelf, from bookcase to lamp. But they didn't make the place seem filthy. They glittered in the dim light as though they were spun from silver and diamonds.

At the far end of the room sat Mrs Pavuka in an overstuffed armchair. She was tiny, wrinkled, pale, and entirely human as far as Chris could see. She wore a red velvet dress with a wide skirt and a pinafore with a black widow print. Her white hair was done up in curls. Next to her sat a cup of tea and a radio on a little table. The radio played *White Christmas,* the Frank Sinatra version. A classic.

Mrs Pavuka was crocheting something, but she paused to pull her spectacles down and study him over the most impressive nose he'd ever seen.

"Do you know who I am?" she said.

Chris looked around. Mrs Pavuka nodded to the chair across from her and he took it, checking it over for spiders while trying to look as though he wasn't checking it over for spiders. The chair groaned as he sat. He was pretty sure he felt springs digging into his thigh. "Winter said you were the Christmas Spider."

"And do you know what that is?"

"Not really, no," he confessed.

She gestured with her crochet hook. Next to her sat a little Christmas tree in a pot, strung with the same glittering webs that adorned the rest of her sitting room. "It was long ago. Though not so long; Nicholas was wandering the earth and his traditions had come to my own country. I lived in the house of a peasant woman, though I was not as you see me today." She shifted, and for a moment Chris thought he saw two arms emerge to take up the crocheting as she picked up her tea and took a long slurp. "The peasant woman had little food and less money and couldn't waste it on things like trees and baubles. But one year a pine tree grew in her garden, and she chopped it down to bring a bit of joy into their hut as her children ate thin soup and spun tales by the fire. I loved hearing the stories, and I loved chasing the fat flies that tried to spoil her meat. I loved that family. So, while they slept I decorated their little Christmas tree, spinning web upon web. And when Nicholas saw it, he laughed."

She shook out the lace. It was a long triangular piece, finely worked, with little beaded spiders adorning delicate webs. "He granted me something for my hard work. The peasant, too. All my strands turned to silver and gold, as soon as the light touched our cabin on Christmas morning." She ran her hand over the lace, and it rippled beneath her.

The white turned yellow and began to shine. Chris stared. Mrs Pavuka held it up again. "My story grew, as they do, and I became legend. Nick is the bigger legend, the Myth. But I am a part of his story, a Little Myth. And this is why part of his magic is here with me."

Chris forced himself to stop gaping and get to the point. "Do you know what happened to him?"

"I felt it when he fell. If you are looking for the truth of why, I cannot help you. But I do not think you're looking for a why. I think you are looking for a *how*. How to bring him back?"

"We were told you had something. Something that could help."

Mrs Pavuka didn't answer for a long moment. Her bright eyes

were focused on the lace. She made another loop with her crochet hook and as the yarn became part of the pattern, it shimmered and rippled over to gold. The lace *shirred* in her hands like chains. "An Apollonius knife," she said.

"Do you have it?" It felt rude to be asking so bluntly, but he could almost hear Winter in the back of his mind. *We haven't got time.*

"Young man, I have kept that knife for many years. Always for myself. Perhaps you see the problem?"

"We'll give it back when we're done with it," Chris offered.

Mrs Pavuka shook her head. "It does not work that way. Once it is used, it is gone. If I give it to you, I am in more danger, for I will not be able to save myself when he comes for me."

When. Not if. "But…" Chris cast about for a good argument. "What will happen to *you* if Nick is gone? Won't that hurt you in some way?"

Mrs Pavuka pushed her glasses back up her nose and worked her mouth. Then she took another sip of tea. "I do not know. It never happened to me before."

Time for a different tactic, then. "You said you knew what was at stake. Surely you know how important it is that we save him." He leaned forward and widened his brown eyes soulfully. Puppy eyes, his mother used to call them, smacking him with a rag when he tried it on her.

Mrs Pavuka pulled her spectacles back down her nose and regarded him. She was unaffected by the puppy eyes—in fact, she scrutinized long and hard, as though trying to determine if he were worth swatting down a peg. Finally, she said, "In fact, I do not. I do not know that it is as important as all that."

"What do you mean?" Chris forced himself to ignore the palm-sized brown spider that slowly descended from the ceiling onto the back of Mrs Pavuka's chair. "I thought Father Christmas was this big force for good. If he dies, won't all that good… poof?" He made a motion with his hands.

Mrs Pavuka snorted. "Of course not. Consider yourself, Chris Demer." Chris frowned. When had he told her his name? "You won't stop being good if Father Christmas is gone tomorrow. Nor will evil magically disappear if you do win the day and defeat Krampus, demon of shadows. Do you truly think all the good in you comes from a Myth, big or little?"

Chris didn't answer. Being good was what he did. What he was. He was Decent Chris. He couldn't imagine turning selfish or evil or horrid at midnight, whether they saved Winter's father or not.

"Myths help things along. People think of them, and they remember how they want to act. And the more they think of a Myth, the more power the Myth has in the world. But people are always people, and we always have the power to decide what we will be today and tomorrow."

She went back to her crocheting and finished off the piece with a little hum. As she finished her tea and put her yarn away, Chris sat. He watched the webs sparkle in the dim light, he watched a spider pick its way over the top of the tiny Christmas tree. He looked at the cabinet behind Mrs Pavuka, dusty and lined with yet more figures.

"You know, it's nice," he said after a while. "That I can decide who I want to be. Because I've thought about it a lot since my family died, and I like being me. I like that I won't be someone different tomorrow. Because I'm the sort of bloke who likes to help people. And right now, Winter needs help. She needs help getting her dad back. She won't say it, but I see it. She's afraid. She's afraid he's gone forever, and she'll never get to tell him she loves him again. And I choose to be the sort of bloke who wants to help her get him back. Because she's too young to lose a father." His throat closed suddenly, and he had to stop.

Something rattled to his right, and he looked down. A cup of fresh tea sat on the side table next to him.

He didn't dare ask who'd brought it. He took a sip, and nodded gratefully, and hoped no spiders had been harmed in the boiling of the water. This was proper tea, no offence to Iain Ross. Strong and tamed with milk and sugar. "I know what she's feeling right now. Except I never got the chance to save my Dad. She does, and it's a rare thing. And I think we should help her. Don't you?"

Mrs Pavuka stared at him. He couldn't work out her expression;

her white eyebrows had lifted but her mouth was pursed. "I see now," she said, and got to her feet.

She was tiny—must be under five feet, and stood half bent. Chris leaned forward to offer his arm, but she waved him away. "I have no trouble keeping my balance, dear." She looked at the golden lace in her hand. "You know, Chris Demer... if you save Nicholas of Myra, you will be giving up power. Power you don't even know you have."

"Not much of a chore to give it up then, is it?" Chris said.

"You could become him. *Be* him. Drive the sleigh, bring the joy, fight the dark. You are a viable mythological heir, which is a rare thing amongst mortals. Are you certain it is not what you want?"

He thought of the life he'd had twenty-four hours ago. Alone, working with dead bodies in the middle of the night, telling himself he was happy because happiness was a choice. Bouncing between his mouldy flat and work with nothing in between. Now he'd touched the clouds. Visited his mother's homeland. Conjured light from nothing and helped bring back the dead. And he'd seen all the things Winter could do...

And he'd give it all up to have saved his family from the fire. He knew how she felt. He *knew*. "Please help us, Mrs Pavuka," he said quietly.

She smiled then, as though he'd passed some kind of test. Something glistened at the edge of her mouth like white mandibles. "Here." She held out the golden lace. Spiderwebs draped from her arms like bangles. "I know it's not exactly what the lads wear these days. Even where I come from it's out of style. But there's a protective spell worked into the pattern. Wear it, and Krampus and his dark elves won't be able to find you."

Chris draped it around his shoulders. "I love it," he said.

"You do, don't you?" Mrs Pavuka shook her head and started to walk around her chair. An extra arm popped out to steady her. She went to the cabinet behind her armchair and rattled one of the drawers. "Sticky thing," she grumbled as it popped open.

She picked up a small stone object. A spider, of course. It

glittered all over in greens and reds, like the knife from the British Museum. "I don't hold with knives, so I changed it. If your Winter can overcome her silly phobia, she can bring it to life. And it will take care of Nicholas."

She held it out. Chris stepped forward with a rush of gratitude. "Thank you. Thank you so much for your—"

He stopped. Her hand had closed back over the relic like a reflex. "Mrs Pavuka?"

The spectacles slid from her nose and smashed to the floor. The room darkened and Chris almost turned to see if the storm had deepened. Then he realized it wasn't the light *outside* that was changing.

The spiderwebs on her arms and shoulders no longer glittered and gleamed. They dripped with black. Shadows lengthened behind her. Eight spindly limbs emerged from her back, ending in points.

Chris stumbled back. "Winter?" he shouted.

The lamp shattered. The last of the light in the room was gone.

A clicking sound echoed around the apartment. Chris threw up his hands and light burst out, making the shadows dance like flame. Mrs Pavuka's face was a rictus of horror. Black smoked from her eyes. Her head bent back. Two long bones burst from her mouth, clacking in a frenzy.

He sure as hell wasn't getting near *that*. "Mrs Pavuka, throw it! The relic! Please!"

She heard him. He knew she did, for she brought her arm back like a cricket bowler. The relic gleamed in her palm. Then the shadows swallowed it up.

The clicking became a rustling, and the spiders burst forth.

They came from behind the bookcases and the decorative plates and the cabinet, from behind the dusty piano in the corner. They poured in from the hallway, scrambling over each other. They reared up against the shadows.

They had no chance. The shadows absorbed them into one writhing mass. Chris pushed with all his might, trying to make his light stronger, brighter—but he'd crossed continents and raced through two museums today, and whatever magic he had felt spun out to a thin thread.

Then the thread snapped, and everything went dark.

He ran for the door. Chittering surrounded him, growing louder and louder. He shoved his feet in his shoes, praying he wasn't squishing anything along the way. He wrenched the door open and tumbled down the stairs. Spiders flew off him as he crashed through the front door and out onto the lawn.

Winter was waiting for him with a cigarette in her hand. Her eyes widened as he ran up to her. "What the hell—" She hopped back. The spiders had started to flee the building. "What the *hell*!"

"Run," he panted. She didn't need to be told twice. "Don't step on the spiders, they tried to help."

"Yeah, that's my first priority, thanks for the tip," she snapped. "What did you do? She's gone mental."

They pelted out onto the empty Victoria Park Road and toward the sleigh, where Ottie and Rosie waited with their paws on the edge. Ottie started to bark, his little black eyebrows moving up and down in a panic.

Chris and Winter leapt over the side of the sleigh and Chris slammed his hand on the ignition, praying he had enough scraps of power to get them airborne.

The sleigh rattled to life. Hope stretched with a sound like a small rockslide. The runners scraped against frozen grass, and then they were in the air.

Winter shoved herself against the edge of the sleigh, gulping air. Chris picked a garden spider off his sleeve and gently pushed Diedre's beak away as she tried to eat a spider off the cuff of his trousers.

"Do not touch me," she said. "Not until you've had a proper shower and I know there's no trace of them left."

His legs gave out, and he collapsed against the side of the sleigh. A shiver ran along his spine. His skin crawled and he couldn't stop twitching. He didn't blame Winter for her phobia now. It'd be a good while before he looked at a spider the right way again.

"What happened?" Winter asked.

"She's gone," he said. It sounded so final, but he knew. "The dark elves attacked. She didn't make it."

Winter looked stricken. "Mrs Pavuka's... gone?"

Chris nodded.

She rubbed her face with her hands. Eyeshadow smeared down one cheek. "She can't... it's just..." She sniffed and palmed at one eye. "This is going to sound like shit, but you have to tell me. Did you get it?"

Chris shook his head. The wind blew cold as they rose in the air, and the dogs howled.

CHAPTER THIRTEEN

They set the sleigh down in Wanstead Park next to a long, frozen lake. An old manor house stood dark and empty across the water, unadorned. The trees were dark and ragged against the snow that blanketed the ground. It felt odd, to be in the middle of the city and see no one. To hear nothing but the wind, singing low and ruffling Chris's hair with icy fingers.

Winter heaved her dad's body out of the sleigh and checked every corner. She inspected the inside, then slid beneath it to examine the bottom and the runners. Rosie trotted up to Chris with a stick and he hurled it across the lawn. The dogs and Diedre left neat stitch-like footprints in the snow as they tore after it. When Rosie claimed the stick, Ottie snuffled until he found one of his own. Diedre promptly took it off him and clipped him with her wing. The little sausage dog trundled off into a clump of heather, grumbling.

"They might have hitched a ride to Mrs Pavuka, but they're not here anymore," she said. She pointed at the golden lace still draped around Chris's shoulders. "Could be thanks to your fancy protection spell. Or it could be that Krampus doesn't need to follow us anymore." She sat heavily on the ground and took her father's lifeless hand.

"There's got to be something we can do." Chris tugged the stick out of Diedre's mouth and tossed it. She flapped after, honking with excitement. "His condition is, erm, still the same?"

Winter unbuttoned Nick's coat and looked at his chest. "The veins are spreading," she said. "But he's still alive."

So, there was still a chance. "Maybe we can steal the knife back," Chris said.

"How, exactly?" Winter looked at him like he'd suggested they fly to the moon.

"There must be something else we can do, then. Don't your lot have special doctors or something?" Chris said.

"Not really. We don't get sick. We're either healthy or dead. Dad being mostly dead is a bit of an anomaly."

"So mostly dead is pretty good." Chris tossed Rosie's stick next. Ottie intercepted it with a neat leap and took off. Rosie chased him, yapping in fury. "It's frustrating. It feels like every time we figure it out, Krampus is stronger than we thought."

Winter sat back on her haunches and flicked her hair back, scowling. "Of course, he is. My dad's getting weaker, and as he gets weaker, Krampus gets stronger."

Diedre trotted back up. She'd snapped the stick in her hooked beak, and she looked somehow mournful. Chris crouched and stroked her skull. "Might it be the other way around, too?"

"Hm?" Winter was staring off into the park, sucking on her cigarette like it was the only thing keeping her sane.

"If Krampus got weaker, would your dad get stronger?"

She sighed and picked at a blade of grass poking valiantly through the carpet of white. "Yeah, well. In case you hadn't noticed, we can barely take on the dark elves and survive. Pulling Krampus back might help, but I don't think it would heal Dad. Just keep him from… totally going." She wouldn't say it, and she wouldn't look at Chris.

"Maybe that's what we need right now. To keep your Dad holding on until we can figure it out." He thought about what Mrs Pavuka had said, that good wouldn't disappear from the world if Nicholas did. "Surely Christmas will still be here tomorrow. The trees and the presents and the crackers and the dinners—"

"It won't be the same," Winter said. "I'm not going to abandon my Dad. And you're not his mythological heir, so…"

Chris put up his hands. "Hang on, I'm not trying to be."

"No? With all the powers and the grand speeches and this and that about the children? It rather *sounds* like you're trying." Her voice had filled with bitterness.

Chris didn't know how to reply, so he didn't. He watched the trees dip their branches in the wind instead. Winter made a

135

snowball. Rosie chased Ottie in a wide circle. Diedre clacked and scratched the frozen ground for insects.

He liked thinking that he was meant for something. He liked the idea that not only did he have a purpose, but his purpose was special. Something he got for being himself.

But he'd meant what he said to Mrs Pavuka, too. He liked being in control of his own destiny, deciding to be the best him. He didn't want to become some mythological heir if it changed all that.

He also meant what he'd said about helping Winter.

"Listen," he said gently. "I'm sorry—"

Winter snorted.

"*I'm sorry* about your father. But I do think that if he were here, he'd tell us what to focus on first. And I think you know what he'd say."

Winter scowled at him. Then she threw the snowball. It hit him in the chest with a soft puff of snow that dusted his chin and shoulders and startled a laugh out of him. "Yeah, well. I still don't know how we're supposed to help the kids if we can't defeat a few measly minions."

"The trick isn't to face him head-on. The trick is to pull the rug out from under him," Chris said. "Make him lose his power *first*."

Winter blew her hair out of her eyes again. "What do you have in mind?"

"Well, your mum said Krampus steals kids, right?"

"Yeah." Winter made another snowball but tossed this one from hand to hand. "It's kind of his thing. He thrives off their fear."

"So, we steal them right back. We take them somewhere safe. Surely with your powers you can get into wherever he's keeping them."

"They'll be guarded," she said.

"Anything a blue whale can't take care of?"

"And I don't know where they are." She dropped the snowball between her legs and looked at him. Her expression was unshielded and full of worry. She didn't think she could do this. She knew their time was running out, and she was afraid she'd blow their last chance.

"You found one with your mum. You can do it again." Chris held out a hand. "I'll help you."

Winter looked at his outstretched hand. Then at him. "Aren't you tired?" she said.

He chuckled dryly. "Yeah."

She scooted over the grass until she was close enough to clasp hands with him. "I'm completely bollocked," she said. "And you must be worse—you were basically a living battery in the museum. But you never complain."

"Got nothing to complain about," said Chris as their fingers twined.

"I hate goody-goodies like you," she grumbled, closing her eyes. But the edges of her mouth were curled up.

He *was* tired. And it was showing. He searched for that thin thread of power, but it took him a little while to find it, curled up somewhere deep inside himself. He coaxed it out with thoughts of squishy marshmallows and squishier hugs, unravelled it gently and started to feed it to Winter. It went grudgingly, and he felt a warning pressure on his chest. But he pushed forward. If they could do this— if she could find the kids—then they could both finally rest.

"It's not working." Winter's brow was furrowed. She wrinkled her nose. In the distance, Rosie barked. Winter blinked and looked out over the park.

"Focus." Chris tugged on her hand. The world around him was fuzzing at the edges. They didn't have time to waste. He leaned forward until their foreheads touched. He didn't dare close his eyes. "Focus," he murmured, as much to himself as to her. "On one thing at a time."

This close he could see her makeup flaking and feel her breath on his chin. This close, the cinnamon clove scent of her was so strong he could almost taste it. He could also feel something else— her magic, maybe?—moving in her like a sea. He urged his thread to meet that sea, to wind it in.

She inhaled sharply and jerked back. Her brown eyes were wide as they latched on to Chris, and he felt a jolt in his stomach that had nothing to do with magic. "I know. I mean, I think I know. No, I know. I saw the boy again. I can find him."

She leapt to her feet and called for Rosie and Ottie. Chris climbed into the sleigh. He ran his fingers over the craggy surface of Hope's tail fin. "Ready for one more ride?" he said.

Hope wiggled. Her vertebrae ground together with a sound like teeth sliding against each other. She seemed eager. It must have been boring at the Natural History Museum, with no variation from day to day.

"It's good to have you on the team," Chris said. He tried to put the thought of the suffering kids out of his mind and conjured up memories of sleigh bells and ice skates. The sleigh rumbled to life. He opened his eyes in time to see Rosie hurtling toward him. He caught her with an "Oof!" and set her down gently as she tried to lick his chin. Her wet-dog scent assaulted him.

Ottie barked at Chris's hand when Chris bent to lift him into the sleigh. He hopped valiantly until Winter scooped him up. "No time for that," she said as he growled. She put Diedre in next, then clambered in herself. She nodded crisply to Chris, and he urged Hope up once more. Wanstead Park fell away until the lakes were nothing more than a frozen brown tangle in the snow.

"Where to?" Chris said, hand poised over the map.

Winter leaned around him to frown at the dash. Then she pointed to a spot and nodded, as though convincing herself. "There. Tower Heights."

***

Arthur was crunching through a slightly soggy meal deal and contemplating Missy's latest text. *Happy Christmas. Thinking of coming to London for a weekend in Jan.*

His stomach twisted sourly in a combination of hope and fear. Missy hated London. Was she bringing the boys in an attempt to play happy family? Was she warning Arthur to stay out of the way?

Or maybe she'd tired of waiting on him to initiate divorce proceedings. Maybe she was coming to make it all official. Maybe she'd found someone else—someone father-approved this time, someone who made asking for divorce worthwhile.

Never mind that. Arthur unstuck cheap bread from the top of his mouth with his tongue and managed one more swallow of egg sandwich before wiping his mouth and throwing his lunch remains out. He'd been the scumbag who left; Missy should date who she wanted.

He went back to the case file and the notes that had exploded over his desk. He had a pretty comprehensive list of what was missing now, and it was more than photos. Locations had been changed, too. Where the kids had last been seen. Arthur had only caught it because he remembered the abandoned Lamiroux tyre factory where they'd found the cloven hoofprint. Except the digital case file said Lamifoille, and the only record of a Lamifoille he could find was in Belgium. He rubbed his temple in an attempt to fend off the oncoming headache. It was too close to Christmas for this, and by *God* he wanted a sweet stout, and—

Izzy stomped into the station. She had a very distinctive tread when she was angry. Arthur did his best to ignore her until her shadow loomed over his desk, and he couldn't pretend that she wasn't mad at *him,* specifically.

"Hayne was useless. Said he'd already told you everything and he wouldn't listen to us slander his favourite employee."

"I did try to tell you—"

"Shut it, Stowe. We're supposed to be working through this together. Instead, you ran off on a stupid side mission and antagonized a character witness. We *have* to make a break in this case." The fire in her eyes said, *if not for your own sake, then for mine.* Her bun was half falling from its tight knot at the base of her skull.

Now might be a good time to interject. "Well, I may have. Look here." He passed over the list of locations.

Izzy scanned it, face twisting in frustration. "So?"

"None of those places actually exist. Harper Primary's listed location is a Waitrose. Lamifoille tyre factory never existed—"

"For Christ's sake, Arthur. They were abandoned spots. So, someone knocked down the old building and put up a new one. It's not rocket science."

139

No, but it had happened with every spot, and wasn't that odd? "They were all bought by Snell," he said.

She paused at that. "Say again?" She started re-pinning her hair.

He went through the list. He couldn't reconstruct every change, but many of the sites were only a few letters off. Antonius Snell's property acquisition was public information, so once Arthur had compared the two lists, he'd found more near-matches. And every newly purchased property near the last known sighting of a victim had been bought by Snell. "You know there's something in this, Izzy," he said.

"I mean… Snell's been buying up the bad lots in town for years." But Izzy's frown was thoughtful now, not angry. "It could be coincidence."

"I don't believe in coincidence." He believed in bad men who got away with bad things. "It's worth taking to the Boss, isn't it?"

Izzy looked from one paper to the other, worrying her lip with her teeth. Then she nodded decisively. "Let's."

Montague always worked Christmas. He said it was because he didn't like to make his team do what he wouldn't do himself. Arthur knew it was because Montague couldn't stand his sister-in-law and she always did Christmas in London. Arthur and Izzy exchanged a look outside his door, then Arthur knocked.

Montague waved them in with a scowl. He'd been tidying his desk, Arthur noted as he caught the scent of lemon cleaner.

The Commissioner's scowl did not let up as Arthur showed him the missing photographs and changed names. "So, you think Antonius Snell is part of a vast conspiracy to abduct children while he's moaning about it on the news? You think he's some supervillain trying to throw us off the scent?" He turned to Izzy. "And you believe this?"

"Arthur, er, seemed to think it was important." Izzy was visibly deflated.

"Christ, Iz, thanks for the backup," Arthur muttered. He gripped old Dad's truncheon until his palm throbbed.

"Are you drunk, Stowe?" Montague fixed him with one hard brown eye.

"*No.*" Why did everyone always ask him that?

"Are you interested in losing your job?"

Arthur waited for Montague to keep ranting, but the Commissioner stopped there, waiting for an answer. Montague had a glare that could erode steel. "No," he said sullenly. He felt like a child caught with the biscuits. Of course, he didn't want to bloody lose his bloody job. It was the only thing he had left.

"This is real life, Stowe, not a detective movie. Why would Minister Snell fund an investigation that would indict him? Why would he pay officers to arrest him? He's always made his money in property development. That's no great secret. You know why he bought those places? Probably because nobody else wanted to after a kid went missing."

Montague's mobile rang. He answered it and said, "Just a moment." Then he put it on mute and leaned on his desk. "Stop running around talking about conspiracies and cover-ups and nonexistent witnesses and Cessnas. And stop obsessing over Snell. This is real life. You're not uncovering a vast conspiracy, you're a mediocre officer in the London Met."

He flapped his hand as he picked up the call again.

Arthur felt like he'd been punched in the gut as they left Montague's office. *You're a mediocre officer in the London Met.* He'd always known he wasn't the best, but…

No, Montague was right. He was a poor detective, and his wild theories would only drag down a promising officer who shouldn't have to rely on him.

The memories came unbidden. *Think nothing of it, officer. That money was for charity, officer. Drop it, officer.* He'd heard all this when he lived in Letherford. Back when he'd had a chance and the choice: be a good policeman, or be happy?

Arthur went back to his desk, too deep in thought to reply when Izzy muttered some half-arsed apology. *If I were a Member of Parliament and I wanted to cover up a big crime, I would absolutely pay the police who are investigating it.* With the power to sack Arthur and Izzy and maybe even Montague, if Snell wanted to push them a certain direction—say, toward a homeless Father

Christmas—who would have the guts to refuse?

He ran his thumb over the top of his truncheon and scratched at his ginger-blond stubble. He was missing the *why,* of course, and without it he'd never get the backing of the Met. Even with it, he probably wouldn't get the backing. Montague had made that clear.

"All right. I've got three possible hits for who our John Doe could be." Arthur jumped. Izzy stood in front of him, arms crossed. Her voice was clipped. She obviously didn't want to be talking to him, but as she'd been having a go at him earlier for not working together, she couldn't really leave him out of this one.

Arthur followed her back to her desk. The fluorescent lights were starting to give him a headache. But he gamely leaned in to look at the mug shots.

"No," he said. None of them looked anything like the victim at Saint Paul's.

"Turkish descent, estimated mid-sixties in age, white beard, white hair. This is all I'm pulling up on the database. You sure?" Arthur nodded. Izzy heaved a sigh. "Now what? Do we try canvassing? See what homeless shelters around St. Paul's say about him?"

"Could do. Or we could check out the old Lamiroux tyre factory."

Izzy's nostrils flared. "We've got to drop it, Art," she said.

"You're not calling me Art. And I'm not dropping it. You know there's something to this. You *know.*"

A couple of the others looked their way. "Shh!" Izzy warned, and Arthur realized his voice had risen. She scooted her chair a little closer. "Yeah, all right. But what are we supposed to do about it? The Commish said to leave it. He knows what he's doing, Arthur."

"There's no evidence that some homeless person ring is conspiring to kidnap children. Unlike Snell, they don't have the resources to pull it off."

Izzy looked conflicted for a moment. Then she shook her head. "You can throw your career down the toilet, Arthur. I'm going to do what I've been told by a man who's got more experience than both of us combined."

"Don't you care about these kids?" he said.

He hadn't meant to. It was a low thing to say, and Izzy recoiled as though he'd spat on her. She paled in anger. "Of course, I care," she said, enunciating each word through clenched teeth. "That's why I'm following orders. I don't need to be right or get my ego stroked. I'm going to put in the work and follow my boss's advice. And I'm going to solve this case. Because that's what being a detective requires. Not that chip on your shoulder, Arthur. Work. And cooperation. You're so busy seeing the worst in Snell and Montague that you can't see they're trying to help."

"Snell's not trying to help," Arthur said. "At best he's trying to save his own arse."

Izzy rolled her chair away from him. "You do what you want, Arthur. I'm going to help Montague win this. And maybe when it's all over, you'll realize not every politician is a *complete* wanker."

I'm going to hate proving you wrong, Arthur thought as he put on his navy coat and hat.

The cruiser was freezing and smelled of petrol, but he welcomed the chance to sit inside it and puff the cold air alone. He was sick of being around people. He'd really thought Izzy was different. Driven to help others and do good in the world. And Hell, maybe she thought she was. But at the end of the day, her first priority was herself.

He smiled wryly as the car rumbled to life. You could always rely on Arthur Stowe to utterly bollocks his own career. But at least he'd do it for the kids.

Lamiroux tyres was a bust. The building had been knocked down and the lot was a big square of snow-covered dirt behind a chain link fence. No footfalls marred the pristine white, nothing disturbed the area. Arthur consulted the map on which he'd marked Snell's properties, then drove on to the next.

The building there was intact, if you could call a roofless square intact. Arthur clipped the link fence with some bolt cutters from the back of the car and prayed no one would report him for it. He'd have a hard time convincing Montague of probable cause. There was nothing there, either.

Nor at the third site, a burned-out apartment block. He didn't have to be nervous yet, Arthur told himself as he got back in his car. There were a lot of places to check. And if he was wrong, well, he'd be sacked for sure. But he thought of the shadow horns and shadow tail that had sprouted from Snell at the British Museum, and he didn't think he was wrong.

It was nearing five in the afternoon when he pulled up outside Harper Primary. He knew immediately that this was the place. The footprints were the clue: two perfect pairs, headed up the stairs to the closed double doors of the school.

Arthur checked for his truncheon and his handcuffs, then slid out of the car. Whatever the truth was, he'd find it inside.

He did a quick loop around the school. The windows were closed, and the door was bolted. As he worked on the door with his bolt cutters, he added one more question to his ever-growing list. How had they gotten inside?

The lock fell to the ground with a *clang*. With one last furtive look around, Arthur pulled on the squealing door and slipped inside.

It took a few moments for his eyes to adjust to the gloom. The school was dark and smelled like dust. As his eyes grew used to the dark he saw the murals on the walls, cheerful and chipped, full of animals and trees and books. The floor crunched with years of built-up dirt. Cubby holes gaped like dark open mouths against the wall. Arthur shuddered as he passed a grinning squirrel, checking for light under each closed door that lined the hall. Nothing. He kept his torch off, hoping that in the twilight he didn't kick a stray stack of books and make a ruckus—or worse, fall and crack his head.

Then he rounded a corner in the hallway, and he began to hear the noise. It was a lone wail, pained and young and frightened.

His heart skipped a beat and his hand went for his truncheon. He should call for back up. But who was going to believe him?

A stair at the end of the hall led to a cellar. As he approached, he saw the strange red light that curled from beneath. The light from hell. The same light he'd seen at the British Museum. He touched his still-tender neck and tasted fear in the back of his mouth. Surely one brush with death was enough for today.

Then he thought of the kids, and he started down.

CHAPTER FOURTEEN

Chris draped Mrs Pavuka's lace shawl over the sleigh. Its thread-thin edges glimmered in the fading light. "Stay well hidden, friends," he said. Rosie gave him a derisive look and hopped out of the sleigh. She clearly thought she was going with them.

"Mum wouldn't want you to," Winter said. Rosie didn't dignify that with a response, choosing instead to circle Chris until he picked her up, wet dog smell and all. Winter sighed. "What about you?" she asked Ottie. Ottie barked and leapt for her arms. She caught him with a grunt. Diedre had already nested down, quite content to chew on the stick she'd found in the park. Her hooked beak clicked and clacked.

Winter grabbed Chris's free hand. That was all the warning he had before they were off the roof and on the ground. He staggered, stomach convulsing as it caught up with the rest of him. "Sorry, but how do you stand that?" he asked.

"Lots of practice." Winter set Ottie down and pulled her black hair back into a ponytail. Even her hair tie had a little silver bird skull on it. She touched the empty sheath where her axe had been, sighed, and pulled the other one loose. "Now, we have no idea what we're going to find. So be on your guard."

Be on my guard to do what? Chris looked at his long-fingered, fine hands. He barely knew how to make a fist.

Harper Primary was a small and unassuming building. Chris would've taken it for an old farmhouse if not for the wooden sign out front in peeling paint and the metal playground sign decaying in the school's courtyard. The bricks, now smudged with London dirt, had probably been a cheerful red once. He followed Winter up to the double doors at the head of the building. A padlock the size of Chris's hand kept them closed. Chris whistled.

"Come on. Is that really supposed to stop me?" Winter pressed on the door, and it opened as though the padlock didn't even exist.

Chris stared as they went through. The padlock was there. It still held the doors shut. Yet they were walking through. "Magic gives me a headache," he said.

"Fair. Don't try to get back through on your own."

They conjured light and slowly walked down the hall, feet squeaking on the linoleum tile. Winter shuddered as they passed dusty picture frames with portraits of staff long gone, flaking murals, a lone backpack forgotten in the middle of the hall. "I hate school," she muttered, kicking the backpack to the side. It skidded and *thunked* into a door. "I always hated going, but an abandoned one is somehow so much worse."

"You went to school?" Chris had liked school well enough. He had had friends there, and many of his teachers had been kind to him, especially after the fire.

Winter made a face. "My dad thought it'd build character." She said the word *character* as though it carried a particularly vicious disease.

Winter led them around the corner and to the top of a wide set of stairs. The bottom of the stairwell was an impenetrable black against their conjured lights. "Of course." Winter rolled her shoulders. One fist clenched and unclenched.

Chris was slammed by the sudden urge to turn tail and run as far as he could. He swallowed his nerves and took a deep breath. He wasn't the sort to run. He'd convinced Winter to do this and he had to see it through. Besides, where could he run to? He couldn't get through the door.

"Do you think he gets stronger off our fear?" he said.

"Probably." Winter started moving down.

Chris thought that the school itself was eerily silent, but the cellar was even more so. It seemed to suck all the sound out of the air—the slap of his shoes on the tile was muted and his heart, so loud in his ears at the top of the stairs, barely pulsed now. At his feet, Rosie began to whine. He held up his conjure-light.

The hall stretched away from him without end. More magic,

he knew abruptly. The wide space had been cut through the middle to make a slim corridor—or perhaps, more accurately, it had been filled on either side with long rows of cages. The cages ran floor to ceiling, with locked doors in the middle. He pushed his light against the nearest cage and peered inside.

He'd known what they were looking for, but his stomach still plunged at the sight.

She was smudged and smelly, crouched with her arms over her chest. Her hair hung limp. She looked at him with dull, hopeless eyes. She was ten, maybe.

He crouched to be on her level. She scrambled backward. Her breath came in short, terrified pants. "It's all right," Chris said, keeping his voice calm though something tightened in his chest. "It's okay. What's your name?"

"He keeps them afraid, remember," Winter said. "She's not going to up and answer you."

"Have you got a mum?" Chris asked. His light flickered. Her eyes gleamed from beneath a curtain of dirty hair. "Shall we take you back to your mum?"

He turned to Winter. "Get it open," he said, and was surprised by his own voice. He'd never heard it go so low or feel so full of steel. Something hot seemed to boil up from his belly, spreading to every limb.

Winter was tugging on the mesh of another cage. She looked over at him and shook her head. "My powers aren't working."

"A bloody good time for them to go on the fritz," he said. He was breathing heavily now. He wanted to open his mouth and breathe fire.

"My powers don't fritz," she grated. "They're being actively countered. Obviously."

"What?" That made no sense. "If they can be countered, how could we get through the lock upstairs?"

"Because I wanted you to get in."

Chris turned. This was a new voice. It was a voice of smoke and slicking oil. It was the voice of every man who'd ever stood in Parliament and told him that his brown skin was his own fault, and that if his family didn't want to die in a burning apartment block, they could've lived somewhere three times as expensive and saved themselves all that hassle.

The voice belonged to a tall white man, impeccably dressed in a pinstripe suit and maroon tie. Shadowy horns sprouted from his head. At his feet, a red glow began to spread, and the air filled with the scent of ash.

"Krampus," Chris said.

The man inclined his head. "I thought I might see for myself the two whelps who are trying to steal Nick's power. The building's hidden from most prying eyes, but I set up a warning spell for anything that got through the door upstairs."

The heat in Chris boiled over and he realized what he was feeling. He tasted bile in the back of his throat. "I don't like you," he said. "I've never met anyone I couldn't like, but I don't like you."

Krampus cocked his head and looked Chris over. "You really are out to save the world, aren't you?" he said dryly. "No wonder you got tapped. *You,* on the other hand—"

He wheeled around and raised his arm. A shadow lashed like a whip. Winter brought up her axe. The shadow-whip wrapped around the shaft. Several of the kids screamed. One started to wail. "Everyone knows that Nicholas's daughter hates Christmas. This must be the last place you'd like to be."

"Yeah, well." She wrenched the axe free. "Anything for the opportunity to kick your ass."

Before she could move, a third voice rang out, clear but definitely tinged with a *what-the-hell-am-I-doing* tone. "All right, that's enough. London Met, you're all under arrest. Hands where I can see them."

Chris turned as another figure descended the stairs. The policeman from the museum. The marks on his throat were livid in the new light. His eyes flickered from Winter to Chris to Krampus. He held a wooden truncheon up like it was going to do him any good.

Krampus spread his hands. "Arthur! Perfect timing, old chap. Slap these unruly youths under arrest and we'll be back at the station in time for a presser."

"You're under arrest too, Snell," Arthur said. "There's no point in resisting. You're a face of the nation and it's not like we don't know where you live." He stepped forward and rattled the mesh on one cage. A kid gasped.

Arthur looked him over. "Aruj Kunil," he said softly. He looked in the next cage. "Geordie Jones." He nodded and something filled his eyes. Rage, Chris thought, and he felt an answering emotion surge in him. Anger was good here, yes. Anger was what they needed, not decency. "Now. Be a good fellow and toss over the keys," Arthur told Krampus.

"What keys?" Krampus's grin split him from ear to ear. "You can't possibly think that *I* have something to do with this."

"Why not? It's your property." He looked down the length of the hall. "I've got eyes on two victims and I'm willing to bet I'll find the rest. And you've had time enough over the years to go into my station, tamper with my case file, and falsify data."

Krampus pressed his hands together as if in prayer. Another shadow-whip struck as Winter brought her axe back, wrapping around the shaft an inch below the blade and stopping her blow. "Art, you're a copper. You've got a fairly simple view of things: find crime, solve crime. You think that if all crime were solved, everything would be perfect. But that's not true."

Krampus ran a finger along one cage. The steel rustled. "A nation is not orderly when there's no crime. A nation is orderly when its people are *afraid*. The problem, Art, is that a happy man quits his job and dosses around. A happy man likes what he has, so he doesn't need to buy more, so he doesn't stimulate the economy. A happy man feels safe, so he doesn't try to move to a better part of town or install a better security system. But a man who's *afraid*... oh, that man will keep his head down so he doesn't get fired. A man who's afraid that his wife will leave him buys presents so she'll stay. A man afraid of his neighbours buys better locks and better cameras. And when I say there's a kidnapper stalking our streets, people don't merely obey a curfew. They clamour for one."

"I don't believe you," Arthur said. The hand holding his truncheon shook.

Krampus pointed at Arthur. "Look at your job. When people are afraid, they come to you. You make them feel better. So, we make them afraid, and your job is secure. And think: when we appear together with all thirty-three children and three culprits, you won't be the loser copper with nothing at home but empty bottles. You'll be the hero who always did what was right. Isn't it time you were recognized for that? Why does doing the right thing have to ruin your life? I can clear your name, Art. You got run out of Letherford, but I'd make you a hero for all Britain. You could get your life back. Your wife back. Your children back."

Arthur stumbled back as though Krampus had physically pushed him. Hope flickered for an instant on his face—hope, and fear. "No, I can't," he said. "Missy hates me."

"She wants you to write. She wants you in the boys' lives. Wouldn't you like to come home with a commendation from Parliament? Wouldn't you like to show her old man where he can stick it?" Krampus stepped forward. "Wouldn't that be better than rotting on the pavement without a job or a home to go to?"

"You can't," Chris burst out. The detective's sharp eyes snapped to him. "You know he's behind all this. You know it, don't you?"

Arthur looked at the truncheon in his hand. Then at his feet. For a moment he seemed to teeter on the edge of a decision.

"Everybody's a bad person, somehow," he said quietly. He looked up at Krampus. "And I was almost the worst sort of person. Your deal sounds lovely. So, I'll be sure to add bribery to the list of charges brought against you." He pointed to Winter, then Chris. "You're all coming in. And if you come quietly, it'll go better for you."

"Oh, Art," Krampus sighed. But his mouth pulled back, baring his even white teeth. He pulled something from his pocket and tossed it into the air. Chris had just enough time to register them as small, yellow-brown bones.

Then they hit the floor, and where they hit the floor, the shadows pooled and lapped. The bones seemed to unfold and multiply, clicking and shuffling into place. Shadows held their bones in place like tendons. A snake, a bird and a wildcat all slunk toward Winter, while behind them yet more bones rose from a tarry mire.

Winter twisted her axe free and lunged for the snake. "Free the kids," she shouted. Then she blocked one strike, then another, and she didn't have time to say anything else. Around them, a chorus of screams went up. At the sound, the shadows grew thicker. The horns at Krampus' temple hardened into reality.

Chris pulled at the mesh of the nearest cage. The wire was strong and unbending. He had a pocketknife, didn't he? No, he'd left it at the mortuary when he'd run after Winter.

"What the…" Arthur said. Then something smashed into Chris from behind, bruising ribs, and sending him *clanging* into the cage. He turned around to see the rhinoceros skeleton from the Natural History Museum. Shadow dripped from its mouth like spittle.

"You again," he said, vaguely impressed that he'd managed to sound resigned.

The rhinoceros was too big for the space. That was the only advantage. He jerked to the side as it tried to gore him with its horn. The horn slid into the mesh and stuck fast. As the rhinoceros bucked and tugged against the cage, Chris grabbed its head. How hard could it be to twist off a couple of vertebrae?

Bloody hard. A plated shoulder slammed into him and stole his breath. He was pretty sure he heard a crack. What a way to go. Trampled by an undead rhinoceros in a primary school cellar.

Rosie leapt up and fastened her tiny teeth around the rhinoceros's back knee joint. She scrambled with her front paws, growling.

It kicked her off. She flew across the hall with a howl and a yelp as she hit the floor. "Rosie!" Chris shouted. He dropped the head and tried to move for her. But the rhino slammed him against the cage again. Its head hit his nose. The cage clanged and blood flowed into the back of his mouth. He choked and spit and lunged to the side. The rhinoceros pulled mightily against the cage and for a moment Chris hoped the creature might actually help him.

Its horn slid free instead. Its head crashed into Chris's stomach, and he couldn't concentrate on anything but the searing pain in his side, his back, his ribs. He grabbed the horn and barely redirected it as the rhino tried to gut him.

Then the rhinoceros jerked. Bones clattered over the floor, and Chris sagged under the unexpected weight of a skull. The lower jaw dropped to the floor, shedding teeth. Black oozed around the skeleton in a shapeless mass, herding the bones gently together.

Arthur stood beside him, breathing hard. He held his truncheon in his hand. It looked like he'd managed to separate the vertebrae after all.

Behind him Winter flashed through the air, moving her axe and a knife too fast to be seen. Streaks of golden light ribboned in her wake and bones cascaded away from her.

"Thanks, mate," Chris groaned, and spat more blood over his shoes.

"I figure I owe you." Arthur held a long pair of wire clippers and moved in toward the lock. "You're still under arrest, but things are looking better for you than they were a minute ago. I think your girlfriend had the right idea."

As he set the clippers against the lock, Chris said, "She's not my girlfriend."

"I really don't care," Arthur replied, and heaved.

The lock snapped. The shadow-skeletons froze.

"Dear me," Krampus said and clapped his hands once.

The skeletons disappeared. So did the children. Chris pushed the door open onto an empty cage.

"Bring them back," he snarled. He'd never been so angry about something in his entire life. *"Bring them back."*

"Hm." Krampus tapped a finger against his lips. "No."

"Game's up, Snell. You're surrounded." Arthur moved to block the stairs. "I don't know what you just did, but I've seen a lot of weird stuff today and I'm beyond caring."

Winter was panting. She lifted her axe.

Krampus looked at her. A vindictive smile played on his lips. He held up a closed fist. "You know, I'll let you choose. You can have the children back... or you can have this."

He opened his hand. A glimmering stone knife sat in his palm.

Winter gasped.

Chris didn't like the way her dark eyes gleamed. "The kids. Winter, the kids." It wasn't even a choice. Their fear and their misery, their torment... no one could prolong that, not for any reason.

"Give up the kids, Snell," Arthur said.

Krampus cocked his head. "Your choice," he said to Winter.

"I..." she said. Her eyes were black pits. She stared at Krampus's open hand. Ottie howled.

She stuck out her hand. "The knife."

"*No!*" Chris shouted.

"Snell, bring those bloody kids back—" Arthur lunged forward.

Krampus's smile twisted, cruel and triumphant. His hand closed around the knife again—

—and he threw it to the floor.

It shattered, sending rainbow shards across the corridor. Winter screamed in heartbreak and fury. Arthur swung.

His hand hit empty air. Krampus was gone, and only his oily laugh remained.

CHAPTER FIFTEEN

Arthur looked from cage to empty cage. *Impossible.* Thirty children simply didn't disappear. Then again, shadows didn't spring from the ground, and MPs didn't sprout horns. He was so far out of his depth he might as well be swimming.

With Snell's laugh a fading memory, it was hard to believe he hadn't had some kind of psychotic break. *Had* he been coming to work drunk for the past day and a half? Was all this a figment of his imagination?

If it was, one of his figments was getting a mind of his own. Chris shook as he faced down Winter. "I can't believe you."

Winter stared at the floor, arms crossed and held tight against her stomach. Her lips moved, but no sound came out. She looked like she was ready to cry.

"We had those kids. They were *right here* and now Krampus knows we're after them and he knows what kind of powers we have, and our best chance to save them is completely gone."

Sirens sounded on empty streets in the distance. Arthur's gut twinged. He imagined Snell on the phone somewhere, babbling about intruders. He still didn't know whether these kids were real or not, but they were coming with him. He'd figure this one out even if he needed to stay out of the station for a while.

He was certain that whoever Snell called in would have no love to lose for him.

He grabbed Chris by one shoulder and Winter by the other. Neither resisted, which was fortunate, because Arthur was certain Chris could outrun him and Winter could break his kneecaps. "You lot appear to have information. We're going somewhere where I can get a pint and write it all down." If now wasn't the time for a drink, he didn't know what was.

"We really don't have time to explain the whole thing," Chris said. "We've only got 'til midnight."

"You're a suspect in thirty-three kidnappings, mate. You'd better make time."

The sirens were around the corner now. There was no way they'd all get in the squad car before the Met was on them. But Chris sighed and said, "Come on," and stomped up the stairs.

There was a swift trotting sound behind them. Arthur whipped round. Two dachshunds appeared from the gloom, one red and one brown. They followed Chris and Winter. "What the hell are those?"

"Rosie and Ottie," Chris replied. The brown one growled at him.

He had to admit they didn't look like servants of some hell spawn. The red one even licked his trouser leg as she went by.

He prodded the near-catatonic Winter up to the door and out around the side of the building. They were lucky with the snow; it had built up over the course of a day and a half into a fluffy carpet that would impede pursuit. All the same. "Did you come on foot?" he said. Escaping on foot would be out of the question.

Winter looked up to the roof of the school. Ah. The so-called Cessna. And… Good *Lord,* what was attached to the end of it?

"I've gone mad," he realized softly. "Or else I've died, and this is the special Hell they've made for me."

"Come on, Winter. Don't want to cross paths with the police." Chris glanced at Arthur. "No offence."

"They can't see us anyway," she mumbled.

"Winter, I'm cold and I'm sore and my suit's had enough of this weather. We need to make a plan. Find out what's next. Come on. Just—get us up to the sleigh. I'll handle the rest."

He put a hand on her shoulder. Something seemed to pass from him to her. She took Arthur's arm, and then they were on the roof.

Arthur stumbled. His stomach flipped over, and he barely kept himself from heaving over the side of the sleigh. "What in the ever-loving name of—"

"Keep your hands and arms inside the sleigh at all times." Chris hauled him back. "Take a seat. Sorry about the dead bloke, but you get used to him."

155

"Homeless Father Christmas," said Arthur, dazed.

Something nipped at his trouser leg: a gigantic bird skeleton. It cocked its head, then nipped again. Arthur pushed it away with his foot. How was this not the strangest part of his day?

"Don't kick Diedre," said Chris as he pressed his hand to a button on the dash. The button glowed green, and the jumble of bones resolved itself, stretching its incredible snout toward the sky. Its fluke slapped the air and sent snowflakes flurrying around them. They began to rise. "Now. Where to? Maybe we can find the kids—"

"We can't," said Winter.

"Winter," Chris began.

"We *can't*," she shouted. "Don't you see? Even Dad couldn't find them after searching for months and months. We only found them because *he* wanted us to, he wanted to cause us pain and tear us down."

"Well, we can't give up," Chris snapped.

"All right. Enough with the lover's quarrel," said Arthur.

"*We're not together,*" Chris and Winter shouted at once.

Arthur couldn't care less. His fingers and toes were working on falling off, in addition to less savoury parts of him. He was hooked up to a whale skeleton and flying over London with no permit, no seatbelt, and no parachute. "We're going to a pub. And when we get there, you're going to tell me everything." He pointed at Chris. "Does this thing have SatNav?"

"More or less," Chris said. Winter rolled her eyes.

"I want to go the *Blue Whale*. Lewisham. If they've got dead aquatic mammal parking."

They swept across the Thames, dodging skyscrapers and skimming the bottoms of the clouds. At some point, Arthur realized he'd forgotten to be flabbergasted by the fact that he was in a flying sleigh pulled by a blue whale skeleton and was actually enjoying the view. London was charming from above, a mad scramble of buildings studded with parks. Some areas were a riot of fairy lights in red and white and green. But other urban areas were dark, unable to afford Christmas lights or maybe light at all. Arthur could only hope they'd managed to keep the heating on.

Chris stood at the helm, a pilot attending to his craft. Winter slumped in the seat next to Arthur, saying nothing and looking at nothing. The corpse sprawled next to her, but evidently she didn't mind. Goths, he thought. They even had to bring skeletons and dead bodies to St. Nick's sleigh.

They sailed into Lewisham and Chris brought them down into the alley behind the *Blue Whale*. Their actual blue whale didn't fit; she lounged on the roof as though it were a rock and she were sunning herself. Arthur checked his watch. Flying by sleigh sure beat traffic.

I must be barking. He'd laugh, except the whole situation wasn't remotely funny.

The pub greeted them with a blast of warmth and a mixed stench of old cigarette smoke and sour beer. Queen's *Thank God it's Christmas* played from the radio over the bar. They found a booth at the back and Chris volunteered to get the drinks as Arthur massaged his fingers and pulled off his coat.

"Get me a Guinness," he told Chris.

"We're working," Chris admonished gently.

Winter did not look at Arthur, nor speak to him. She sat and stared at the oak table with its patina of spilled booze and dirt. Arthur got out his notepad, tapped his thumb against his truncheon, and waited.

Chris came back with three steaming cups on a tray decorated with a sprig of holly, and no sweet stout. He set the cups out and then flopped down with a sigh that seemed to carry the weight of the world. Arthur knew that kind of sigh well, and Chris was too young for it.

Winter stirred at last, looking at the tea. "How much alcohol's in it?" she asked as she picked up her cup.

Chris looked at her strangely. "Er, none. It's tea."

"I've had nothing but tea all day. If I don't get something to put in it right now, I'm going to flip the table." She stood up and stalked off.

"She's not going to do a runner, is she?" Arthur said, leaning around to watch her.

"Nah, she can't drive the sleigh." Chris took a deep sip of his tea and leaned back, closing his eyes. "When you feel like you have nothing, you can always make yourself a cup of tea. That's what my mum always said."

Arthur didn't miss the use of the past tense. He didn't press for details, either. They sat in awkward silence until Winter came back with six shots. She poured one straight into her teacup.

"What is that?" Chris said.

"No idea, I swiped it from the bar." She took a long drink, then choked. "It's disgusting." She took a gingerly sip of another shot and made a face. "Ugh. Jägermeister."

Arthur didn't need a drink *that* badly. "All right. We've got drinks, we're out of the way, nobody's paying attention. I want answers. What's going on?"

"Well, we're trying to save Christmas," Chris said. At Arthur's look he clarified. "Father Christmas. Though I suppose saving *Father* Christmas will also save the *holiday* Christmas—"

Winter sighed. "Hush." She downed a clean shot, then turned to Arthur. "Father Christmas is my dad, right? And he died last night at St. Paul's. Except he's not really dead, and if we can save him we can stop Krampus—that Snell guy who's kidnapped a load of children and is trying to destroy the Christmas spirit forever."

"Except now the kids are gone." Chris folded his arms and looked at Winter. "We agreed we had to save the kids. Why did you do it?"

Winter stared at the table. "He's my dad, Chris."

"You know what he would have wanted you to do. You know what he would have done in your place."

"*I'm not him,*" Winter shouted.

Arthur and Chris leaned back. Winter's eyes were blazing. Arthur half expected her to go for her axe, but after a moment, when she sagged, he realized the shimmer in her gaze wasn't anger. It was tears. One of those tears slipped out and rolled down her cheek, making a track in her makeup. She smeared it away.

"If we'd gotten the knife, we could've got Dad back. And he would have known what to do." She spoke quietly, tracing a stain on the table. "He always knew what to do…"

She lapsed into silence. Chris and Arthur made awkward eye contact. Surely this couldn't be happening. Arthur was mad, utterly mad. So mad he was contemplating the Jägermeister. So mad Izzy'd track him down and find him singing to himself amidst six empty shot glasses.

"So, you're telling me that Father Christmas is a real person," Arthur said.

Winter glared at him. "You just took a sleigh ride. Where do you think we got it?"

"And you're telling me that Krampus is masquerading as a Member of Parliament and kidnapping kids." He'd heard of Krampus; David had done Krampus for a year three project on Christmas traditions. "Well, that part I can believe." All MPs were basically the devil.

"You can't believe in one and not the other," Winter said.

"Sure, I can. I can believe in the power of hate without believing in the power of love." Arthur shrugged and took a swig of his tea. The warmth went straight down to his bones. He still wanted his sweet stout, though. He'd get the next round and make sure to buy himself an adult drink.

"You can't get the one *without* the other," Winter said.

"Sure, I can. The world is full of bad people, so it's easy to believe in bad things." He tapped a coaster on the table.

"What about good people?" asked Chris.

Arthur thought for a long moment. Chris had wide eyes that gave him this innocent, eager look. But it was more than his eyes. His whole face was open. He looked one moment away from smiling, even though he'd fought demons and watched thirty kids disappear. He looked like a kid himself, nineteen or twenty. Arthur had to wonder what the next twenty years would do to him.

"Maybe there's no such thing as a good person," he said. "We've all got a darkness in us, waiting to get out." Politicians started out with ideals and ended their careers with bank accounts full of bribe money. Detectives started out with the view that justice prevails and ended up chased out of town, paid off by their father-in-law to leave their own family.

Snell had offered him his old life back. And for a moment, he'd wanted to take it. He'd been willing to trade thirty-three children for it. So no, he didn't believe in the inherent goodness in anyone.

"Well, I believe," said Chris, lifting his chin stubbornly.

The television over the bar switched abruptly to the news. The anchor, a woman in a smart red jacket and a green bow in her hair, read from her notes, wide-eyed. "This is a special broadcast, coming to you live from London. For over a year, parents all over the city have been gripped by terror in a case of serial kidnappings. Thirty-three children have been found tonight, and a new suspect has emerged in the case. We are live in Westminster."

The television cut to the press conference room at Westminster Palace. Antonius Snell stood at the pulpit, smiling his unctuous smile. Behind him stood a line of assistants and aides, headed up by Kuiper.

And standing next to Snell, trapped to his side by one of his long arms, was Geordie Jones.

Snell leaned into the microphone.

"Good evening to you all. For over a year I have spearheaded the *Save the Children* campaign, which has sought to prevent our vulnerable children from falling prey to crime and extreme poverty all over Great Britain. Our efforts to find the thirty-three victims of a serial kidnapper were a part of this program. This evening, at around five o'clock, I am happy to report that I personally discovered the children in an abandoned warehouse. They are home, with their families, celebrating their safe return. My team and I couldn't be prouder of our efforts and unfailing faith that these children *would* be found."

Arthur felt his jaw go slack. Winter leaned forward. "He did *what?*"

Snell continued. "Unfortunately, corruption is at the heart of this case. I myself feel like a fool; I trusted a man and considered him my friend, and he used his position of power and authority to hide this most evil of acts and gain access to dozens of homes and crime scenes. Metropolitan Detective Inspector Arthur Stowe is officially wanted for thirty-three counts of kidnapping and should be considered dangerous. News outlets will be circulating his likeness shortly. If you encounter Stowe, do not engage him. Ring 999 immediately. Thank you."

The floor erupted with questions, but Arthur couldn't hear a single one. He stared at the television. His mind was utterly blank.

"I don't understand." Chris looked from the television to Arthur, and back again. "He let them go?"

"Yeah." Arthur's voice was far away. "He let them go. And *then he framed me.*"

Everything. Everything he'd worked to rebuild after fleeing his old life was gone. The Met would find him, arrest him, and he'd spend the rest of his days in a cell.

"But… why did he do it? He's just lost his advantage. No kids means no fear, right?" Chris said.

"Oh, people'll be afraid." Arthur's hand found his truncheon and squeezed. "It's quite clever, really. The London Met's going to be bombarded with hate for this. There'll be an inquest, investigation, audits, the whole circus. And everyone in London will know by the New Year that the Met kidnaps kids." His voice started to shake. "So that woman who gets beaten by her husband, she thinks, 'No, I can't call the Met, they won't help me, and they'll take my kids away.' She'll be too scared to even call."

And he had done this. *He* had done it. He should have taken Snell's deal and figured out how to double-cross him. He should have talked Snell down. He'd been a damn fool to think Antonius Snell would respond to the authority of anyone but himself.

One of three drunken patrons leaned toward the bar. "Isn't there an Arthur Stowe that comes in here?" he asked.

"Three times a week. If he comes back, I don't think the rozzers'll get here in time to save him from my justice." The bar man slammed a pint glass down on the bar. "Imagine doing that to kids…"

Arthur slid down in his seat.

"They can't see you," Winter said. "As long as you're with me, you'll be safe."

His mobile rang.

It was Izzy. Arthur looked at Winter accusingly. "I didn't say they wouldn't be able to call you," she said. "Don't pick it up. I'm off to see if I can swipe some more satisfactory booze."

"Your Dad would tell you not to steal," Chris called after her. She gave him two fingers as she left.

Winter was right. He shouldn't answer. But it was Izzy. They'd worked on this case for over a year. She'd see the holes in Snell's story immediately—all the times kids had disappeared when Arthur was at work, all the evidence they'd toiled over together. Surely she'd know it wasn't him.

She's not your friend, Arthur reminded himself. Besides, there were no good people in the world. And Izzy wanted to get ahead more than she wanted anything. Would she take a deal with Snell to set him up in exchange for the career of her dreams?

But it was *Izzy.* She still had a strong sense of right and wrong. He picked it up. "Stowe."

"Arthur?" Her voice shook. "Arthur, where are you? Did you see the news?"

"I saw it," he said, ignoring her first question.

"What the hell's going on? You disappeared and now Snell's saying you did it all? Is this some kind of special operation?"

"I'm going to be lying low for a couple of days, Izzy," said Arthur. "I didn't kidnap those kids, I swear it. But I need to take a breather. Figure out where we go next."

"If you didn't do it, you've got to come in," Izzy said. "To the station. We'll sort it out."

Arthur's mouth quirked up humorlessly. "You know I wouldn't last five minutes in the station."

"I'll come to you, then," she said quickly. Too quickly. "Where are you?"

"I'm staying with friends," he said. That ought to throw her for a loop. He didn't have any friends.

At that moment, the bartender dropped a glass. It shattered. "*Wahaay,*" cried a group of men.

"Are you at a pub?"

"Got to run, Izzy. Give my love to Montague." Who was no doubt standing right next to her, listening in. Arthur hung up. Then he turned to Winter and Chris. Winter was sipping a Holly Jolly cocktail. "We need to get out of here."

"I told you they can't see us," Winter said.

"This place'll be crawling with uniforms in five minutes and I'm not taking chances. I saw you, even when I wasn't supposed to. Maybe one of them'll see me."

Chris stood up and pulled his coat on. "Where do we go, though?"

They slipped out into the alley and activated the sleigh. As the blue whale pulled them up, Arthur narrowed his eyes. "Is this that skeleton from the Natural History Museum?"

"Focus. Chris is right. We need some kind of new plan."

"Let's plan to get out of this bloody cold," grumbled Arthur. She hadn't answered his question, he noted.

She gave him a sidelong look. "It's your fault we're here in the first place. Couldn't trust me to hide you."

"Why don't we go back to your Mum?" Chris called over the rising wind.

"Never get to her in time," Winter replied.

The wind howled and stung Arthur's ears. A dog had taken refuge behind his legs, and he was frankly jealous he couldn't do the same.

His phone buzzed. It really was a marvel of modern technology that he got signal up here. Or was it a curse?

It was a text. From Missy.

Saw the news. Got yourself into trouble again no mistake, but I don't believe a word of it. Please call. Want to help.

Had Montague called her? Had Snell? Pain stabbed through Arthur like a knife. Bad enough that his father-in-law meddled in his relationship with his wife, but would others do so too?

Of course, they would. Montague would want to catch his crooked copper. Snell would stoop to anything. And even if they hadn't... well, he wanted to believe Missy wasn't trying to catch him for Montague or Snell. But he couldn't count on it, could he?

And if she *wasn't* trying to trick him, then it was better she stay out of this mess. Life would be hell enough for her and the boys as it was. No need to make things worse.

Chris and Winter were still arguing. "—Don't have time to run all over London just in case someone wants to let us in," Winter was saying.

"All right, then." Chris gave the sleigh a new course. "If we have no choice, we have no choice. My flat it is."

CHAPTER SIXTEEN

Chris lived in a rundown block of dirty grey flats in Tower Hamlets. As he let them into his studio flat, Winter used Arthur's mobile to phone her mum. The flat didn't give much privacy; there was a single mattress on the floor, a kitchenette in one corner, and a water closet Chris couldn't turn around in without banging his elbows on the beige-tiled walls.

He went over to the kitchenette and put the kettle on as Winter sat on his bed and murmured into her phone. There were three packs of instant noodles in his cupboard and, having no bowls, he divided them among mugs.

"Nice place," said Arthur, and Chris couldn't tell if he was being funny or not. Aside from the bed, the only furniture was a lopsided Ikea table and two metal folding chairs he'd fished out of a skip. The walls were the buttery colour of last-new-coat-applied-twenty-years-ago. The lino floor was cracked, and mould collected on the windowsill. The place was cold and damp-smelling. Like most of his neighbours, Chris kept his radiators on the lowest setting and found another sweater when it got cold. Chris had tried to decorate for Christmas; a stuffed, possessed-looking reindeer stood in the corner, and the door to the toilet had a wreath on the handle as he wasn't allowed to hang anything on the walls.

"Best location in London," Chris replied. "Not too far from the job, and as long as you keep mould spray on hand, quite livable." The same story he told himself each day.

They'd propped Nicholas against the wall like a ghastly mannequin. Ollie stood guard. Diedre had opted to follow them inside and was now clacking about in the toilet, trying to dismantle the pipes and scraping her featherless wings against the tile with a *schicking* sound. Rosie stuck close to Chris. Hoping, no doubt, that

165

he'd drop a snack.

"Hm." Arthur frowned and peered out the window. The sleigh sat on the green outside, collecting an icing-sugar dusting of snow. Five or six children were having a snowball fight around it without even realizing it was there. Their shouts drifted up to the window and made Chris think of Mrs Pavuka. There would always be good in the world. "I'm surprised you got a spot. They usually reserve the studios for homeless military veterans, people like that."

"I was one of the Bluebell kids," Chris said.

He didn't really like talking about the Bluebell Tower fire. Everyone got so sympathetic that they didn't know what to do with him. Was he a poor thing? Was he stronger for it? Was he the victim of senseless tragedy, of circumstance, or of the evil and uncaring government that hadn't checked that Bluebell was up to code? Arthur's face flashed with pain. Then he got an odd look, and his mouth turned up on one side in an angry smile. "You know who the Minister of Housing was back then?" Chris shook his head. "Everyone's favourite Christmas killer. Snell swore up and down that it was nothing to do with him. And then someone leaked the memos…"

"Oh, yeah. The brown people memos." Chris remembered that. Snell had moved funds from the upkeep of places like Bluebell to grants for construction companies that wanted to build flats for the rich. *Who cares about a few hundred brown people?* the memo said. Only Snell hadn't called the Bluebell Tower victims brown people.

Chris had lived his life with the philosophy that anyone could choose to be good. He'd always been certain that even the most hardened criminals had the ability to change. But Antonius Snell might prove him wrong.

Or maybe he did make his choice, over and over again, and because he was so powerful the consequences were devastating for everyone else.

Winter came over and handed the mobile back. "Mum's not helping," she said, face drawn. "She keeps telling me that she knows I'll do what's right." She folded her arms and looked out the window.

Chris thought of Mrs Pavuka again. "Maybe... it's because there's nothing left to do."

A storm was brewing in Winter's brown eyes. The skin around her mouth tightened. "I'm not giving up on him. There *has* to be something."

"But what? Mr Ross said there were three knives, and now they're all gone. We had a plan to save the kids. *They're* gone. Maybe it's time..." He stopped and swallowed. How could he make his point without making her angry?

He hadn't stopped soon enough. Winter's nose wrinkled and her mouth twisted bitterly. "Time for what? Time for you to step up and become that hero you always knew you were meant to be?"

Her mockery stung, and he spoke before he could stop to think about the wisdom of his words. "No, it's time for *you* to step up. All this time, you haven't been trying to do what's right. You've been trying to bring back your dad. Because at the end of the day, it's scary to lose a father, and it hurts, and I *know* what it's like. But you don't want to make the hard decisions. You don't want to deal with being the spirit of Christmas, or a Myth, or whatever it is you call yourself. You want to bring your dad back so that he can rescue you and you can feel like a kid again. But you can't. That's over."

Suddenly he was out of words and out of breath. He stared at Winter. She stared back.

Finally, she said, "Wow. Eff you, Chris." She collapsed on a chair and slouched over his table.

"I'm sorry," he began, then stopped. Arthur poured water into the instant noodles and set them out. For a long minute they were silent, watching steam rise from each cup.

Chris *wasn't* sorry. He meant every word. The same way he'd meant what he said to Mrs Pavuka, about becoming a Myth himself. His words came from his heart, and just because he didn't have the chance to soften them first didn't make them less true. And he didn't need to say sorry to smooth things over. Now, more than anything, they needed to act, and they needed to be clear about how they acted.

"Yeah, well. You're right." Winter took a cup and a fork.

She jabbed the fork and started to twirl noodles as though they'd personally wronged her. "I'm not used to making decisions like that. I kick arse in the moment. I get to focus on this Christmas. Never had to think about next Christmas, or the one after that, or the one after that. And Dad… Dad was always this moral compass. He *knew* what was right without having to think about it. That's not me. And I always knew that no matter how I messed it up, Dad was there. Mum and I fought like crazy, but Dad… he let me be me."

Winter stuffed a forkful of noodles in her mouth. As she chewed, her expression became more and more horrified.

"It grows on you," said Chris, and took a bite of his own. It was salty enough to shrivel his tongue. Noodles mushed around in his mouth.

"Until you grow out of it. And realize you're a sad old man whose Christmas dinner is pot noodles with a couple of teens," Arthur put in. He took a morose sip.

"I'm almost twenty," Chris said. "And she's not a teen at all. She's a mythological heir."

"No, I'm not," Winter said reflexively.

Chris sat across from her and leaned in. "You are if you want to be," he said seriously. "And now's the time to decide if you want to be."

She set the cup down and stared at him. Her hair was an unruly cloud around her face and there was more lipstick on her fork than on her lips now. Emotion filled her brown eyes, but he wasn't sure which one. There was sorrow in it, and the kind of melancholy that came with acceptance. But there was also determination and strength. And maybe even hope. "I want to be…" She sighed and looked out at the sleigh. Hope drifted a few feet above the ground, bobbing in her sleep. "I want to be the kind of person who saved the kids. I want to be strong —"

"You are strong," Chris said.

"And I'll be honest, I want Krampus to shit himself when he sees me coming." Her voice grew in conviction. "But I don't want people to be afraid of me like they are of him. I want people to see me and think, 'She does good things.' I don't want to do what's easy."

Chris's eye was drawn to her hand. A thread of light like a wispy vein wound its way up her little finger and curled around her wrist. As he watched more light began to spread, starting at her fingertips, flowing up her hand, joining with other threads until her arm glowed. Winter didn't notice. Her eyes were hard and bright, her face set. "I want to do what's right."

Her hands blazed. Chris shut his eyes and heat flashed against his face. "Good Lord," Arthur muttered behind him. Rosie and Ottie barked once, then twice, then howled in tandem.

Mrs Pavuka had been wrong. Chris had never been a mythological heir. Not even a possibility. This was Winter's legacy, and her responsibility.

The light dimmed and Chris opened his eyes. Winter was staring at her hands, half in wonder. She closed her fist and extinguished the light completely.

"Nice," she said.

"Holy hell," Arthur breathed. He was staring through the window. In the snow beneath Hope's slumbering form, little skeletons frolicked. Squirrels, rabbits, crows—they bounded and hopped together, and as Chris watched more birds winged in to join them.

Chris tried to summon a light of his own. It flickered weakly, like a lamp on a dodgy line. So, Winter's powers were growing, and his were fading. This was a good thing, he told himself, though he couldn't deny the longing that stabbed at his heart. Winter needed all the power she could get. Although Iain Ross had said there was something else to him…

He touched her arm. Her body flared with light, and the earth rumbled. Winter's breath caught and her eyes lit up.

"All right, whatever *that* is…" Arthur said, and Chris let go. So, he lacked Saint Nick's powers, but it looked as though he retained one or two tricks. He was still a conduit. And if he was still a conduit… "Maybe now you *could* defeat him."

Winter nodded—slowly at first, then with more conviction. "But we have to come up with a plan. Think it through."

"Get in, get out, hide the body?" Chris suggested with a smile.

"Krampus played us. I might be more powerful than I was, but he's still an old Myth, and he's been fighting my father for hundreds of years. If we can catch him by surprise and put him on the defensive, we'll have a better chance at winning. And..." she looked over at Nicholas. "I have to try one more time. If it comes down to choosing between defeating Krampus and Dad, I'll do the right thing... but I have to try."

She looked back at Chris. Her eyes held that deep sorrow again, the sorrow Chris knew too well. It was a sorrow that might never leave her. But he saw acceptance there, too. She *was* ready to do the right thing. He took her hand and squeezed it. Her warm fingers pressed against his.

"Thank you," she said softly, and Chris realized she was relieved. Somehow she'd gone from a grudging acceptance of his presence to wanting him around. The thought flushed him from head to toe.

She turned to Arthur. "You don't have to come with us."

Arthur snorted and walked over to put his cup in the tiny stainless steel sink. "Where else should I go? Besides, Snell tried to put me away and it's only fair that I return the favour."

"You're out of your depth," Winter said bluntly. Chris smiled again. Some things would never change.

Arthur laughed. "Never stopped me before."

Winter looked at him for a moment as she tapped one black-lacquered fingernail against another. Then she nodded and blew a strand of hair out of her face. "Yeah, well. Good. 'Cause I've got an idea."

Chris nodded at her. "You can do it. I know you can."

She took a deep breath. "Actually, *you're* going to do it."

170

CHAPTER SEVENTEEN

Arthur stared at his telephone. He'd never liked the bloody thing, and now it felt like a sleeping adder in his hands. His fingers were wooden, unwilling to cooperate. "Are you sure this will work?" he asked Winter. He didn't exactly have a habit of trusting the plans of eighteen-year-old girls, even if they did claim to be semi-immortal.

"Of course, I'm not sure." At least she was honest. She sat in one of the dodgy folding chairs, reapplying her make-up with the aid of a pocket mirror. "But we know what he wants, and he doesn't know what tricks we have up our sleeves. So, stop stalling and make the call."

Arthur swallowed and found Snell's number.

The ring tone blared in Chris's small, silent apartment. Chris sat on his bed with his hands and legs folded. Winter continued with her make-up as though she were headed out on a normal Saturday night. When Arthur put a finger to his lips as a reminder, she rolled her kohl-lined eyes.

Snell picked up on the second ring. "Art, old chap. Need a recommendation for a good lawyer?" He laughed a smoky laugh. Arthur wanted to reach down the phone line and choke him.

"No need for one yet, as I'm sure you know."

"You of all people should know how difficult it is to hide from the Met for long." Snell was clearly enjoying this.

Arthur kept his voice cool and calm, the way he did when he was trying to talk down a man with a gun. "I don't need to hide from the Met for long, Snell. I'm ready to make you a deal."

"Hah." Arthur imagined Snell shaking his head at Kuiper. "It's too late for that. I made the offer, you said no. Regret's a bitter thing, isn't it?"

"You say that as though I have nothing to trade," Arthur said.

"You don't." Was it Arthur's imagination, or did Snell sound a tad unsure?

"What about the old man we found dead? What about his sleigh?"

"What about them?" Snell said.

"Well, I have them both, and I'm willing to trade them to you," Arthur said. He glanced at Winter. She nodded.

There was a pause as Snell considered. "I don't see why it's necessary. Good old Nick will be dead soon, and his name will be tarnished in the news as your accomplice. Enjoy the murder charge coming your way, by the by. I don't see how I could kill him any better."

"His daughter said something about another knife," Arthur said. Winter nodded again.

Snell paused again, and Arthur knew he had him on the hook. "That's impossible." Snell affected a drawl of boredom. Arthur's gut twinged. "They've all been destroyed."

"That's the funny thing, isn't it? She said, 'As long as he doesn't know about the fourth knife, we've still got a chance.'"

"And where would this fourth knife be, if it even existed?" Snell asked, falsely casual.

Arthur shrugged, forgetting for a moment that Snell couldn't see him. "I'm in way over my head, mate. All I know is what I heard. And they told me to watch the sleigh while they hared off to get it."

Snell was silent for a few moments. "You've done a lot to get this far," Arthur pressed him. "Wouldn't you rather finish the job? Squash the goodness from this world once and for all?"

Snell chuckled. "My word, Arthur, the melodrama. When you get out of prison, think about pantomime as a serious career choice. Of course, I don't want to 'squash the goodness out of the world.'" His voice dropped and crackled like fire. "I want *power*. I want Christmas to be my holiday. I want people to do things for me. And people don't do things out of the goodness of their hearts or other saccharine reasons. They do things because they're afraid and they're greedy."

"Bold claim," Arthur said, looking at Winter and Chris. Chris was tapping his knee nervously. A light flickered weakly on one palm.

"Is it?" Snell sounded smug. "Why are you calling me, detective? Because you're afraid of getting arrested. Because you want what I had to offer in the first place. You think you're a good man, but you're the same as everyone else."

No, thought Arthur. He wasn't the same as everyone else. He knew he was a screw-up shithead. He didn't waste mental breath trying to justify all the things he'd done wrong in life.

"Well, *old chap,* you're greedy, too. So, do we have a deal? Saint Nick in exchange for clearing my name, and the sleigh in exchange for my family?"

"And what of the daughter?" Snell said. "The young lady who belongs on a medieval battlefield."

Winter's chin dipped once. She made a motion with her hands. *Close the deal.*

"Sure," Arthur said easily. "What's she to me?"

"Hm." Arthur heard Snell tapping on a keyboard. "Let's say I'm intrigued."

"I'll be at Saint Paul's in forty minutes. Come alone." He hung up before he had to hear one more oily syllable slip out of Snell's mouth.

His mouth was dry. He opened a few cupboards and found a glass, but nothing to drink. "Where do you keep your cider?" he said. "Or your beer."

"I don't," Chris said.

"Trust me to team up with the only nineteen-year-old boy in London that doesn't drink," Arthur grumbled. The water from the tap tasted slightly mildewy. Arthur held his nose and drank it down.

"You should have a clear head for tonight," Chris said, and though Arthur wanted to throttle him for that, he had to admit that Chris was probably right.

"Are you sure he'll come?" Arthur said, putting the glass in the sink. "He didn't sound convinced. And he's had lots of chances to get the body."

"Not after we put Mrs Pavuka's shawl on the sleigh. He can't find it." Winter stood and reached for her coat. "I think he'll come. He wants to make sure the job is done. Like you said, he's come this far. And now he has me to consider." She lifted her chin, determined, but Arthur spotted a spark of fear in her eyes.

Chris had changed out of his mourning suit and into a pair of jeans, a shirt, and a threadbare hoodie. From the look of his wardrobe, he didn't own much else. "Are you sure we have to kill him?" he said as he came over to them. He didn't sound happy. Arthur didn't blame him. The way Winter explained it, Chris would be the one doing the actual killing.

"How else are we supposed to stop him? Do you really think you can write him a strongly worded letter and get him to change his mind?" Winter said.

"I just... no one's all bad," Chris said in a quiet voice.

"He's a Myth. He's a literal personification of evil. I can assure you; he *is* all bad."

Arthur wasn't sure whether Chris's naivety was foolish or endearing. Antonius Snell had been responsible for the kidnapping of children and the deaths of hundreds of people, and he still thought the man could be turned?

"Think of it this way." Winter raised a hand and then froze, as though she'd caught herself in the act of trying to comfort another person and it made her supremely uncomfortable. She tucked her hands behind her back instead. "You're not killing him. You're giving life back to my father. You're being a conduit, transferring Krampus's life force to Dad. Snell won't even know it, in the end. He'll disappear like all Myths do when they finally die."

"And you're saving Christmas. Could be worse," Arthur said.

Chris rubbed an eye. "Yeah," he said. He looked doubtful.

CHAPTER EIGHTEEN

Snow fell over the city of London, and the sleigh fell with it.

They alighted behind St. Paul's since Arthur wouldn't be able to get down from the roof without obvious help. The strains of *Merry Christmas Everyone* drifted from a pub down the road. A red velvet bow flapped against a light pole. Winter picked up her father and walked toward the church, looking all manner of confident in her Doc Martens. Rosie and Ottie and Diedre followed, slipping on the slick stone and chasing snowflakes.

Arthur watched her go. "Good Lord," he said. "Are her arms made of concrete?"

The city was quieter than Chris had ever heard it. Lights twinkled softly behind curtains of snow. He stuck his hands in his pockets. His only pair of gloves was still at *Hayne & Sons.* "Have you ever killed anyone?" he asked Arthur.

"Er, no," Arthur admitted. "When I lived in Letherford I mostly investigated petty crime. Small towns, you know. I've had to arrest a couple of blokes with guns, but…" He trailed off, then patted Chris awkwardly on the shoulder.

The world was full of strange things. Chris had always tried to be decent, yet he was going to be a killer at the age of nineteen.

Winter waited for them at the door to the cathedral. She pushed it open, and they squeezed past the combined bulk of her and her father.

"Have you ever killed anyone?" Chris asked.

"A few people," she said. "They all deserved it. And he does too, Chris. I promise."

Her voice was soft in a way he didn't like. It meant she knew he was upset about this. Yet she was pushing him to do it anyway.

"Think of it one thing at a time. We start by getting Snell into the building, okay?"

One thing at a time. "Okay."

They walked up the nave, illumined by a ball of white light that floated behind Winter like a familiar. Their shoes and paws clicked on the floor. As they passed the first chandelier, she looked up. Her light zipped up and the chandelier started to glow.

"You really are amazing," Chris said.

"Save your praise for when we win," Winter told him, but her ears turned pink and the corners of her mouth turned up. She made a small motion with her hand and the Christmas tree flared to life, sending flecks of light shivering across the floor like scattering embers.

Chris wanted to linger—who knew when he'd visit Saint Paul's again, after all? He wanted to feel the smooth wood of the pews, admire the Christmas stars and trappings that dotted the choir and ambulatory. He wanted to light a candle for his family. He settled for looking up as they walked under exquisitely painted domed ceilings. The largest dome, *the* dome, had been hastily covered with a tarp, and buckets stood on the floor to catch leaking water. Somewhere above the dome drifted Hope, set free in case Snell somehow got hold of the sleigh.

"Put him on the altar," Arthur said. "That way we can hem Snell in when he gets here."

Winter nodded and stepped over the red velvet ropes separating the choir and the altar. The altar was covered by a rich red and green cloth. The perfect cloth for Christmas. She lay her father gently down.

"Ottie, Rosie, and Diedre. You need to hide." Winter ushered them into the ambulatory to one side and dismissed her light. Chris stepped behind a pillar on the other side. "Now stay," she warned them. She held out her hands and Arthur slid his handcuffs over them. The ruse would be obvious if Snell looked closely, but the plan was to act before he had the chance.

She peeked through a stained-glass window. "There's a car outside. It's him."

Chris thought he heard the slam of a door. He shrunk back into the ambulatory. Winter *hmmm*ed. "I'm pretty sure I see someone else in the car."

"All right. Come back over here." Arther jerked his head, and she headed over, looking irritated even though it was her plan. Winter wasn't exactly the helpless type. It was almost enough to make Chris smile. Almost.

"I'm still not sure about this," he said.

"You can do it, mate." Arthur nodded to him. "I have faith in you." He looked vaguely surprised.

The doors at the end of the nave opened, and the long form of Antonius Snell appeared.

"I told you to come alone," Arthur called as Snell's polished shoes tapped toward them. He pitched his voice low and gruff and angry.

"I did come alone." The minister's voice echoed mockingly up the nave.

"Who's in the car outside?"

"Kuiper. Just Kuiper," Snell chuckled. "He's waiting for me. He'll come if I call, or if I take too long. Never can be too careful, can you?" He reached into his pocket, scattering bones like seeds as he walked up the nave. Chris clenched his hands, ready for the shadow-skeletons to spring up.

"That's enough of that," Arthur snapped.

Snell's smile turned condescending. "Security, Art. You've taken precautions, I'm sure. I'll be taking precautions as well."

Chris tried not to breathe too loudly. He peeked out from the pillar as Snell made his way up the choir and to the altar. The minister wore a new suit; a charcoal grey jacket with a tie that shimmered red and orange.

He shook Arthur's hand, then wiped it on a red handkerchief and looked Winter over with the expression of the cat who'd cornered the mouse. "Not so scary without your precious axes, are you?" A muscle in Winter's jaw twitched. "Not to worry, dear. I saved the other one. Your pair will be reunited when you come with me. Where's the sleigh?"

Arthur folded his arms. "I'll show it to you when you've fulfilled your part of the bargain. For now, it's hidden. But nearby."

"See? Precautions. For everyone." Snell turned away to

examine the body on the altar. His mouth stretched wide, revealing too-red gums and too-white teeth. Chris's stomach turned over. A man was going to die because of Snell, and the look on his face was of pure joy. *He deserves this,* Chris thought. He should dart forward now, grab Snell by the wrist and complete the circuit. But his legs were stiff as wood. He couldn't move.

Snell picked at a bit of fluff on Nicholas's coat. "Gives a new meaning to the phrase 'Christmas comes early.'" He cocked his head. "This really him?"

Odd. Why wouldn't he know?

"You saw the body before I did. You tell me," Arthur said.

Chris needed to move. He needed to move.

"The fourth knife." Snell looked back at Arthur. "I'll take that, too."

Winter and Arthur glanced at each other.

"I see," Snell said softly.

"Yeah, well." The cuffs clattered to the floor. Winter's axe was in her hands before Chris could blink. She swung heavily and her axe stopped in midair. Something dark had grabbed the handle. Light flared and they both fell back.

Snell shook his head. "So predictable, honestly. 'Come alone?' I knew you were up to something." He snapped his fingers. Shadows began to slither out from behind the choir. The chandeliers dimmed. Things clacked and clicked from the gloom of the nave. Snell laughed. "It was also when I knew you had no idea how powerful I am. Come alone? As if I need security."

A wall of skeletons formed up in front of them, animals of all shapes and sizes, prehistoric, large and small, from the Natural History Museum. Snell had brought them here as his security detail, it seemed, along with his dark elves who had woven themselves into the creatures. Something leapt at Arthur, something with bone legs and sharp teeth that looked vaguely dog-like. Winter lunged around the side of the altar and chopped it in half. Bones and black tar scattered.

"Hold this," Winter said, handing the axe to Arthur. His eyes widened as he took it. Black-and-bone skeletons were winding up the choir. Chattering echoed down the nave.

Winter stepped back and made two fists. Squaring her shoulders, she breathed deep. This time she didn't need a conduit: Chris felt power roll off her in waves through the walls and ground of St. Paul's.

"Trying to scare me, little heir?" Snell mocked. Shadows swarmed around him like a flood. "Even your father couldn't defeat me, and he had a thousand-year head start. Believe me, I wouldn't have told Arthur to bring you if I thought you were capable of half the things Nicholas was."

Winter said nothing. She narrowed her eyes. Her arms flexed. From outside the church, Chris heard a sound like pouring rain, like a waterfall of pebbles. She needed her own army.

The window behind Winter shattered in an explosion of jewel-coloured glass, and bones poured in.

Gleaming bones and dirt-smeared bones. Bones in tattered rags, bones half decayed. The bones of the dead of Saint Paul's stood clumsily, fixing ribs and jaws back into place. Their ligaments and tendons were thin slivers of light, as golden as the light on her axe. They clutched muskets, swords, paintbrushes and crowns, the artefacts that defined them in death all lined up in an orderly fashion in perfect ranks. And they all turned their heads—what was left of them—to Winter.

"Attack," she said, and her lips curved.

Winter's army sprung forward to meet a wave of creatures that only had existed in myth in their times. A cacophony of noise erupted as the Battle of St Paul's commenced. Human hands grabbed animal limbs. Human skulls crashed against animal ones. Rusting guns fired ghostly shots. Light twined and tugged with shadow.

Snell's eyes widened. He backed away.

"Chris!" shouted Winter. If Snell ran or got wise to their plan, Chris wouldn't be able to touch both the minister and the Myth.

Chris jumped out from behind his pillar and was immediately slammed back by a long shadow limb. Its touch sent a wave of fire through his body, making him convulse. Black dotted the edges of his vision. Something long wound about his throat. He hauled on it fruitlessly, gasping air that tasted like ash and seared the inside of his lungs.

A skeletal hand closed around the darkness that was throttling him. A fellow in a tricorn hat was squeezing the shadow tighter and tighter until his bone fingers slid through it like jelly. Bright red spots speckled the bone. The shadow flopped as the dark elf let out an unearthly howl and its severed limb slithered from Chris's neck to the floor, where it lay motionless. Chris clapped a hand to his neck.

"Thanks, mate," he rasped.

The skeleton gave a half bow. A telescope and a sword dangled from the remaining scraps of a naval uniform adorned with huge star medals that hung from his frame. He offered Chris what might have been a salute had he not been missing his right arm before swinging away to join half a skeleton in a brittle crown. Chris only had seconds to think he seemed familiar from his history books at school. Somehow, he knew him.

Arthur swung Winter's axe like he was trying to chop wood. A prehistoric bird dove for his head while a crocodile skeleton lunged at his leg. And those were only the animals Chris recognized. Creatures with fins, creatures with long back legs and short front legs, creatures with too many teeth and creatures with no teeth at all. Creatures with shining white bones and creatures with fossilized, flaking ones.

Winter and Snell faced off like rival conductors. Winter directed her skeleton army in a frenzy, sending them crashing into the shadow-fossils that teemed about the altar. Rosie leapt out and snatched a femur from a small dinosaur that caused it to fall over and scatter across the floor. She galumphed down the ambulatory with great pride, dragging an enormous bone with her. Diedre ran after the skeleton of a snake that slithered its way across the marble floor, nipping away at its tail. Snell snarled wordlessly and made a motion with his hand. His dark elves split and oozed, losing all semblance of something human. The shadow nearest Chris stretched up and the skeleton in the mouldering tricorn hat turned back to him. He held a saber in his left hand. Spots bloomed on his bones like a fungus, eating away at his fingers. Chris tried to conjure his light, but it did little more than flicker in his hand like a candle flame. That power had gone over to Winter now.

Sweat trickled down Winter's temple. A shadow-spewing elk skeleton slammed into Arthur and sent the axe flying. Snell was grinning.

Winter's axe smashed into a pillar. She lunged for it. Arthur screamed as a bony foot pressed on his chest. "Chris, *now,*" she cried.

But a malevolent darkness boiled in the space between him and Snell. There were too many of them.

"I—" Chris stopped. He couldn't say *I can't.* "I need help," he shouted instead.

Light wreathed Winter's hands like gloves. She leapt over Arthur's prone form and a globe of light burst from her with a sound like a thunderclap. Shadows sizzled and disappeared in its wake. Bones were flung out over the altar and choir, breaking apart as the light hit their tarry tendons and raining down on the stone floor.

Winter threw out an imperious hand. Her skeletons abandoned her, flowing over each other like a river of misshapen marbles. Hands emerged from the jumble to pull down more shadows, more animals. Skulls bit and fingers scrabbled.

Then they hit a wall of bone and shadow. Teeth and claws rent the light that held the bones together. Tendrils slid between gaps and began to wind about the dead army, creating bright splotches of red. The skeletons broke apart, each taking on a shadow. Killing themselves, Chris thought, as brittle bones started to snap and crumble. They were utterly killing themselves—

No. They were making a path for him. The space between him and Snell was slowly clearing of dark, writhing shapes. They were giving him a chance.

Think about one thing at a time. He wasn't killing Snell; he was slipping through the corridor of dark and light. He wasn't killing Snell; he was getting behind him. He wasn't killing Snell; he was taking the minister's wrist in the tightest grip he could manage. And

181

then he was lunging, spreading the fingers of his other hand.

His hand hit Nicholas of Myra on the chest, and the connection was complete. And then Snell started to scream, and Chris couldn't lie to himself anymore.

Snell flopped to the floor, but Chris held on. *He's not a person, he's a Myth.* He'd disappear, and then it would be like this had never happened. He might look like a man, but he wasn't a man. He might scream like a man, but he wasn't a man. And even if he was, didn't he deserve to die? He kidnapped thirty-three children. Shouldn't he pay for that? Shouldn't he pay for all the lives he took when he refused to enforce the code for Bluebell Towers? What else had he done that Chris didn't know about? What kind of man was he?

He was a man in pain. Snell's screams became raw yet Nicholas showed no sign of waking up. Well, Chris had lived through his fair share of pain, too. *Think of Mum and Dad,* he thought.

He imagined them watching this. His mother, who had taught him to be sweet and kind. His father, who had taught him that strength comes from righteousness. His sister, who teased him when he wouldn't even squash a spider. None of them would tell him that this was right. They wouldn't even say it was justified.

Mrs Pavuka's words came back to him. *We have the power to decide what we will be today and tomorrow.*

Chris wasn't sure what he would be tomorrow. He wasn't even sure he'd be alive. But he wouldn't be a killer today.

He wrenched his hand from Nicholas' chest. Power snapped through him like a rubber band. Snell's screams cut off and Chris fell to his knees. The world swam around him.

The minister had fainted. Chris wanted to faint, too. Sweat plastered his T-shirt, cooling quickly. He shivered.

"Dad?"

The cathedral was quiet—too quiet. No rustling bones, no whispering shadows.

Chris gathered the strength to look around. Plaster dust, bone dust, and marble dust mixed on the floor. The chandeliers blazed merrily down the length of the nave, banishing all shadow. The creatures from the Natural History Museum had collapsed into heaps of tar-smudged skeletons.

Winter stood over Arthur, glowing like an angel. The glow faded as she stumbled over to the altar. Her hair stuck to her face, and she was breathing hard. She looked at her father.

"He's not..."

"I'm sorry," Chris said. The world started to spin around him.

Winter looked at Snell, then at him. Her face was a mask of confusion. "But you have to finish. You have to bring him back. Krampus is still here." She came around the side of the altar and knelt. Her hand was as heavy as the whole world on his shoulder. He barely heard the axe clatter to the floor.

"I can't," said Chris. He was starting to feel sick. "I can't kill him. That's not me."

"Chris." Her expression shattered, and his heart shattered with it. "It's him or my Dad. Don't go on at me about hard choices when you can't make one of your own." Her hand slid down his arm. Their fingers twined. "We got so close. The dark elves are gone. It's *one* more step, Chris. We'll take it together."

She took one of Snell's motionless hands and placed it on Chris' knee. Then she leaned up, guiding their clasped fingers toward the altar. Chris pulled away.

"No," he whispered, but he wasn't sure he had the strength to fight her.

"You can't leave me on my own like this. Please," she said. Her voice quivered, and he wasn't sure whether it was with fear or with rage. Her eyes were wet. "If he doesn't deserve to die, who does?" What was a little more power, transferred from one life to another?

But Chris couldn't do it. It was death, and he'd seen enough of it for one lifetime. He was not the man to bring it, now or ever. He mustered the courage to say *no* one more time.

There was an unmistakable creak as the grand doors at the end of the nave opened, and he came in.

CHAPTER NINETEEN

Chris peered down the nave, swaying. His head swam. He put his palm down on the marble, using its cold smoothness to focus. From the other side of the altar, Arthur groaned and sat up.

"Did we get him?"

Footfalls echoed on the floor. As they came closer, the sound changed, from the soft clip of an Oxford to a harder *clop*. As the footfalls drew nearer, Chris's mind finally made sense of a figure at the end of the choir.

It was another man in a suit, a suit so identical to Snell's that Chris had to look back down at the minister to be sure it wasn't him. But this man was taller, paler. And beneath his thatch of golden hair, shadows wound about his head like a crown. As he walked up the choir he began to clap, slowly and mockingly.

"Kuiper," Arthur said. He sounded dazed. "I see."

"Stay back." Winter raised her axe. "You don't understand what's going on here."

"Well done, you. Really. Fantastic job with Snell, I didn't honestly think you could defeat him. He was the best mythological heir I've had in a long time." The man moved forward. "Of course, there's a downside to borrowing that kind of power. He couldn't handle it when you burnt him out."

He was a few feet away now. Snell groaned softly as consciousness began to return to him. Kuiper put one foot delicately on Snell's chest. Only, foot wasn't the right word anymore. It was a hoof. A cloven hoof.

"You're Krampus," Arthur said. He hadn't moved. "This whole time. You were Krampus, and... *he* was your assistant?"

Kuiper—Krampus—laughed. He leaned down until his nose nearly touched Snell's. Snell's eyes fluttered but didn't open. "Oh, how he'd hate that word. *Assistant.* He wanted to be me. Of course, that led him to act too much like it, which is what got him in this predicament."

"But… *why?*" Arthur said.

"That's the thing about people, Detective Stowe. You must *lead* them to be good, but you need only give them the opportunity to be bad. Antonius Snell wanted power, and he had a lot to hide. It wasn't hard to make a bargain. And as you've seen, being a mythological heir has certain perks."

Winter lunged for him, but he wasn't there. A strange sensation hooked into Chris's belly and *twisted,* and suddenly Krampus stood at the other end of the choir again. Chris was struck by a strange dèjá vu, as though the last minute had been a dream, or a story he'd made up in his head.

"Your father's not the only one who can manipulate time," Krampus said, wagging a finger. "I used to run from house to house, too, collecting children to take down to Hell. Unlike the old man, I found more efficient ways to make people afraid of the dark. I pick legislation. I write speeches. I find scapegoats for when things go wrong. That's the problem with being good, Detective Stowe. You will fight your whole life, and you might save one or two people. I can build an empire in a few years. A legion of men who will make *my* world in exchange for a few pennies, a few buried bodies." He started making his way up the choir again, leisurely. "Children are kidnapped, so their parents keep them home out of fear. They learn to keep their heads down and be obedient. Society prospers. Surely you understand, Detective Stowe? A society that fears is a society that obeys."

"That's not why I became an officer," Arthur said.

Krampus shrugged. "As you will. Yet you have acted out of fear before. You left your wife because you feared you'd make her homeless. You obeyed her father's law. You do understand me, I think."

Arthur got to his feet. Blood trickled from his nose. He held up two fists. "It was the biggest mistake of my life," he said. "You're not going to tell me it's the way to build a society."

Snell gave a little sob from where he lay. Krampus looked at him. Chris wasn't sure what he expected, but it chilled him to see not one ounce of sympathy in his eyes. "Don't kill him," he blurted.

He got that strange hooking feeling again. Then Krampus was standing over Snell. He regarded Chris with his head tilted to one side. "Even knowing all the evil he has done? Even knowing he did it willingly, in exchange for a bit of power and money? Even though you hate him?"

"I don't hate anyone," Chris said.

Krampus looked at him for another long moment. His features were still mostly human: the snub nose and pale cheeks, the flop of hair over his forehead. But he was taller than any man, and his pupils were long horizontal slits, like a goat's. "I believe you," he said. "And I never kill without reason. But the man *has* outlived his usefulness."

He bent down and placed his hand on Snell's forehead. Snell's eyes shot open. He spasmed, then stilled. Black smoke drifted from his mouth, up and up until it touched the shadow on Krampus' brow. There it grew darker, more solid, curving up and around until two slim, wicked horns replaced the shadowy crown.

Chris grabbed Snell's wrist. His pulse was faint.

Krampus straightened, and he'd somehow grown taller still. Eight feet? Nine? He contemplated hands that had sprouted wicked black claws, then looked at the body on the altar. "I never kill without reason," he said again. "Unfortunately, the existence of the three of you—" he pointed to Winter, then Chris, then Nicholas— "makes enacting my plans much trickier. I do hope you understand. We are all faced with difficult decisions in difficult times."

And then he wasn't standing over Snell anymore. He was behind Chris, and his hand was around Chris's throat.

A nail punctured the skin above his collarbone. Krampus' fingers were warm as they pressed into his neck. Chris smelled ash and brimstone and his own sweat. Something wet soaked the neck of his shirt. Winter's eyes widened—

Then she was gone, too. Krampus hissed and the hand dropped from Chris's throat. "You," he grated.

186

"Yeah, well." Chris spun in time to see Winter attack, driving the giant back with jabs from her axe. The side of his suit was soaked in blood. "Dad can do the time thing, you can do the time thing, everyone can do the bloody time thing. You're not special."

He vanished and reappeared between two pillars at the edge of the ambulatory, and she followed. He disappeared again. Chris heard a snarl from the shadows. Then Winter was at the top of the nave, ducking as she spun her axe, anticipating that Krampus would follow. He slid back to avoid her blade and she took the opportunity to blast him with a blaze of light. There was a great crash as he hit the Christmas tree, and it all went down. Wood cracked and glass tinkled as it broke.

Winter stood in the nave, axe raised, eyes narrowed. Then she spun as Krampus appeared. He'd availed himself of a candlestick as tall as a man and was using it as a staff. He blocked her next swing with a *clang,* baring his teeth. Baubles dangled from his horns. Winter would have found this funny if her life were not at stake. He shook his head and they went flying. Blood dripped from his wound, hissing like hot oil as it hit the floor. Winter's throat bobbed as she looked at the pitted marble.

He grinned. "Better beware."

He shoved off her axe and swung the candlestick. She dodged back, then back again. She disappeared and reappeared behind him, but he moved the candlestick easily to parry her next blow. He jabbed her in the chest and she stumbled, then he twisted the world and appeared next to her as she blocked an opponent that was no longer there. She barely turned in time to avoid a blow.

They backed off. Both were breathing hard. Krampus put a hand on the gash at his side. "We can do this as long as you like, you know," he said. He was trying to keep his tone light, but it took effort to speak. "Your father is slowly dying. The longer you're distracted, the closer I am to winning."

Winter's eyes flicked to the altar. He took advantage of the distraction to press forward, backing her against a pillar with a flurry of short jabs. She teleported again, stumbling to one side. Maybe *Krampus* could do this all day, but she clearly could not.

"We have to help her," Chris said to Arthur.

"Stay out of my way," she snapped.

"She's right," Krampus said. "You'd make a marvellous shield." He stepped back and swung the candlestick wide. They danced back and forth as he pressed in and she tried to slip past his guard. Their weapons clashed. When Winter got close enough to jab with her axe, Krampus flicked a hand. Blood flew from it to speckle her dress, arms, and face. She hissed a curse and fell back, rubbing her cheeks. Chris thought he saw little marks like barely closed cuts. Sweat dripped from her chin.

"Can you feel it, my dear?" Krampus asked. "Your father's life, slipping away piece by piece? It won't be long now. When Christmas comes and he doesn't fulfil his duties, the link will be broken."

Winter's eyes slid to Chris and widened, as though she were trying to tell him something. Some way he could help. She attacked with renewed vigour, perhaps trying to push Krampus back toward the altar—but Krampus laughed and vanished.

Winter stood panting and alone. She lowered the axe and raised her head, as though he might be hiding somewhere in the ceiling. "Why are you toying with me? Don't you have anything better to do? Or have you finally realized that you can't kill me without an Apollonian knife?"

"Oh, the knife made it easy." Krampus's voice echoed around the church. He sounded pleased with himself. "But that's certainly not the only way to kill a Myth."

She spun, anticipating him behind her. "And what's another way to kill a Myth?" she called. "Just if, you know, I happen to meet one."

"Simple." And he was behind her. One long hand closed around her throat. "You remind her she's not a Myth yet." He lifted her off the ground. Her feet kicked wildly. She lashed out with the axe, and he tore it from her hand and tossed it up the ambulatory.

Chris and Arthur both dashed for her, but Arthur got to Krampus first. Krampus stopped him with a bloody hand, striking him in the chest so hard that he flew across the floor. His head hit a pew with a terrible *crack,* and he lay still. Krampus's eyes, flashing golden and inhuman, found Chris. *Don't even think about it.*

He drew Winter closer. "You and your father will die the same night. No Myth, no heir. No more spirit of Christmas."

"No," Winter choked. She flailed, fingers scrabbling at his arms.

This couldn't happen. The season was hope and light against the darkness for so many people. This season was the season to find something to believe in. Even when you had nothing, no family and no money and no house and no future, hope could see you through it. Sometimes hope was all you had.

Chris looked at Snell's prone form. What would he do to keep hope alive? Winter's words came back to him. *If he doesn't deserve to die, who does?*

A booming toll resounded above them. And Chris realized the answer.

The bell of St. Paul's Cathedral rang the midnight hour. Chris stepped away from Krampus, away from Winter. He turned to the body on the altar.

"One thing at a time," he whispered.

He took Nicholas's hand and then did what Iain Ross told him never to do. He used himself as a conduit. And this time, with nothing to draw on, his power drew on him.

At first, the pain was too intense to register anything else. His entire body was being pulled in different directions, from his bones outward. He clung to Nicholas's hand. He heard a high, shrill sound like an alarm, and then his voice gave out and he realized he'd been screaming. He was *still* screaming; he just couldn't make noise anymore. He squeezed Nick's fingers, heedless of breaking them, pushing one thought through the pain like fire. He only had to do one thing at a time, and that thing was to hold on.

He was dimly aware of a roaring, of Winter shouting something. He heard a crack like the earth breaking, but a moment later he realized it was the altar collapsing. He had no choice but to collapse with it. Dust filled his mouth.

The pain began to lessen, washing over him in waves rather than a tide. His stomach spasmed but he didn't have the strength to retch. He tasted blood and bile; maybe he'd retched already. As the pain ebbed and flowed he became aware of his own breathing, bubbling and raspy. He couldn't feel his legs anymore.

Did it work? he tried to say, but he could barely wheeze. Maybe it wasn't finished yet? He couldn't let go. He could no longer tell where his fingers stopped and Nicholas's began.

"Chris," said Winter. Something like ice touched his forehead.

Hi, he tried to say. His breath grated like sandpaper.

"What did you do?" she whispered.

There was one thing he had to tell her before he died. He opened his mouth. *You're the coolest girl I've ever met.*

But nothing came out.

And the darkness rose to claim him.

CHAPTER TWENTY

It had been a lovely sleep, but it was time to come back to the land of the living.

The man, the Myth, the saint allowed his consciousness to drift up toward the cold and wild world. Pain was a faint memory, as though his hurts were so long ago they should be forgotten.

Bloody cold, though. Why couldn't dear old Krampus have done him in over Brazil?

Nicholas of Myra opened his eyes and sat up, disentangled himself from the body holding his hand, and took in the chaos.

He had all of his limbs. That was a good start. He still had his beard, though it was unruly and stuck out in three different directions. He smoothed back his hair, and his fingers came away grey with grit. He'd been lying on the wreckage of a table. Close to him were two figures he didn't recognize—and one he did.

"Dad?" Winter whispered. He couldn't tell whether her face was pale out of surprise or because of that ghastly makeup she always insisted on using. Her black dress was torn at the shoulder and her face was dotted with little cuts. Her dark hair stuck up in a tangle. A bruise had started to form next to her collarbone.

Her lower lip trembled. She threw herself into his arms and he got the best thing anyone—man, Myth, or saint—could dream of: a hug from his daughter.

Beyond her stood a long, lanky, and very recognizable shape at the end of the choir. Krampus's features were twisted in fury. He raised a fist, summoning dark elves from either ambulatory—

Nicholas flicked his hand and called the light. It rolled through the church in a wave as bright as the full moon, chasing the shadows before it. He shook his head in warning at Krampus. Some things you didn't interrupt.

"My dear Winter," he said, and she pulled back, wiping her face. Nicholas chuckled. It felt good to be back. He couldn't remember anything after the fall, and the fall itself—well. He just remembered thinking of her. "I always had faith in you."

He looked around. The church was a shambles: bone and chunks of marble lay scattered over the floor, candlesticks had been toppled, two windows had giant, gaping holes and glass was strewn about like a disassembled rainbow. Leave it to Winter to enact utter destruction in the name of all that was good.

Nicholas's laugh rumbled down the nave. He loved that laugh and used it as often as he could. "Let it be known, however, that I do not condone the destruction of esteemed institutions."

Winter cracked a wobbly smile. "Don't visit the British Museum or the Natural History Museum for a good few weeks, then."

That was his girl. Always getting herself into some kind of trouble. Always getting herself out of it, too. And this time, she'd gotten *him* out.

Krampus had lowered his head as though he intended to charge.

"You've gotten bolder, my friend," Nicholas said.

Krampus' lip curled. "This is impossible."

"It's the season of miracles," Nicholas replied. And it was the season of faith. A little faith could go a long way, and he'd had much to choose from: the faith of his daughter, buried but constant; the faith of the detective, newly blossoming, and the faith of the young man, unchanging and evident.

"Miracles won't save you forever," Krampus snarled. "The world changes. And one day, you won't have your spawn around to protect you."

"Indeed, no." He certainly hoped he wouldn't. Winter was meant to be his heir, not his assistant. It was the way of things that one day he would slip away, and she would be the Myth.

But that didn't mean he had to rely on anyone else now. Nicholas climbed to his feet, ignoring his grumbling knees and the twinge in his back. There'd be plenty of time for complaining later. For now:

He summoned the light.

This was no gentle moonlight. He shone like the heart of a star, brighter and brighter, making the windows blaze. Winter clapped her hands over her eyes. Krampus hissed. Nicholas felt movement behind him, a whisper of air that should not be displaced, and twisted time as he turned. It was difficult to fight time travel with time travel—you had to know exactly *when* someone would be, and not just where. But Nicholas knew Krampus like a brother and knew he'd want to cause maximum hurt. He turned in the middle of the hug with his daughter and caught the hand that swung toward him, claws out.

"Enough," he rumbled in his serious voice, his *You get coal* voice. And the light blazed brighter.

Krampus shrieked, and the hand slid from Nicholas's grip. When Nicholas finally dimmed, the Myth was nowhere to be seen.

Winter stared at him, open-mouthed. "Wow," she managed. "You brought the big light."

"He interrupted a hug from you." Nicholas put a hand on her shoulder. "I don't get many of those these days."

"*Dad.*" Winter rolled her eyes. But she leaned in for another hug.

"Though, really, you put this place in a state. What would your mother think?"

An anxious yapping sounded from behind a pillar. Rosie and Ottie rushed forward and flung themselves at him. Nicholas caught them with a surprised, booming, "*Ho!*" and let them lick his face until they'd settled down.

"Thanks for keeping an eye on her," he told them seriously.

It was ridiculous, Rosie replied, sniffing around his knee and settling down. *The number of times she tried to get herself killed.*

You should have taught her common sense while you had the chance, Ottie said. He sat, ears perked up on alert.

And she has a new pet. Rosie snuffled delicately. *It's a bird. We can't even eat it.*

"Can we fix it?" Winter was looking at the dead boy next to her on the floor. The boy who'd been clutching his hand. Her eyes were filled with sorrow, and she touched his shoulder with a tenderness she didn't give to a lot of things.

Nicholas chose to answer the question she'd asked, not the question she meant. "It'll take a lot," he said. "But we shall see what we can do."

It was fiddly and difficult work. He had to find the exact moment to put back the glass without trapping Winter's skeletons outside. The skeletons themselves were, in some cases, beyond repair, but he sent what bones could be picked out of the dust grumbling back to their graves. Winter picked up candles and other objects that had fallen in the fight.

Sometimes during a time shift the dead came back to life. If their death had been accidental or easily prevented, it was more likely. The policeman Arthur Stowe sat up with a "What the—!" But the young man didn't so much as twitch as the altar table rose beneath him and knit itself back together. If Nicholas was reading the situation right, he'd chosen his death, and chosen it with courage.

When Nicholas had finished with the pillars on the ambulatories he turned around, gusting a sigh. That had been a lot of work, and he still had the busiest night of the year ahead of him. "Next time, try to have your epic battles before the twenty-third of December," he said.

"Is it really you?" said Arthur Stowe. Nicholas nodded. "I tell you mate, you didn't half put me through the wringer."

"Difficult situations are an unfortunate side effect of tangling with Myths," Nicholas said.

Arthur looked around at the church, nearing its former pristine state. "Is he really gone? Kuiper? Krampus?"

"For now." No doubt he'd found a hiding spot to lick his wounds. He'd be back, with another man who'd trade his soul for a seat in Parliament. He was right about one thing: the times were changing. Perhaps there was something to his deputizing strategy.

"You know, I thought this government couldn't get any worse." Arthur nudged the prone Minister with the toe of his boot. "Then they try to cancel Christmas."

Nicholas laughed. "At least I'm robust." He patted his belly. It was good to be back.

Winter was silent through all this, holding the boy's hand. Arthur's expression turned serious. "I'm sorry," he said.

She palmed one eye and glared at the boy. "What kind of person does that?" she asked.

"The selfless kind." Nicholas put a hand on her shoulder. "Antonius Snell is a bad man, but he is still a man. That was all that mattered to him."

"I don't know, I think 'man' is a fairly generous term," Arthur said darkly.

"Why does Chris get to do the choosing? Since he chose wrong." Winter sounded petulant. She truly was an adolescent despite her years.

"It was his life. And if he hadn't chosen to do what he did, he wouldn't have been the person you so value."

"This is why I don't value people." Winter brought one arm against her belly in a half hug. But she didn't let go of Chris's hand, not even to wipe away the stray tear that slipped from her eye.

Poor Winter. She'd grow out of her teenage years someday, and when she did, she'd realize that it was perfectly fine to show people you cared. But until then, she needed the gift of gentle parental prodding.

"There are ways to get him back, for people like us," he reminded her.

She worried her lip between her teeth. "But he will not be completely whole ever again," she said at last.

"He can be somewhat living, or he can be all dead. Why not let him choose?" Nicholas said.

Winter hesitated. Then she closed her eyes. A gentle glow suffused her, a different kind of light than the light Nicholas had used to banish Krampus. She'd come a long way from the rebellious girl intent on separating herself from all things Christmas.

The boy called Chris stirred on the table. Winter's eyes flew open. She threw herself over his chest and squeezed tight, heedless of his bloody shirt.

"Uh, wow," he said in a rusty voice. "Hi." He brought his arms around her and held her gently.

"You idiot," Winter said, voice muffled by his chest. Chris laughed weakly and, after a moment, so did she. Arthur turned away, sticking his hands in his pockets. The scene touched him, Nicholas could tell—and it embarrassed him, and it saddened him.

Nicholas slung an arm about his shoulder and directed him gently down the choir. "You know," he said, "Christmas is a time for new beginnings. For grand gestures. For renewed hope."

"For extra work and high heating bills and presents you can't afford," Arthur added.

"Christmas is complicated," Nicholas acknowledged. "And alas, I do not have the power to fix everything."

They turned at the bottom of the choir and made their way back up. Winter was pulling Chris to his feet. He faced her when he could finally stand on his own, holding her hand gently.

"So, I'm not dead?"

"You can be, if you want. I mean—" she blushed. "Not that I'm trying to kill you. Not that I'm offering—bollocks." She looked to Nicholas for help, but her father shook his head. Winter needed to learn this part of the job, too. The talking to people part. They didn't have to do it often, but that made what they said doubly as important. "You're like Hope, or Diedre. You just… have all your bits on."

"I appreciate that. I like my bits," Chris said seriously.

Winter narrowed her eyes at him. Then she cracked a smile. Chris laughed softly.

Nicholas cleared his throat in that official, time-to-remember-your-father's-here way. Not that he minded two Christmas lovebirds, but they had a cracking mess to clean and a world of houses to visit. Winter started back and flushed from her ears all the way down her neck. Chris stared at him, mouth slightly open.

"Yes. I'm what all this fuss was about."

"A real pleasure to meet you, sir." Chris stuck out his hand.

Nicholas shook. The boy's hands were soft, but his handshake had a determination to it that Nicholas liked. Then he turned to

Winter. "Are you ready?" he said. Was she ready to take the reins? To truly become his mythological heir? To put her life of chaotic good behind her and weave herself into the story?

She breathed deep, straightened her shoulders, and sighed. Then she patted down her pockets. For a moment, she looked concerned, then she pulled a box from an inner pocket in triumph. She took out a cigarette. "Just so you know, I still have a life of my own. I liked what I was doing before. I'm not going to give it up."

"Of course not," he said. Best to let her ease into things, anyway. "And don't even think about lighting that. Your mother would go absolutely mad if she caught you smoking, and I won't have cigarette burns on the side of my sleigh."

Winter stuck the cigarette behind her ear with a guilty expression that told him all he needed to know about his child, his sleigh, and cigarettes.

"Now. I think our first stop tonight should be our traumatized friends. Think you can find them?"

Winter hesitated, then nodded. Chris held out his hand and she took it, closing her eyes.

They would make a good team, Nicholas decided. Stranger things had happened.

Arthur had handcuffed Snell and was sitting the unconscious man up. He grunted as he tried to heave Snell by the armpits. "I could use a bit of your freakish super strength right now," he said to Winter.

She opened her eyes. "They're at the children's hospital," she said, and sauntered over to Snell. She picked him up and slung him over her shoulder. His head flopped against her back. "Where are we taking him, if not the garbage heap?"

"The Met station, Lewisham," said Arthur. "I've got some explaining to do to my boss."

Winter headed for the grand entrance of the cathedral. Chris slid off the altar and trotted after her and they fell in line, talking softly. That left Nicholas and Arthur, the two old men, to bring up the rear.

"Tell me to have hope," Arthur said. He stared down at his

scuffed shoes, hands stuck in the pocket of his camel coat.

Nicholas put a hand on his back and called his power forth. The hand glowed for a moment, leaving a golden imprint on Arthur's coat. And though the glow faded, Nicholas knew the warmth would remain for a long time. "All will be well," he said.

The air outside was still and cold and fresh, and seared Nicholas's lungs. The snow had stopped, and the clouds had cleared away to reveal an indigo night dotted with stars. A perfect night for a sleigh ride. Nicholas smiled, and for three blocks in each direction, the Christmas lights brightened.

He came to a dead halt as they rounded the corner of the cathedral. "What the bloody hell is hanging about my sleigh?"

***

Chris shook Arthur's hand as they parted outside the Lewisham Met station. It felt odd, in a way, as though the world should feel less solid than it did. He was half dead and half alive apparently.

Winter folded a note around Snell's tie. It read, HAPPY CHRISTMAS. She'd wanted to add a crude drawing too, but Chris had talked her out of it. Arthur shuffled his feet at the door.

"I don't know what to say to you about all this madness," he admitted. "Except, thanks. And I'll see if I can get your reindeer bones out of evidence."

"Call your wife," Chris said.

"Second," said Winter.

"You make it sound so bloody easy," Arthur grumbled. He turned and faced the doors of the station.

They waited until he was inside, and officers had come out to retrieve Snell. Then they took off, making their way toward the children's hospital.

"Can I ask you something?" Chris said. It had been bothering him for a few hours now, though he hadn't had much time to think on it.

"You may," said Nicholas gravely.

He swallowed the temptation to say, *Do* you *think your*

daughter's the coolest person you ever met? "Those knives. They bring you back to life, but they also kill you."

"Correct."

"So... why did you keep them around? Why not get rid of them?" Chris asked.

Nicholas nodded, as though appreciating the question. "Because they bring me back to life."

Yeah, but they also kill you, Chris thought, but he held his tongue. Below them, London was soft and silent, more peaceful than he'd ever seen it before.

"They're not the only things that can kill a Myth. We are hard to dispatch, but not invincible. The knives were an insurance policy, of a sort. I had them protected and hidden. It was my hubris to think that Krampus wouldn't be able to break my protections. I shall have to take extra precautions in the future."

"But... he already found all three. They're gone," Chris said. No point in protections now.

Nicholas's eyes twinkled. "Who said there were only three?"

They landed Hope on the helipad and went down to the ward. The hallways were decorated with cheerful images, butterflies and trees and lions, but the sterile smell, the hard beds and chairs, the machines that beeped and trilled, all served to remind Chris that this was not a fun place to be.

Most of the kids had family with them. Many sat up and watched telly, or played a game, or ate. But some lay listless, staring at nothing. Remembering, perhaps, or trying not to remember.

Nicholas started with one of them. He brushed his hand over the child's forehead and eased away the fear, the dark memories of being trapped and cold and helpless and hungry.

"Your turn," he said.

Chris thought he was talking to Winter. Then she nudged him. "You're the one with fancy memory powers," she said.

"I thought—" he stopped. He'd thought that when it was clear that Winter was the mythological heir, all of his powers would fade, like the light-bringing one. Yet he was still a conduit. Did he dare to hope that after all this was over, he'd be more than just Chris?

Well, if he got to keep these powers, he'd better learn how to use them for good. He thought of Christmas lights and snowmen and cold days wrapped up in warm blankets. Then he leaned over the bed and pressed his fingers to the forehead of the girl in front of him.

The ghost of a smile touched her face as she slipped into sleep.

CHAPTER TWENTY-ONE

Christmas Eve. Father Christmas's sleigh sat on London Bridge. Chris patted Rosie goodbye and gave Ottie a nod, man to dog. He even hugged Diedre, getting a nose full of musty smell and a happy honk in his ear. Then he climbed out onto the pavement.

Winter followed him, walking with him to the edge of the bridge. "Are you sure we can't drop you at home?" she said. Wind toyed with her hair.

"I'll be fine." Chris stuck his hands in his pockets. "It's nice to be in the city on Christmas. Watch the lights, look at the snow. Who knows when it'll snow like this again in London?" The Thames twinkled, a ribbon of night studded with neon stars. He'd buttoned his coat all the way up to hide his bloody shirt, and when Winter handed him Mrs Pavuka's shawl, he wound it about his neck.

Winter couldn't quite meet his eye. "Listen," she said. "I hate people helping me. I hate people, actually. But I don't hate you."

Chris grinned. He wasn't likely to get a better compliment than that. "Thanks. It was a pleasure working with you, too."

"Only, I need to step up now. Do more. And, well, Krampus got me thinking. I can't go it alone like I thought I would. I mean, I can, obviously." She blushed, and Chris turned his laugh into a hasty cough. "But it's probably more efficient not to. Have to keep ahead of the forces of evil. You know."

Chris nodded. "The next time Christmas needs saving, you know where to find me."

Winter hesitated. Then she stepped in and wrapped her arms around him. She still managed to smell like cardamom and cinnamon, even though she hadn't changed her clothes in almost forty-eight hours. Chris was almost afraid to hug her back, but then she said, "Don't make me do this alone," and he couldn't help himself. He laughed and squeezed her tight. He tried to remember the last time someone had given him a real hug. As Christmas presents went, it was rather nice. Her cheek rested against his, and her breath was like the tide. He could feel her heart against his chest and her ribs against his forearms. He liked it a lot.

She pulled back and rested her forehead against his. "We'll see each other again," Chris said. "Can't really go anywhere, can I? I mean, I'm a little bit dead."

Winter snorted. Then she leaned in and kissed him on the cheek, so quickly he had to wonder if he'd imagined it. "We'll see each other again," she replied.

"You're the coolest girl I ever met," he blurted as she got in the sleigh.

She half turned, her sharp profile slicing through the view, and she smiled. "Wait 'til the next time you see me."

Hope fluttered her tail, and the sleigh rose into the air.

Chris watched it go, hands in his pockets, whistling a tune. *All I want for Christmas...*

All he wanted for Christmas was a slice of Turkey and mince pie; he'd got a whole more than he had asked for. He stood on London Bridge until the sleigh was nothing more than a speck amongst the stars. Then he turned around and set off, humming.

He didn't want to go home. He draped the shawl around his shoulders, heedless of the way it made him look like an old lady's end table. He had one more errand to run.

Downing Street blazed with a merry light behind a large iron fence. Chris managed to reach a finger through the gate and touch the unsuspecting guard on the side of the face. He called up an image of the kids in the hospital. "Remember what's important in life," he whispered.

The guard frowned in confusion. He looked straight past Chris in his shawl, then twisted around. Gingerly, he opened the gate to peer out. Chris slid in past him and trotted past pale brick townhouses until he found the dark façade of Number Ten.

He touched the doorknob and thought the same thing. *Remember what's important.* The latch clicked softly, and the door swung open.

The pristine hall was lined with paintings by artists with old and foreign names, and sculptures on plinths. It smelled like roast turkey, mulled wine, and sweet and sticky toffee. Chris sidled past an ancient Greek vase, holding a breath he wasn't sure he needed anymore. If he didn't get on the naughty list for breaking and entering, he would surely do so for destroying priceless artefacts.

As he moved down the hall he began to creep past dark rooms and closed doors. He moved upstairs, resisting the temptation to open every door he came to. When would he ever get the chance to come to Downing Street again?

Finally, he spotted golden light emanating from an open door. He peered in. It was a small library, packed from floor to ceiling with books. Two armchairs and a coffee table sat in front of a crackling fire. Only one of those armchairs was occupied, by a balding white man Chris had seen on the telly countless times. He was flicking through papers, stopping occasionally to pick up a glass of dark liquor.

Chris came in and the man looked up. "Just a moment, love, I'll be—" He stopped. His mouth parted and for a long moment he stared right at the spot Chris stood. Then he shook his head. "Too bloody tired," he muttered, palming one blue eye.

Chris looked at the Prime Minister. He thought of the kids, shivering and fearful in their cages on Christmas Eve. He thought of them again, peaceful in the hospital. Smiling. He touched the Prime Minister lightly on the shoulder. He thought of Winter's face, savagely determined, fighting for her father and the children and the legacy of the season. He thought of Arthur, staring down Antonius Snell as he refused his offer.

"You've got to remember what matters most in life," Chris said. More than money, or getting reelected, or promising his friends nice contracts or good positions in government.

The Prime Minister shivered. Then he looked up, furrowing his brow. He frowned into the distance.

Chris hoped he was thinking about it. He slipped away.

Outside Number Ten the snow was as fresh and soft as new carpet. Chris nudged at it with his shoe. Funny thing, he wasn't making footprints anymore. He fingered the golden edges of Mrs Pavuka's shawl. "Did you make me invisible or did death?" he mused aloud.

"A little bit of both, I expect."

Chris looked up. By the golden light of the lamp, he could just make out the outline of a white man in a pinstripe three-piece suit with an old-fashioned cut.. He was bald on the top of his head, and the ring of salt-and-pepper hair above his ears was trimmed close. His moustache was likewise orderly. He held a pipe in one translucent hand and tapped it against his chin. "Pleasure to meet you, Mr Demer. We've a mess on our hands, and you're just the man for the job."

The man stood and extended his hand. The farther he was from the lamplight, the more solid he seemed, but Chris was still surprised to feel solid, warm flesh beneath his palm as they shook hands.

"Nice to meet you, er. Mr…?"

"Attlee. Clement Attlee." The man smiled. "You may not know me, but I used to be the Prime Minister once a long time ago when I was alive. It was my government that created the National Health Service you see today. It appears your wish to hear all those stories of those that came before and have left your earthly world has come to pass."

Chris smiled back. "Pleasure to meet you. So I can see the dead now? Ghosts exist, then?" An embarrassing hope flushed through him. "Did Winter send you?"

"Yes, you can, Chris and yes, we exist, and we can be useful again if people just asked us. I'm afraid our problems are… a little more down to earth and this is not at Winter's request," Attlee told him. He gestured with his pipe. "It's best if I show you. Come along, young Chris. The witching hour is ours."

Chris almost objected. He'd agreed to the morning shift at *Hayne & Sons,* after all, and surely he'd had enough adventure for one lifetime…

Good thing I'm not alive anymore, he thought, and grinned, and followed the man in the pinstripe suit.

***

Boxing day. Arthur stood in Montague's office, even though he'd been scheduled off. Somehow, spending three hours as the most wanted man in London didn't make him want to putter around Lewisham or go to the shops. He'd found a powder packet of hot chocolate in one of the station kitchen cupboards. Sipping on it reminded him of Colchester when the kids were young. He stared at Montague's orderly desk and waited for his boss to speak.

Montague looked as though he'd slept as little as Arthur the last few days. He'd been dealing with the case round the clock: the Snell case, it was called now. Someone had snapped a photo of Snell handcuffed outside the station and sent it to *The Guardian,* and now every newspaper in Britain was ringing the commissioner's phone off his desk.

"You didn't have to come in, though I don't blame you for wanting something to do." He looked through the drawn curtains of his office window. Behind him, Arthur saw at least one journalist waiting for a good photo. He missed Winter's powers of invisibility right now. "If you insist on working, I'll place you on desk duty. 'Til it all blows over."

Arthur licked his lips. The hot chocolate was making his teeth feel fuzzy. "Actually, sir. I was wondering if I might have some leave."

Montague took a long swallow of coffee and made a face. "Lord knows the Met owes you. Fill out the paperwork and go when you like."

It was seven in the morning. Even Izzy wasn't in, probably sleeping off a Christmas hangover. Or maybe someone had convinced her to take a personal day. They hadn't spoken since her phone call. Arthur wasn't sure what he wanted to say to her, if anything.

"Don't blame her." Montague had caught him looking through the open door at Izzy's desk. "We all thought bringing you in would help. And we were afraid of the mob mentality. What if the public had caught you first? They mightn't have waited for exonerating

205

evidence." Montague turned back to his desk and rearranged a paperweight. "But… I am sorry."

Arthur kept his face carefully blank. "What for, sir?" Personally, he felt there were many options.

"For letting Snell interfere with the case. For pushing you to follow his vision." Montague shifted. He still wouldn't look at Arthur. "He's got a very convincing manner. Guess that's why he's a politician."

"Not for long," Arthur said.

Montague nodded at that. "Here." He turned his laptop around. The BBC had a clip of Snell being transferred to a private prison. His normally immaculate figure was in disarray—his suit hung lopsided, his hair stuck up, and his face was blotched and sallow. He was escorted by four guards, and he turned his face away as the cameras tried to get a good shot.

"They'll be talking about this one for years, Stowe," Montague said. "It's going to absolutely make you."

And Izzie, and you, Arthur thought. Though he had no idea what he'd say when he was called up to the witness stand at trial.

He leaned in. "Isn't that Kuiper?" he said, pointing.

Montague leaned in and cocked his head. "Who?"

"Snell's aide." He stood in the background, looking as washed-out and unimportant and bored as ever. If Arthur hadn't been actively looking for him, he probably wouldn't have noticed at all.

"I suppose so. Bad luck to be that bloke's employee. But politicians always land on their feet." The clip ended. Montague moved a few more things on his desk. "Anyway, Stowe. You've had a rough Christmas, deserve the time off. Don't let me keep you."

Arthur nodded and moved toward the door. No accolades, no prizes. Maybe he'd get a promotion somewhere down the line. Ah well. He hardly needed it.

"Oh, and Stowe?" Montague said.

He turned back, arching an eyebrow.

The Commissioner looked unhappy. He stuck his hands behind his back and forced himself to meet the detective's eye for the first time that morning. "I lost faith in you. It won't happen again."

A warmth spread in his belly, better than any kind of booze. Arthur allowed himself a faint smile. "Not to worry, sir. I lost faith in myself." He let the door close behind him and whistled as he gathered up his things. *All I want for Christmas...*

He wasn't the world's best man. But he was getting better, and the next time he thought it couldn't be done, all he had to do was remember Winter, who was so aggressively good no one could stop her or her axe. He could remember Chris, whose goodness was so utterly incorruptible that even spiders and slimeballs received equal compassion.

Arthur checked his watch. If he drove now, he could reach Colchester before lunch. He just had to check something first.

His mouth went dry on the first ring. On the second, he almost hung up. But the line clicked on the third, and he steeled himself. *All will be well.* His heart pulsed in his throat.

"Hello?" said a woman's voice on the other end of the line.

"Missy?"

***

December twenty-seventh. Off the Irish sea, the skeleton of a blue whale crested joyfully, then dove into the deep, sending up salt spray like chips of ice. A sleigh zipped through the air, pulled by the oddest assortment of skeletons: a sabre-tooth tiger, a huge tortoise, some ancestor of the rhinoceros, half a mammoth, an aurochs, and a giant sloth. At the head of the peculiar company was a dodo, waddling as fast as her legs could carry her and magically assisted so that she was none the wiser. The whale breached again, trumpeting. Two dogs howled in reply as the sleigh flew away. And over the quiet roar of the sea, two voices could barely be heard:

"This ride was smoother with the reindeer."

"Try something new, Dad. Live a little."

"Speaking of trying something new: ready to learn? You've got a long way to go before you're ready to take over."

"And many years, too." The sleigh bobbed a little, disappearing into the gloom.

"Better to be prepared than… *Winter Noelle Christmas, get your boots off the dash.*"

"Wow, Dad. 'Tis the season, you don't have to get all worked up."

"I'll give you worked up. I'll give you the season. I'll give you the season with polish and a rag if you're so keen."

"Ho, ho, bloody ho."

And then even the voices were gone.

THE END

Printed in Great Britain
by Amazon